Though scandal followed her everywhere, Lady Philippa Wyckfield was really a most sensible young lady. After all, she hadn't *really* stolen Lady Oxbrough's sapphire—and the affair of the horse called Salvaje was easily explained, if anyone cared to listen... which it appeared, they did not.

No one was more surprised than Pippa at the rumors and gossip which seemed to accompany her every act, no matter how well-intentioned. But Fate held the greatest surprise of all: Love, and from a most unexpected quarter!

PASSING FANCIES

A Regency Love Story by
ELIZABETH MANSFIELD

Books by Elizabeth Mansfield

WINTER WONDERLAND
MY LORD MURDERER
THE PHANTOM LOVER
A VERY DUTIFUL DAUGHTER
REGENCY STING
A REGENCY MATCH
HER MAN OF AFFAIRS
DUEL OF HEARTS
A REGENCY CHARADE
THE FIFTH KISS
THE RELUCTANT FLIRT
THE FROST FAIR
THE COUNTERFEIT HUSBAND
HER HEART'S CAPTAIN
LOVE LESSONS
PASSING FANCIES
THE MAGNIFICENT MASQUERADE
A MARRIAGE OF INCONVENIENCE
A SPLENDID INDISCRETION
THE GRAND PASSION
A GRAND DECEPTION
THE ACCIDENTAL ROMANCE
THE BARTERED BRIDE
A PRIOR ENGAGEMENT
A CHRISTMAS KISS
A BRILLIANT MISMATCH

A REGENCY HOLIDAY
(with Monette Cummings, Sarah Eagle,
Judith Nelson, Martha Powers)

JOVE BOOKS, NEW YORK

PASSING FANCIES

A Jove Book / published by arrangement with
the author

PRINTING HISTORY
Berkley edition / September 1983
Jove edition / October 1987

For information address: The Berkley Publishing Group,
200 Madison Avenue, New York, New York 10016.

ISBN: 0-515-09175-8

Jove Books are published by The Berkley Publishing Group,
200 Madison Avenue, New York, New York 10016.

PRINTED IN THE UNITED STATES OF AMERICA

10 9 8 7 6 5 4 3 2

Passing
Fancies

Prologue

LADY STURTEVANT, bustling into the entryway of her disheveled townhouse just past five of a rainy September afternoon, was too irritable and distracted to take note of the letter which lay in plain sight on the pier table against the wall to her left. She handed her pile of parcels to the butler, who juggled them clumsily in his arms, dropping the two topmost boxes to the floor. Lady Sturtevant cast him a dagger-look, picked them up herself, placed them atop the pile he'd managed to keep a grasp on, and waved him off. Then she turned to the mirror which hung over the table and pulled off her hat, still not noticing the white envelope which lay right before her.

Her headpiece was an impressive creation, festooned with silk flowers in various shades of blue and, in addition, sporting a number of long plumes attached to the back of the crown and curling over the brim. Lady Sturtevant usually took the greatest care in removing it.

Today, however, she snatched it off with careless disregard for its trimmings or the coiffure upon which it rested. She glared at her reflection in the glass and made a face at herself. "I look like an old sow!" she muttered aloud.

Her self-disgust was not warranted. Georgina Sturtevant, though approaching fifty years of age, was still considered a handsome woman. In spite of a stone of extra weight, a tendency to choose garish colors for her clothing and a too-bright-red dye for her hair, she had an admirable appearance. Her carriage was imposing, she had a pair of lively, intelligent eyes, a deep, warm laugh that made everyone within its hearing smile, and a way of gesturing with her hands when she spoke which gave her a unique charm. If some members of London society thought her manners too casual (and even somewhat vulgar), most of the others were wise enough to admire her generosity of spirit and her absence of pretension.

Her ladyship's self-disgust was a temporary condition occasioned by a visit to her favorite milliner's shop, where a hat which she'd admired in the shop window had looked positively ridiculous when she'd tried it on. The experience had made her uncomfortably aware of the wrinkles around her eyes and the puffiness under her jawline. "I must put myself on a diet," she muttered, lifting her chin and brushing at her jowls with the back of her gloved hands. "Nothing but dry biscuits and vinegar for a fortnight."

"You won't stick to it for a morning, much less a fortnight," came a voice from behind her. Adolphus Sturtevant, the youngest of Lady Sturtevant's five children, was coming down the stairs, dressed to go riding. The fashionable cut of his riding coat, the light color of his breeches and the gleaming polish of his boots were more suited to a mature Corinthian than to a freckle-faced seventeen-year-old.

"Are you off riding again?" his mother asked. "At this hour? I suppose that means you won't be back in time to sit down with us for dinner."

"Told you yesterday I wouldn't be. Taking a late dinner with Doodle," he reminded her, coming up beside her and peering into the glass to adjust his neckcloth. "I say, Mama, what's *this*?"

Lady Sturtevant, who'd already turned from the looking glass and started for the stairs, paused. "What's what?"

"This letter. Addressed to you."

She took it from him with brows upraised. "That looks like . . ." She broke the seal hastily and read the brief contents, her brow clearing and a smile appearing on her face. "It *is*! It's from Pippa! She's coming *home*!"

Adolphus turned from the glass in pleased surprise. "Is she? At last! When?"

"Next week. Isn't that the most delightful news, Dolly? It's been so *long*!"

"It's splendid! Really splendid. She's just the person I've been hoping to see. There's something particularly important that I've been wishing to speak to her about."

His mother's smile faded. "If you're going to try to persuade her to lend you money, Dolly Sturtevant, I shall wring your neck."

Adolphus drew himself up with all the dignity a snub-nosed, freckle-bedecked dandy could summon. "I've *never* borrowed money from her. Our dealings in financial matters have always been purely business transactions."

His mother threw him a look of complete disdain. "Ha! What gammon! But I'm much too excited to stand about bandying words with you. I must go up to tell Sybil—"

"Sybil ain't back yet," Adolphus said, turning back to the looking glass to make a last check on his appearance. "Went driving with Surridge." He sauntered to the door. "Why my sister ever permitted herself to become betrothed to that mawworm I'll never understand."

Lady Sturtevant paused on the stairway. "Do you

mean that no one's home but Simon?" she asked, disappointed. Simon, her second-born, would be as glad to hear the news of Pippa's imminent arrival as anyone else in the family, but his responses were always so stoic and unimpassioned that it wasn't much fun telling him anything. Silent Simon. He'd probably only mumble "That's fine," and not even look up from whatever scientific experiment he was working on at the moment.

"Don't despair. William's come," Adolphus informed her over his shoulder as he opened the door. "His monthly going-over-the-accounts visit. You'll find him in the study, as usual. Goodnight, Mama."

"William's here? He's just the one to whom I wished to tell the news," Lady Sturtevant said to no one in particular, Dolly having already closed the door behind him. She lifted her skirts eagerly with one hand and waved the letter excitedly in the other. "*William*, my love! Wait 'til you *hear*—!"

William Sturtevant, the eldest of Lady Sturtevant's offspring, was sitting at his deceased father's desk, frowning over the stack of bills. Ever since Edgar Sturtevant had died, William had been attempting to bring his family to some semblance of order in the running of the household and the management of the finances. It was not that his father had left them impecunious—on the contrary, their income was more than adequate for their needs. But William hated the wasteful way in which his mother, his sister and his youngest brother squandered funds. Their irresponsibility and lack of interest in business matters, as well as the careless, slapdash way they ran their lives, was very disturbing to him. That was why he'd moved into bachelor quarters in Cleveland Street two years before. At least his own surroundings were neat and orderly.

His mother's voice interrupted his fiscal calculations. "What did you say, Mama?" he asked, looking up.

"*Pippa's* coming home," she answered, entering the room breathlessly. "Next *week*! Isn't that the most marvelous news?"

William stared at his mother, his hand arrested in the

air. *Pippa was coming back.* He didn't know how he felt at hearing the news. To the rest of the family, Philippa Wyckfield was like a sister, but he'd never become as close to the girl as the rest of them had. When she'd first come to live with them, a dozen years ago, he'd been away at Oxford. Then he'd spent some years in a cavalry regiment on the Penninsula. When he'd finally returned home, Pippa and Sybil had just turned eighteen. Pippa had seemed to him as bookish and shy as his sister Sybil was aggressive and loud. He'd been very attracted to Pippa's soft-spoken, gentle manner and lovely smile. But a number of incidents, in which she'd joined Sybil in mischief and mayhem, had convinced him that his first impressions had been false, and now, he had to admit, he thought of her as just another nuisance that his mother had foisted upon him. "Wonderful," he responded to his mother drily. "I'm overjoyed at the prospect of contending with another feminine troublemaker on your premises."

His mother studied him in annoyance. It had been her dream for years that William and Pippa (Lady Philippa Wyckfield, if one could think of her by rank and wealth rather than by affection) might make a match of it. Pippa was the daughter of her dearest friend, Camilla. When Camilla had married Captain Collinson and gone off to sea with him, Lady Sturtevant had welcomed her friend's daughter into her household with loving warmth. Pippa had been like one of her own. The girl was superior in intelligence, breeding, appearance and manner. A man like William—past thirty as he was—might well consider himself fortunate to win such a wife. And for a while, when William had first come home from the wars, she'd believed the two were attracted to each other. What had gone wrong? "Don't you *like* Pippa, William?" she asked curiously.

William did not have the opportunity to respond. A female voice, calling from down the hallway, interrupted them. "Mama? Dash it all, Mama, where are you? I have something to tell you which—"

Lady Sturtevant threw her eldest son a look which

said, *We will speak of this anon,* and turned to the doorway. "In here, Sybil. Where have you been all afternoon?"

"Riding with Surridge in the park," Sybil answered, appearing in the doorway looking statuesque and dashing in her riding costume. "He was in a foul mood, accusing me of flirting with his friend, Lord Hepburn, whom I absolutely despise, so I—" Her flushed cheeks paled. "Good God! William! *You* here?"

"You needn't act as though you'd seen a ghost. I'm here quite often, am I not? It is my house, you know, even though I don't choose to live in it."

"Yes, I know. It's just that, of late, you never come home unless it's time to go over the bills, and that's always such a to-do," the girl explained, uncharacteristically nervous. Sybil, now almost twenty-two years old, had not yet lost her youthful, tomboyish quality. She was tall and athletically built, her red hair tied back in bouncy curls, her green eyes usually alight with mischief, and her manner brusque and direct. At the moment, however, she seemed ill-at-ease at seeing her brother. William wondered what she'd done that caused her to feel such discomfort at the sight of him. "Have you spent a fortune on some frippery, my girl?" he asked suspiciously.

"No, hang it, I haven't. If you'd seen the bills, you'd know—"

"Then why did you jump so at seeing me?"

"You startled me, that's all. Besides, when you hear my news, you're quite likely to make one of your ugly scenes."

"I don't make ugly scenes," her brother said coldly.

"What news do you have that would upset your brother?" Lady Sturtevant asked, frowning at her daughter in anticipation of the worst.

Sybil looked from one to the other cautiously as she withdrew her gloves. "Dash it all, aren't you going to ask me to remove my hat and sit down first?"

"No," her brother snapped. "Tell us without all this shilly-shallying."

The girl shrugged. "Well, then, here it is in a nutshell. I've broken it off with Surridge."

"Oh, Sybil, *no*!" Lady Sturtevant cried.

"Good Lord!" William exclaimed. "Have you gone completely mad? That's the third fellow you've thrown over in the past two years. Do you want the world to call you a jilt?"

"I don't care what the world calls me. Confound it, I won't wed that idiot! He's moody, suspicious and a dolt in the bargain."

Her mother sighed deeply. "I don't know what to do with you, Sybil. They are calling you a jilt already. Every dowager is whispering it behind her fan. Soon all the eligibles will avoid you like a plague-carrier. No gentleman wants to become the victim of a jilt, you know."

"I don't care," Sybil said with a toss of her head, causing her dashing riding cap, with its curled white plume, to fall slightly askew. "It's better to jilt them before the wedding than to suffer with them afterwards."

"I don't understand you, Sybil. Why do you become betrothed to these fellows if you don't like them?" her brother asked curiously. "Can't you tell from the start that—?"

"No, I can't. I liked them all at the start." She kicked aside the train of her riding dress and turned toward the door. "It isn't my fault that they all turned out to be . . . to be passing fancies."

William and his mother exchanged glances. Sybil was too impulsive by half, and neither the mother nor the brother knew just what to do about it. William shook his head hopelessly. "Passing fancies, indeed! Next time, my girl, hold back for a few months before agreeing to a betrothal. Perhaps in that way you can be more certain that the fancy won't be a passing one."

The redhead girl flicked a disdainful look over her shoulder. "Much *you* know about it. Better find *yourself* a betrothed before you offer *me* advice."

"Whether he's betrothed himself or not," Lady Sturtevant said severely, "your brother is quite right. It's the outside of enough to be entangling yourself in these betrothals before you're sure of your feelings."

Sybil paused in the doorway, an entrancing figure in her dark riding costume and high-crowned, awkwardly tilted hat. "I don't see how I can help it. Blast! One never learns a man's true nature until *after* the betrothal. Those dissemblers are models of devotion and charm until they've won a girl's promise. It's only after that promise is made that the truth of their characters becomes plain."

"That can't be true. Most girls seem to manage to go ahead with the nuptials just the same," her brother pointed out.

"Not I!" Sybil declared proudly. "I refuse to be trapped by convention and by what people will say. Confound it, let them call me a jilt if they must. At least I haven't found myself *trapped*!"

While her brother and her mother stared at her speechlessly, the girl waved saucily and made a quick escape. She was halfway down the corridor when her mother's call stopped her and brought her back to the study doorway. She'd hoped she'd heard the last of the scolding. She stuck her head in. "Did you call me, Mama? What else do you want to say?"

Her mother glowered at her. "You needn't take that tone, my girl. I don't intend to scold. It never does any good, anyway. But I, too, have news, and it will please you a great deal more than your news pleased me. Pippa's coming!"

"Pippa?" Sybil's entire face brightened. "*Really*, Mama? When?"

"Next week. Thursday at the latest."

Sybil whipped off her hat and tossed it in the air like a delighted child. "I knew she wouldn't fail me!" she chortled. "I *knew* it."

"*Fail* you?" Lady Sturtevant blinked at her daughter in confusion. "What on earth do you mean?"

Sybil immediately stiffened. "Nothing. Nothing at all." She picked up her hat from the floor and brushed it off. "I only meant . . . that is, I wrote to her that I . . . er . . . missed her."

William's eyes narrowed. There was something havey-cavey about Sybil's behavior. "Are you and Pippa up to some mischief?" he asked suspiciously.

"Don't be absurd," Sybil said, turning away. "Now, please, give me leave to go to my room. I want to change for dinner."

Lady Sturtevant observed her son with critical detachment after Sybil had gone. "Pippa is not the sort to be up to mischief," she said to him after a while. "I think, my dear, that you've always misjudged the girl."

William dropped his eyes from his mother's steady gaze. "Have I?" He shuffled through the papers and resumed his additions of the monthly bills. "Perhaps I have."

"Why don't you like her, William?"

"I like Pippa well enough."

Lady Sturtevant sighed and lifted herself wearily from her chair. "No, it's not well enough to suit me. I thought, a few years ago, that you were taken with her."

"I was."

"If so . . . then, what happened?"

He put down his pencil and blinked thoughtfully. "I don't know," he said after a pause. "Perhaps it was like Sybil's affair—only a passing fancy."

He picked up his pencil and set to work with a decided firmness that told his mother he would reveal no more. Lady Sturtevant sighed and left him to his accounts. Pippa was coming back. The matter was not yet beyond hope; there was much of the tale still to be told.

And speaking of tales still to be told, she said to herself, *who else must I tell about Pippa's return?* Herbert, her third son, was away at Cambridge, so the news did not immediately concern him. That left only Simon. Silent Simon, so wrapped up in his scientific studies and experiments that he seemed not to take note of the world around him, would not be very interested either, but she supposed she might as well tell him anyway. She climbed up to the third floor where Simon had his bedroom, a dressing room which he'd converted into a library and storeroom for his equipment, and the study which he'd set up as a small laboratory in which to perform the various experiments which so fascinated him. No one else occupied the third floor, permitting Simon the privacy he desired.

She wondered as she mounted the stairs (much steeper here than they were on the lower floors) if she'd made a mistake in permitting him to occupy so secluded a part of the house. It only added to his detachment from the rest of the world. But of course the fellow was twenty-eight years old; if she hadn't permitted him to establish himself here, he would have found himself a loft or garret in some disreputable part of town. A mother couldn't control her children's lives once they'd come of age.

She was breathless when she reached the top of the stairs, and she sighed heavily. If only her misanthropic son would show half as much interest in people as he did in his microscopes, his telescopes, his slides, his lenses and his puzzling experiments. Really, sometimes she wondered if she'd made a mull of bringing up her children. In angry self-reproach, she rapped sharply on the closed door of Simon's study. "Simon, are you in there? It's your mother."

"Yes, Mama," came a muffled voice. "Come in."

She opened the door and peered into the dimly lit room. (Her son had informed her that he was engaged, of late, in the study of optics. He was fascinated by the nature of light rays. By what sort of peculiar logic, therefore, was the room so dark?) Her tall, lanky, carelessly clad second son was bent over a long worktable, his right eye fixed on a small hole cut into the end of a long, black box, the other eye tightly shut. The only light in the room came from a single candle placed adjacent to the box, its light refracted from a mirror to a lens fitted into the box's top surface. Lady Sturtevant had no inkling of what his purpose was in staring into the strange-looking box at a reflected candle-flame, but if she asked him, she knew she would receive a lengthy, complicated response which she wouldn't understand, so she held her tongue. Instead she cleared her throat pointedly and waited for him to take notice of her.

Simon didn't remove his eye from the box. "Is it dinnertime already?" he asked abstractedly. "I can change in a twinkling and come right down, I promise."

"No, you've a couple of hours yet, you moonling," his mother answered fondly, unable to keep from smoothing back his tousled, dark-red hair.

"Oh, good," he murmured, not the least distracted from his observations by her motherly caress.

She frowned at him. Her son was becoming too thin, too careless of his health, too abstracted. He spent entirely too much time in this close, airless room. "Have you eaten at all today?"

"Hm? Yes, I think so. In any case, I *am* coming down to dinner, so you may save yourself a scold."

"That's very good of you," his mother said drily. "But I haven't come up here to scold. I've come to bring you news. Pippa's coming next week."

There was a moment of complete stillness, during which Simon didn't move his eye from his box. "That's fine," he muttered after a time.

"That's just what I thought you'd say," Lady Sturtevant snorted. "One would think you didn't even care whether she comes or not."

There was no response from her preoccupied son, so she shrugged and turned to go. "Well, I'll leave you to your . . . whatever it is. But be sure to change your shirt, too, Simon, before coming down to dinner. Don't think you can change only your coat and pretend to be dressed. That will not do. Not at all."

After she'd closed the door behind her, Simon took his eye from the peephole in his box and stood erect, staring out before him blindly. "Pippa!" he whispered hoarsely, running his fingers through his disheveled hair. He stumbled across the room to the window, pulled aside the draperies and leaned his forehead against the glass. "Pippa," he muttered in an almost silent groan. "Oh, God! Not again."

Chapter One

THEY WERE packing her things again. Here in this small bedroom, from which she could look out of the wide casements and see the ocean, Pippa Wyckfield and her once-governess-now-companion, Miss Ada Townley, were once again busily cramming her belongings into her well-worn trunks and portmanteaux. The younger woman turned from the chest of drawers, adjusted her spectacles which had slipped down on her nose, let a partly folded petticoat drop from her hand and looked about her. The bed was covered with folded underthings, a half-filled portmanteau lay open on the floor, and on the opposite side of the room Miss Townley was struggling with the straps of a huge trunk so crammed with fripperies that it would not stay closed. It was a depressingly familiar sight. In the past dozen years (ever since 1804, when she'd been ten and Mama had decided to run off to wed Captain Thomas Collinson) Pippa had packed her things eight or nine times.

Miss Townley looked up and met her eyes. "Yes, I

know what you're thinkin', my girl. This deuced packin'. One would think the task would get easier with practice, eh?"

"Yes," Pippa sighed, turning to the window, "but it never does." The sea looked grey and forbidding under the darkening sky, but she loved to look at it. Mama and Thomas would be sailing on it by this time tomorrow. If she'd only make up her mind, she could be with them. Thomas had assured her that he could make things right with the admiralty. As far as her parents were concerned, she'd be most welcome on the voyage. If she had an ounce of sense . . .

As if she were reading Pippa's mind, Miss Townley remarked, "If you'd decide to sail with your mother and the captain, you wouldn't have to bother with all this. You wouldn't need half these belongin's. You could leave everythin' to me and just sail off without a care."

Pippa threw the older woman a quick look over her shoulder. *Sail off without a care.* If only she could.

For in truth, Pippa was quite sick of it all . . . all the packing, all the moving, all the pain of finding herself uprooted yet another time. The first time she'd had to pack, back when her mother had married her sea-captain and gone off on the first of their voyages together, Pippa had found it rather fun. She'd been happy to go to live with their friends, the Sturtevants. But no sooner had she adjusted to that irregular and frenetic household, her widowed Aunt Ethelyn had taken ill, and Pippa had repacked and gone to live with her ailing aunt at the family estate at Wyckfield Park. After her aunt's passing, Thomas had left the East India Company to take a commission in the Navy, and Pippa had packed again and returned to stay with her mother here in the Southampton house while Thomas had sailed off to fight Napoleon and make a great name for himself. During the ensuing years, Pippa had been shunted between her parents' Southampton house and the Sturtevant's abode (depending upon whether or not Mama could join Thomas on shipboard), finding it a most uncertain and disturbing existence. As she grew older, each uprooting had begun to seem more disconcerting than the last. Especially when she'd had to leave Mama to return to the Sturtevants.

But Pippa had never confessed to Mama and Thomas how difficult her life had been. They were so happy together that she couldn't permit herself to cloud their contentment. Even Miss Townley didn't guess the extent of her unhappiness. All three were convinced that Pippa was content wherever she lived. Happy, adaptable Pippa.

And they had some justification for their illusions, for Pippa truly loved all the Sturtevants. She would never bring herself to admit aloud that the unruly Sturtevant household didn't really suit her.

So why don't I agree to sail with Mama and Thomas? she asked herself, turning back to stare out at the distant, still-glowing horizon. She permitted herself to imagine for a moment the joy of strolling the deck of Thomas's ship, the ocean winds ruffling her hair and the taste of salt on her lips. Her mind toyed with the notion of "sailing off" with the sort of gluttonous eagerness with which an overweight matron might consider the offer of a second portion of chocolate cake—tempting to contemplate but a sign of weakness to accept. She couldn't help sighing again. Wouldn't it be wonderful to be able to sail off with her parents instead of going back to London to face William Sturtevant again?

But she shook her head. She couldn't. It was a temptation to which her conscience would not agree. Besides, she'd already written to Lady Sturtevant that she was coming. And the urgent letter from Sybil still lay on her dressing table. Sybil needed her. The closeness she'd always felt for her girlhood friend had not abated during the ensuing years. Whether they lived together or apart, their mutual affection had remained strong. If Sybil had so urgently requested her return, how could Pippa refuse? "I'm not seriously considering sailing,

Miss Townley," she said, her eyes remaining longingly on the grey sea. "I *want* to see the Sturtevants again."

"Hummph!" Miss Townley sneered. "That Sybil Sturtevant's wound you round her finger again. She always could."

Pippa didn't answer. But it wasn't only Sybil who drew her to the Sturtevants almost against her will. There was William, too. Not that anything of real significance had passed between Pippa and William Sturtevant. It was all so . . . so inexplicable. Whatever attachment existed between them lived more in her head than in any explainable reality.

She could explain it to herself, of course, if she started at the very beginning. The beginning . . . when Mama had first married Thomas and gone off to sea with him. Pippa had eagerly moved into the Sturtevant household on that first occasion. Her home with Mama had seemed to her then to be much too quiet and staid when compared with the tumult and animation of the Sturtevant townhouse in Charles Street. In the Sturtevant house everyone seemed remarkable . . . everyone possessed an exciting character. Lord Sturtevant was an M.P. and in the center of political events. Lady Sturtevant (her beloved "Aunt Georgie") was a loving, easygoing, boisterous, uninhibited woman who encouraged eccentricity in everyone from her offspring to her servants. And there was wild, tomboyish Sybil, whom Pippa adored, and her four interesting brothers, two of them older and two younger than the girls. Pippa had wanted nothing more than to learn to be as unrestrained, as tomboyish, as devil-may-care as her friend Sybil—Sybil, who used swearwords, climbed trees like a boy and created mischief as easily as breathing.

But living in the midst of the turbulence of the Sturtevant house had not turned out to be as pleasing as Pippa had expected. She'd found the noise and disorder confusing and even a bit depressing. She'd begun to long for a quiet corner in which to hide away to read or to think. Only the hours when Simon let her work silently at his side in the laboratory had she really felt happy, purposeful and at peace.

In those early years she'd admired Sybil's ingenuity in creating new and adventurous ways to make mischief, and she'd joined in those escapades with enthusiasm. But after a while, Sybil's exploits began to seem pointless, wasteful of energy and even silly. Not only hadn't she become more like Sybil—she was no longer sure she wanted to!

It had been very disturbing to contemplate. She'd committed her life to the Sturtevants, and she didn't want to admit that she was becoming disillusioned. She'd continued to behave like a contented, involved member of their family, and she'd pushed her doubts and her feelings of isolation into the deep recesses of her secret mind. When she'd felt particularly unhappy, she'd been able to find solace by working with Simon. But what a relief it had been to return to Southampton every time Mama and Thomas sailed into port. It had even been a relief to go to stay with Aunt Ethelyn at Wyckfield Park.

But if she took pencil and paper and added up the months spent with the Sturtevants over the past decade, the total would far exceed the months she'd spent with anyone else. The Sturtevants had been her family, and the whole truth was—the truth she would never admit to a soul—she could *not* be happy with them.

But how could she tell this to Mama and Thomas? They would be overwhelmed with dismay and guilt. Yet none of this was their fault. Besides, there was nothing they could do about the worst of this situation—there was nothing they could do about William.

That problem had manifested itself during her eighteenth year. It had been a turning point in her life. Even now, four years later, she could not recall the events of that year with equanimity . . .

. . . The year was 1812. Sybil and Pippa were presented to society with a great ball. Then, shortly following the elaborate festivities, Edgar Sturtevant passed away, the victim of a sudden, unaccountable heart seizure. William Sturtevant, the eldest son, was immediately recalled from his cavalry regiment to take on his inherited titles and the charge of the family. Pippa, at that time, didn't know William very well. He'd been away at school when she'd first come to stay with the Sturtevants, and then he'd gone into the cavalry. She was impressed with him as she grew to know him. At the time of her come-out, he was twenty-seven years old, a dark-haired, broad-shouldered, strong-willed fellow who immediately attempted to bring a semblance of order into the chaotic Sturtevant establishment.

Pippa found herself much admiring him. He was firmer and more forceful than his father had been in running the household, and although he was not very successful in establishing order in the Charles Street house (his mother's casual complaisance toward the undisciplined behavior of her servants and her children being quite resistant to change), Pippa nevertheless respected his attempts.

Little by little her knowledge of him grew. Sometimes he came upon her as she sat reading in the tiny, rear sitting room, and he sat down and conversed with her. He seemed pleased by what he called her "erudition," and he talked to her at length on subjects as diverse as politics and poetry. She enjoyed the conversations but found herself quite shy with him. She had no idea why this was so; he was almost a brother to her, after all. But he was nine years her senior, and his long absence from home and his military bearing made him awesome. Nevertheless, she relished every moment in his company and sought every possible opportunity to spend time with him, even if it meant cutting back on the time she spent in Simon's laboratory.

But Sybil still demanded most of her attention. Sybil always involved Pippa in her mischievous activities. Not long after Pippa and William began to spend hours in each other's company, Sybil embroiled Pippa in a situation which brought matters to a crisis. It had all begun simply enough—Sybil had run up a huge bill at the milliner's. Not wishing to endure a scolding from her "managing" eldest brother, she had, as usual, prevailed upon Pippa to pay the bill. Pippa, who was heir to a considerable fortune left to her by her father, the long-deceased Earl of Wyckfield, was always happy to pay whatever household bills she could. Neither Lady Sturtevant nor William ever permitted her to pay for anything except her own clothing. So she gladly gave the money to Sybil.

Sybil, however, was not out of the woods by the receipt of Pippa's money; she had discovered that the incriminating bill lay with a pile of others on William's desk. She'd coaxed Pippa into wagering on which one of them would creep into the study when William was out and remove the bill from the pile. They'd tossed a coin (which Pippa later discovered had heads on both sides), and Pippa, of course, lost.

With her heart beating with fear and trepidation, Pippa stole into the study and began to rifle through the papers. Just as she came upon the milliner's neatly written and exhorbitant account-sheet, the door opened. She whirled about so precipitously and with such consternation of spirit that she lost her balance and fell with a cry into William's arms.

If he'd had any suspicions regarding her reason for intruding into his *sanctum sanctorum*, he seemed to lose them at once. He held her close and stared down at her as if he'd never quite looked at her properly before.

"I'm sorry . . ." she mumbled, embarrassed at being there, embarrassed at having fallen against him and embarrassed at their unwonted proximity.

"Sorry?" he echoed absently, staring at her face.

"The . . . the papers. They've fallen . . ."

He let her go—quite reluctantly, she thought—and they both bent down to pick up the fallen papers. Despite the tumult of her spirit, Pippa spotted the milliner's bill, retrieved it and surreptitiously tucked it into the bodice of her gown. When the last of the papers had been gathered, he took her hands and helped her to her feet. "Has anyone told you that you're quite lovely when you're not wearing your spectacles?" he asked, holding on to her hands.

"Since I can scarcely see my hand before my face without them," she responded, blushing, "no one has had the opportunity."

"Then why aren't you wearing them now?"

Her blush deepened. "Good God! They must have fallen off when you . . . when I . . ."

"When I walked in on you as you were stealing Sybil's milliner's bill," he remarked drily, looking round for the missing eyeglasses.

She wanted to sink through the floor. He, meanwhile, spotted the spectacles and picked them up. "I'm . . . very sorry, William," she mumbled again.

He placed the glasses on her nose. "There," he said, and she saw with a new clarity his appealing smile. "No need to look so guilty, my dear. Just take the bill from its hiding place in your bodice, give it to me, and we shall say no more about it."

Wordlessly, her face aflame, she did as he asked. He took the paper from her, his hand closing over hers again. "You know," he said, his smile fading and the interested look returning to his eyes, "I was mistaken earlier. You're just as lovely with your spectacles on."

That day had marked a change in her attitude toward life at the Sturtevants. The days became both more exciting and more troublesome. Aunt Georgie began to tease her about William, remarking that he seemed to stare at her across the dining table or that he showed particular interest in her comments and opinions. "I've always loved you as a daughter," she laughed, "but it appears I may soon love you as a daughter-in-law as well."

Her taunts and sometimes bawdy comments on the developing relationship with William made Pippa uncomfortable. Simon, too, seemed to notice a change in her and accused her of being too absentminded to be of use to him in the laboratory. She tried to ignore these tell-tale signs of her growing infatuation, but she could not ignore her breathlessness whenever William entered a room and looked at her. *Am I falling in love with him?* she wondered.

It was puzzling. Her feelings were so confused that she was not certain whether what she felt was love or mere girlish self-consciousness. But before she was able to decide, an incident occurred which brought an end to all such speculation.

The incident began with Sybil's purchase, without William's permission, of a high-perch phaeton painted a bright blue. William, who was attempting to bring his impulsive, irresponsible family to some sense of responsibility in financial matters, was furious with her. He rounded on her before the entire family, calling her a "spoilt, addlepated widgeon" and ordering her not to dare to employ any of his horses to show off her new equipage. "It's a trumpery vehicle at best, all style and no substance, shoddily constructed and poorly balanced. The only horses you may use to drive it—if drive it you must—are Dover and the old mare."

"Dover and *Darley*?" Sybil exclaimed, horrified. "Dash it, they're nothing but a pair of *slugs*!"

"Just so. Too slow to cause that precarious, rubbishy excuse for a carriage to overturn. Mind what I say, Sybil! If I hear of you taking out my chestnuts—or any of the other horses, for that matter—you'll have more of my wrath to deal with than you've ever faced."

Sybil snorted contemptuously and promptly schemed to do just the opposite of what he'd ordered. She tried to inveigle the groom to ignore his master's instructions and harness William's precious chestnuts to her new phaeton. The groom resisted her blandishments for almost a fortnight, but he eventually surrendered to the gleam of three gold sovereigns. Pippa, a very reluctant conspirator, supplied the funds. Before she knew it, she found herself seated beside a grinning Sybil on the driver's box of the blue phaeton, drawn by the beautiful chestnuts. She was already ridden with guilt.

The phaeton soon began to sway dizzily as they tooled along a busy thoroughfare. "Sybil, love," Pippa remonstrated gently, "let's turn back. The traffic is exceedingly heavy. If any harm should come to William's horses—"

"They are *not* William's horses!" Sybil retorted callously. "They belong to the whole family."

"But he did choose them, you know, and they're his favorites."

"What if they are? Egad, Pippa, you know as well as I that I can handle the ribbons as well as any member of the Four-in-Hand."

"But this equipage is new and unfamiliar to you. And it seems to be swaying a great deal too much—"

"Nonsense. Dash it, Pippa, must you be so deucedly timid about everything?"

Pippa sighed and clamped her lips shut. There was little point in arguing with Sybil once her mind was made up.

Ten minutes later, as Sybil was executing what she hoped would be a dashing turn from New Bond Street into Picadilly, she came upon a pair of horses tandem, drawing a closed carriage along Picadilly, right in her path. She had to swerve. The phaeton, its balance as precarious as William had predicted, swayed for a moment with heart-stopping hesitancy before tipping over to the left. Pippa was aware of a horrid neighing and the sounds of cracking wood and colliding horseflesh before she was thrown from her seat and struck the road.

The owner of the other vehicle in the collision was an elderly gentleman who lost neither his temper nor his head. He ordered his coachman to free Sybil from beneath the wreckage while he himself saw to Pippa. Sybil emerged discomposed and disheveled but miraculously unhurt, and the gentleman took both young women up in his carriage while his coachman and his tiger took care of the horses. Pippa, dizzy from a blow to her forehead and pained by a severe bruise on her shoulder, retained only the haziest of recollections of their ride home, but, as the stranger's carriage departed the scene of the accident, she glimpsed enough of the wreckage to realize that the phaeton was quite destroyed and that at least one of William's chestnuts was bleeding badly.

Pippa slipped quietly into the house and ran upstairs before Aunt Georgie or Miss Townley could see her. It would be better, she knew, to keep both those ladies out of it—at least until her bruises had been attended to. There was only one person in the household who could be counted on to maintain a cool head in a crisis, and that was Simon. She ran up to his study, where he made a quick examination of her bruised shoulder. With quiet efficiency, he strapped her shoulder and gave her one of his powders for her headache. He was, as usual, dispassionately sympathetic and helpful. In addition, he was completely lacking in curiosity about how she'd been hurt. He asked no questions. She didn't have to tell him a word about Sybil's foolish behavior. And when she tried to express her gratitude to him, he pushed her out the door.

That evening, she and Sybil sat in the drawing room, white-faced and frightened, waiting for William to come home. Pippa had never before seen Sybil so terrified. She realized for the first time that much of Sybil's air of confidence came from tomboyish bravado.

They both stiffened when the door opened shortly after nine. But it was only Simon, coming in to inspect the lump on Pippa's forehead and to examine her eyes. "I just want to reassure myself that you're free of concussion," he explained as he knelt before her, removed her spectacles and pulled back her eyelids with the professional detachment of an experienced medical practitioner. "One can sometimes detect symptoms in the eyes, you see."

He was thus engaged when William burst into the room, his lips white with anger. He crossed the room to confront Sybil in three strides. "You maggoty female!" he hissed. "You're nothing more than an idiotic, spoilt, self-indulgent *wretch*!"

"William!" Pippa gasped, appalled.

He threw her a disparaging glance over his shoulder, but, unable to contain himself, turned right back to his sister. "How *dared* you take my horses? And after I'd specifically *warned* you—!"

"Let be, William," Simon put in softly, getting to his feet. "These recriminations can wait until tomorrow. The girls should be in bed—"

"Stay out of this, Simon," William ordered. "You don't know what this miscreant sister of ours has done to my chestnuts."

Sybil put up her chin in self-defensive sullenness. "They're not *your* horses. The stables belong to the family, don't they?"

William grasped her by the shoulders and dragged her from her chair. "One of the horses no longer belongs to *anyone*!" he shouted, shaking her in fury. "We had to *shoot* him!"

"Oh, *William*!" Pippa cried out in sympathy.

"It wasn't my fault," the trembling, pale, guilt-ridden Sybil managed to say as soon as she caught her breath. "The other coachman wasn't watching where he was going. And . . . besides . . ."

"Besides?" William's voice dripped sarcasm. "What other feeble excuse are you about to offer?"

"Well, you see . . . it was *Pippa* who was driving, and she's a bit cow-handed with the ribbons, so . . ."

"Pippa?" William seemed to freeze for a moment. He stared at Pippa in utter astonishment.

Simon uttered a grunt of disgust, glared at his brother and made for the door. "If you put any credence in *that* tale," he muttered, "you're a greater fool than Sybil is in concocting it." And he slammed out of the room.

Pippa lowered her eyes to the floor to keep William from seeing her bewilderment. If Sybil had been so frightened by her brother's fury that she'd resorted to such a lie, Pippa did not wish to give her away. As soon as she'd recovered from her shock, she looked up at William with as much courage as she could command. "I—" she began.

But William had turned back to his sister with a sneer. "What a disgusting fabrication. Did you think you could turn me up sweet with such an obvious rapper?"

"It's *not* a rapper," Sybil insisted, throwing her friend a pleading look.

William took a deep breath. "Is this true, Pippa?" he asked, turning to her.

"Yes."

"It was *you* who drove my chestnuts behind that rig?"

"Yes."

There was a long moment of silence during which William stared at Pippa, his cheeks pale and his jaw stiff.

"Of course," Sybil said at last, belatedly and guiltily trying to share the blame, "it wasn't her idea to take the chestnuts in the first place."

"I didn't think it was," her brother muttered with dry disdain. "If you'd tried to blame her for *that*, I would never have believed you, no matter what your friend said in your support." His eyes had not left Pippa's face. "As to the rest, Pippa, I don't know whether you've told me the truth or not. But it doesn't matter very much. Whoever was driving, you were *both* involved in this stupid and harmful enterprise, and whichever one caused the actual damage, the other aided and abetted her. I am not surprised at my sister's part in this—I've been discovering during my months as head of the house that she is willful, thoughtless and selfish. But it comes as an unpleasant shock to realize that you support her in this sort of behavior."

"Hang it, I don't see why you call me willful and selfish," Sybil objected. "It was only a bit of bad luck—"

"Be still!" he barked icily, throwing her a quelling look over his shoulder. Then he turned his attention back to Pippa. "I don't know what to say to you about this, Pippa. You're not related to me and must be considered, I suppose, a guest in this house. Thus it would be inappropriate for me to reprimand you. But I'm afraid I must include you in the restriction I'm about to place upon my sister. Neither one of you is to ride or drive a horse from our stable until further notice. In the meantime, on those occasions when you must travel about, you will do so in the town carriage with Robbins driving and the tiger mounted behind. Do I make myself clear?"

Pippa nodded, and Sybil, not courageous enough to rebel, merely threw herself down upon her chair sulkily.

William went quickly to the door, but there he paused. He gave Pippa a last, unreadable look. "Dash it all," he muttered, half to himself, "I hadn't thought it of you."

After he left, Sybil immediately cast herself upon her friend in a flood of guilty tears. "I had to do it!" she sobbed. "He would have been ever so much harder on me than he was on you. He l-likes you much more than he does me, you know, and he couldn't inflict a p-punishment on you, since you're not really his sister. You *do* understand, don't you? And you d-do forgive me?"

Pippa, of course, forgave her at once. What else was there to do? Sybil couldn't have guessed that her self-defensive lie would inflict a killing frost upon a romance that had just begun to bud. Sybil, not very observant of the feelings of others, hadn't even noticed. How could she then be blamed? The close friendship between the girls continued unabated.

From that evening on, however, William took only the barest notice of Pippa that politeness required. He no longer sought her companionship, no longer visited her in the rear sitting room, and no longer engaged her in cheerful banter at the dinner table. In fact, he rarely joined the family at dinner at all, remaining in the City on business until late or taking dinner with his friends at his club. Thus Pippa's growing intimacy with William came to an abrupt end.

Pippa had been unable to bear the disappointment and depression which this sudden change in her prospects had inflicted on her spirits. Escape from the Sturtevants had seemed the only solution. She'd told Aunt Georgie that it was necessary for her to go to stay at Wyckfield for a time. "The estate has been so long unsupervised," she'd explained, "that things are falling into disrepair. I must spend some time in Dorset to set things right."

Firmly overruling Aunt Georgie's objections, she'd packed her things and gone with Miss Townley to the country where she'd led a peaceful, if not quite healing, existence until Mama and Thomas had come home to Southampton . . .

Now, four years later, there still hadn't been enough time for her to sort out her feelings toward William. The thought of him still caused a turmoil within her, but the significance of that tumultuous feeling was not clear. Was it regret at the loss of approval from a respected friend? Was it the discomfort that comes from a rift between members of a family? Or was it the pain of a blighted love?

She was twenty-two years old; it was time to learn the answers to these questions, once and for all. And those answers would not be found on Thomas's ship.

She turned from the window, her mind made up. But she found Miss Townley peering at her suspiciously. "You can't fool me, Philippa Wyckfield," the older woman accused. "All this sighin' and starin' out of windows. You don't want to go back to that topsy-turvy Sturtevant house any more than I do!"

Pippa's eyes fell. "Yes, I do. The Sturtevant house is *exactly* where I want to be."

"A likely tale. But if you've decided, you've decided. We'll go, then. I can put a good face on it as well as you."

Pippa crossed the room and put an affectionate arm about her old governess's shoulder. "Of course you can. We can bear it one more time. And who knows? This time the visit may be quite wonderful."

Ada Townley snorted with bitter humor. "Bearable it may be, but *wonderful*, never! Oh, well, give us a smile, lass. Let's leave the packin' for later. Let's go downstairs and give your parents a merry farewell dinner. At least we can be glad that *they* don't have to spend the next few months at the Sturtevant *ménage*."

Chapter Two

THE STURTEVANTS kept a watch on the door of their Charles Street house all week, each of them eager for a first glimpse of Pippa after her long absence. But affection for the girl was not the only reason for their impatience. Each had a personal, particular reason for keeping an eye on the drive—a reason none of them would divulge to anyone else. There was something of urgency in the way they waited for her arrival.

When Thursday rolled round and the girl had not yet come, they reread her letter and concluded that this was the day on which she would surely arrive. Lady Sturtevant seated herself near the drawing-room window right after luncheon so that she might keep her eye on the drive. Adolphus cancelled his plans to go riding with his cronies and stretched out on the sofa in the library; from that place of comfort he could hear any goings-on which might occur in the hallway. Sybil, the most nervously eager of any of them for Pippa's return, paced about her bedroom impatiently, leaving only to supervise the maidservants as they freshened Pippa's room. Simon, although keeping strictly to his normal schedule, found himself unable to concentrate on his light-wave experiment; he was drawn much too frequently for his peace of mind to the window which overlooked the front drive. Even Latcham, the butler, kept himself occupied at the front of the house so that he could respond promptly to the first sound of wheels on the gravel.

Shortly after two, a knock at the door sent all but Simon flying to the front hall. But it was only William's manservant, bearing word to Lady Sturtevant that her eldest son would honor them with his presence that evening for dinner. Lady Sturtevant smiled to herself —it seemed that William was looking forward to Pippa's arrival with the same eagerness as the rest of them.

By four that afternoon, however, the vigil had become dull indeed. Adolphus had long since slipped into a stertorous sleep on the library sofa. Lady Sturtevant, in an effort to pass time, had picked up her embroidery but, wearied by the effort of straining her eyes over the tiny stitches, had by this time fallen into a drowse over her frame. Sybil, having exhausted all her energy in tyrannizing over the two upstairs maids while they aired Pippa's room and relined her drawers with scented paper, had settled herself at the table in the upstairs sitting room with a deck of cards and was desultorily playing Solitaire. And Simon, by this hour completely absorbed in his investigation of the different wave lengths of the colored rays of the spectrum, had succeeded in banishing the entire matter of Pippa's arrival from his mind.

Latcham, too, had given up the vigil. Placing the two footmen on duty in the front hall of his place, he'd gone down to the servants' hall, removed his coat and seated himself before the fire with his feet up. His two footmen, notoriously unreliable, had no sooner taken their places at either side of the front door when they'd spied a pulchritudinous nursemaid passing on the street with her little charge. Off they'd gone after her and were soon happily engaged in flirtatious badinage, their duties completely forgotten. It was at just this time, of course—when the front hall was utterly deserted—that the hired hack from Southampton drew up at the door.

There were two occupants within the carriage, both pressing their noses to their respective windows. Miss Ada Townley was looking toward the street, and Pippa was staring with mixed feelings at the town house which she hadn't seen in years. In the warm afternoon sunlight the house appeared to be quite unchanged. The front door, flanked by two narrow windows and topped with a semi-circular one, still appeared to her to be impressively welcoming, and the second floor window above it, set into a magnificent recessed arch, still seemed an inspired architectural embellishment. The boxlike facade of the house was disguised by the four exquisitely proportioned pilasters which reached from the second-story balconies to the roof pediment over the third floor, giving the structure an aura of both grace and dignity. Only the most punctilious observer would note that the paint of the window frames was smudged with neglect, that the windows were dirty and that the circular stone steps leading to the doorway would have been much improved by a proper sweeping. *No*, Pippa thought with a sigh, *nothing has changed.*

Miss Townley, looking out in the other direction, gasped in irritation. "Aren't those fellows disappearin' down the street her ladyship's *footmen*?" Her hawklike nose twitched in disgust. "Who, I'd like to know, will be available to take care of our baggage?"

Pippa leaned forward and patted the older woman's hand comfortingly. None knew better than she that life in this household could set one's nerves on edge. None of the servants therein was competent at his job. Latcham always dropped things; Noreen, one of the upstairs maids, giggled and chattered endlessly while Emma, the other maid, was conveniently deaf; the footmen were never about when needed; and even the cook—a French chef imported at great expense, whom

Lady Sturtevant insisted was a genius—was much too tempermental and much too liberal with his garlic. However, Pippa promptly dismissed her misgivings from her mind. As the coachman lowered the steps, she prepared to alight with a hopeful mind. The people within were like family to her; the affection she felt toward all of them would see her through these minor difficulties—and any others which might arise. She jumped from the carriage with renewed eagerness. "Hand me that pile of gifts, Miss Townley, please," she asked, turning back to the coach. "I want to distribute them at once."

"Never mind," Miss Townley muttered, disgruntled, "I'll take them. Go on up, since you're so eager."

Pippa didn't wait to be urged again. She ran up the steps and gave a smart rap on the door. But when Miss Townley caught up with her, her arms loaded with the gaily wrapped parcels, the door still hadn't been answered. The two women exchanged puzzled glances. "Didn't you write we were comin'?" Miss Townley asked irritably.

"Of course I did." Pippa pushed open the door and stepped into the hall. "Aunt Georgie? Sybil? Is anyone at home?"

Miss Townley followed behind her. "Where's Latcham? You'd think at least *one* of the servants would be in evidence." Her disgust was apparent in her voice. Ada Townley had disapproved of Lady Sturtevant's casual ways ever since she'd first met her, more than a decade ago. This shameful lack of attention to arriving guests was typical of the woman's lackadaisical management. "I *say*!" she shouted. "Let's have some assistance here!"

The shout roused Adolphus in the library. "Pippa?" he muttered, shaking himself awake and jumping to his feet. "Is that you?" And with uncharacteristic disregard for the rumpled condition of his neckerchief and his coat, he ran out to the front hall.

"Is it *Pippa*?" came a shriek from the upstairs sitting room, and Sybil came flying down the stairs. "Pippa, my dearest, at *last*!" she clarioned. "We've been waiting all *day*!"

Lady Sturtevant, hearing the commotion through a blissful dream in which she was nibbling a piece of very creamy wedding cake, opened her eyes, blinked with delight and ran out to join the crowd in the hallway. "Pippa, my *precious*! Let me embrace you at *once*!"

Pippa found herself surrounded and was soon fully engaged in exchanging embraces, smiles and the fondest expressions of endearment. In the warmth of the welcome, her first impression of a deserted house and a barren reception was forgotten.

Miss Townley was soon included in the greetings, but her irritability did not abate. "Where's Latcham?" she asked as soon as she could fit the words into the confusion. "Isn't there anyone about to see to the baggage?"

"Here I am, ma'am. Right here." The butler came running toward them from down the hall, hastily buttoning his coat as he approached. "Lady Philippa!" he chortled with avuncular familiarity. "We'd just about given you up. And Miss Townley!" He gave the governess a welcoming smile, which she returned with a frown of disapproval. "Shall I take your parcels?"

"Yes, if you won't drop them. About time, too," the elderly woman growled.

"No, give them to me, Latcham," Pippa intervened. "These are presents that I've brought for the family. I want to distribute them at once."

"Let *me* have them, Latcham," Adolphus offered gallantly.

Latcham, juggling them in his arms precipitously, gladly surrendered the pile to Adolphus. "Shall I see to the rest of your baggage?" he asked.

"Yes, of course," Miss Townley barked, "but I warn you, my good man, that you'll get no help from your footmen. I saw them wanderin' off down the street."

If Miss Townley hoped her disapproving remark would have an effect on either Latcham or his mistress, she was doomed to disappointment. The butler merely shrugged, and Lady Sturtevant's beaming expression didn't change. "Why don't we go to the sitting room," she suggested placidly, starting down the corridor. "Latcham, have you brought the tea things?"

The butler, already heading toward the door, stopped and turned. "Tea?" he asked as if he'd never heard the word before.

"Yes, tea. It *is* teatime, isn't it?"

"Well past, if you ask me," Miss Townley muttered.

The butler shrugged. "Not yet, my lady."

"Not yet?" Sybil put in. "It's almost *five*."

"Yes, Miss Sybil, but y' see, I didn't know when the ladies would arrive. I'll see to the tea at once."

Pippa held back a giggle. This scene of confusion was so typical of life among the Sturtevants that it filled her with nostalgic amusement. But Ada Townley was not amused. "Hummmph!" she grunted, pulling off her pelisse with angry determination and thrusting it at the butler, who promptly dropped it. "Take care of this and the baggage, if it isn't too much for you, and *I'll* see to the tea."

Lady Sturtevant, meanwhile, unconcernedly sailed down the hallway, with Sybil, Pippa and Adolphus drifting behind. "You needn't have brought presents, Pippa," Adolphus was saying while eyeing the parcels he carried with interest. "We're all past the age for presents."

"What humbug," his sister retorted. "*No one* is past the age for presents."

They entered the sitting room and settled themselves comfortably, Lady Sturtevant on the largest easy chair, Sybil and Pippa side by side on the love seat, and Adolphus, after placing the parcels carefully on Pippa's lap, dropping down on the ottoman. "Egad, Pippa," Sybil declared, "I'll be frank and admit I'm all agog. What have you brought for me?"

"Since you ask, Sybil, my love, you shall have, as Chaucer said, 'first grist.' "

"First grist? What does that mean?" Adolphus demanded a bit jealously.

"*Whoso first cometh to the mill, first grist,*" Pippa quoted.

"And you, Dolly," his mother laughed, "since you're too old for presents anyway, shall be last."

Sybil's present was a magnificent shawl of fine French lace. She threw it over her shoulders at once and pranced about the room showing it off. Next, Lady Sturtevant unwrapped the largest of the parcels to find within a genuine China vase. She gasped with delight as Pippa explained that Thomas had procured it in the Indies and had purchased it especially for Pippa's beloved "Aunt Georgie." This led her ladyship to ply the gift-giver with a dozen questions about her parents, their health, their states of mind, their plans and their whereabouts. Poor Adolphus had to wait long minutes before he was given his parcel. The contents proved to be well worth waiting for: within the box (the smallest of all) was a gold watch-fob and chain, the fob studded with an amethyst of startling clarity and inscribed at the back with his initials.

One package remained on Pippa's lap. "This is for Simon," she explained, looking about her in sudden realization that she hadn't yet seen him. "Where is he?"

"You know very well where he is," Lady Sturtevant said, shrugging hopelessly. "The irritating make-bait never comes down to tea. But never mind, my love. You'll see him at dinner."

"If he deigns to join us," Sybil added drily.

"He'll join us if I have to send a couple of the servants up to *carry* him down," his mother vowed.

"But I can't wait for dinnertime," Pippa objected, looking down at the last parcel in keen disappointment. The contents of this last of the gifts she'd brought were the result of her most careful planning and greatest effort, and she'd been looking forward to seeing Simon's face when he opened it. She looked up at Lady Sturtevant with pleading eyes. "May I be excused, Aunt Georgie, to go up and say hello to him now?"

"Must you, my love? You haven't yet told us a word about what you've been doing this past age—"

"We shall have plenty of time for that," Pippa promised, rising determinedly from her seat.

Sybil clutched at her hand. "Pippa, you won't be long, will you?" she asked in an undervoice. "I must speak to you. Something of the utmost urgency has—"

"What are you saying, Sybil?" her mother inquired.

Sybil stiffened. "Nothing, Mama. I was only saying that tea will be here shortly."

Pippa squeezed Sybil's hand reassuringly. "I'll return before the tea has cooled, I promise."

She tucked the heavy parcel under her arm and hurried from the room, not noticing that Adolphus rose and followed her out. The boy caught up with her at the bottom of the staircase. "Pippa, thank you again for my watch-fob. It will make the fellows green with envy," he said earnestly.

"Goodness, Dolly, you needn't have run after me just to tell me that."

"That's not why I followed you. There's something else I've been wishing to tell you of."

She smiled at him affectionately but put a foot on the stair. "Can it wait, Dolly? I—"

But Adolphus couldn't wait. By the simple expedient of taking her arm and literally pinning her to the newel-post, he kept her from departing. "You see, there's a prime bit of blood that's caught my attention—"

"A horse? Do you want to talk to me now about a *horse*?"

"Not just a horse. The sweetest goer you've ever laid eyes on!" The boy launched into an eager monologue about the virtues of the animal, telling his captive listener that the horse, magnificently muscled and fleet of limb, was the property of a friend of his, "whose pockets being all to let, would consider selling his prize mount at a most advantageous price."

"Would he?" Pippa murmured, knowing quite well what Adolphus had in mind.

"The animal's a treasure, my *word* on it! His name's Salvaje."

"Salvaje? Doesn't that mean Savage?"

"Yes. He's Spanish, you see."

"But why is he called Salvaje? Is he wild?"

"Oh, no. Spirited, of course, but I wouldn't say wild. I'm certain he'd suit you perfectly as your personal mount." His eyes glowed with enthusiasm and his freckled nose twitched in excitement. "He's prime in all his paces. I'd ride him only when you'd give me leave, of course," the boy added in perfect sincerity.

Pippa hid a smile. "Yes, Dolly, I realize that, but—"

"I tell you, Pippa, you'd be getting the greatest bargain. You'll love him at sight. But even if you don't—which is almost an impossibility—you'd have no difficulty at all in selling him at an enormous profit."

Pippa patted his cheek fondly. "You've quite convinced me, Dolly, I assure you. I fully believe the horse to be a wonderful investment, and we must certainly speak of this in greater detail. But for now, dear, I'm most eager to go upstairs to give Simon his gift. May we postpone this discussion until later?"

Adolphus, about to remonstrate, caught the glint of laughter in her eye. A sheepish grin spread over his face. "Pushing at you a bit, am I?"

She grinned back at him. "Just a bit."

"Well . . . I'll let you go for now. But we will continue this, won't we?"

She started up the stairs. "After dinner, I promise."

He turned back to the sitting room. "But I warn you, Pippa," he called over his shoulder, "if you delay too long, this chance may be lost forever."

Pippa's smile remained on her face through the climb up two of the three flights of stairs. Dolly's infatuation for the horse, and his obvious machinations to acquire it for himself through her, were very amusing. But as she turned to the third flight—where the stairs were narrower and steeper—her pace slowed and her smile faded. Would it be right to indulge Dolly in this matter? Was it good for his character to make the acquisition of an undoubtedly expensive animal so easy for him? Would his mother approve? Or . . . William?

But as she approached the top of the stairway, and

her eye fell on Simon's door, the problem of dealing with Adolphus faded from her mind. She would have to deal with the problem of Dolly and his mount before long, she knew, but now she was about to see Simon. In his special way, Simon could be a problem, too. She looked down at the package she'd carried so carefully up the stairs and then flicked a glance at the closed door in front of her, hesitating. What difficulties were in store for her next?

Chapter Three

HER COURAGE deserted her. She couldn't immediately tap on the door. How would Simon greet her? Why hadn't he come down earlier to welcome her with the others? Had she done something, however unwittingly, to offend him? Now that she thought about it, she suddenly realized how strange it was that he hadn't written to her during all the time she'd been absent, in spite of the fact that she'd included messages to him in all her letters to the family.

She hoped nothing was wrong. Of all the Sturtevants, Simon was the one she most respected. Absorbed in his studies and scientific investigations, he was somehow aloof from the stresses, the petty squabbles, the hysteria of the life below him. He had a pleasing steadiness of disposition, so different from the volatile natures of the rest of the family. There was a gentle concentration in his face whenever he listened to the problems of the others—a concentration so rapt that he became the sought-after confidant of his brothers when they were really perplexed. Pippa, too, had found him a soothing companion when, in the past, her life in this tempestuous household had seemed too difficult to bear. The times he'd permitted her to assist him in the laboratory had been very satisfying and were among her happiest memories. It would be a blow to discover that something had occurred to blight their warm relationship.

But she was letting her imagination run away with her. Just because he'd seemed strained and withdrawn when she'd seen him last . . . or because he hadn't written . . . these were not necessarily signs of estrangement. Everything was probably just as it had always been with him. She squared her shoulders and knocked firmly at the door. "Simon? It's I, Pippa. May I come in?"

There was a long silence. Then the door opened slowly. Simon, framed in the opening, looked abstracted, shabby, tousled of hair and lean of cheek. Quite the same as ever. He stood blinking down at her as his eyes adjusted to the brightness of the corridor (for the light from the setting sun streamed into the west-facing window at the top of the stairs) which contrasted sharply with the darkness of the room behind him. "Pippa!" he said, his face brightening with a slow, hesitant smile.

"Hello, Simon." She grinned back at him. "Still working in the dark?"

"Not as much in the dark as when you saw me last. I've learned a thing or two." He stepped aside to let her in. "There have been some amazing advances in optics, you know. I've been working on some new ideas. Trying to analyze light waves."

She stepped across the threshold while he went to the windows and threw open the draperies. As the light flooded the room, she studied him curiously. "Light *waves*?" she asked, puzzled by the word.

"Perhaps I should call them undulations," he explained, tying back the draperies. "You see, it's becoming apparent that light must consist of undulating waves rather than a stream of particles as Newton assumed. Do you remember my speaking to you of Thomas Young? Well, I've been meeting with him at the Royal Society and writing to a fellow in France as well. A scientist named Fresnel, who's been making mathematical measurements which seem to agree with mine, showing that—"

Finished with the windows, he turned to face her. As his eyes met hers squarely for the first time, his flow of words abruptly ceased. He stood stock still, scrutinizing her face with a look so piercing that she almost blushed. "Is anything the matter, Simon?"

"Good God, Pippa, you're . . . you're—!" His eyes swept over her with unnerving intensity. "You've quite . . . grown up."

"Oh, is *that* all?" She sighed in relief. "I don't see why you're so surprised by it. It's bound to happen if one waits long enough. I'm almost twenty-three, you know. Time to be at my last prayers, they say."

His slow smile lit his face. "Whoever says that is a fool. Our knocker will be sounding all day with suitors, I imagine, as soon as the word is out that you've come."

"Do you think so? Thank you for those kind words, although I don't set any great store by them. I haven't the flirtatious spirit to attract a flock of suitors that your sister has. Too owlish and pedantic, I'm afraid, with my spectacles and my bookish ways."

"Rubbish," Simon retorted, averting his head.

He seemed unusually ill-at-ease. Her earlier suspicion that he might perhaps be angry with her returned to her mind. "You haven't invited me to take a seat," she pointed out gently. "May I sit down?"

He lifted his eyes and stared at her for a moment. Then, without speaking, he pulled one of the room's two stools out from under the table. "Why do you bother to ask?" he muttered as he set it beside her. "You've always made yourself at home up here before."

"Yes, but . . ." She threw him a troubled glance as she placed the parcel she'd carried carefully on the table before her. "Perhaps . . . you don't wish me to make myself quite so much at home any more."

He avoided answering. He merely perched on the other stool. "What have you there?"

"It's something I've had made especially for you," she said, pushing the box across the table to him.

He took it awkwardly, with the self-consciousness of one not accustomed to receiving gifts. "See here, Pippa, there was no need to bother—"

"I know. As Dolly said, you're all too old for gifts. But since I've already 'bothered,' you may as well open it."

He undid the wrappings neatly and efficiently, his long fingers working at the string and paper with the same care he used for his work. He lifted the hinged lid of the wooden box he'd uncovered under the wrappings and removed two heavy objects swaddled in soft cloth. "What on earth—?" he asked, unable to guess what lay within. Further investigation revealed two perfectly matched, triangular prisms, each standing ten inches tall from base to point. "Pippa!" he gasped in immediate appreciation. "They're wonderful! I've always wished for a pair of matched prisms of this quality. How did you know—?"

"I remembered your frustration when we performed those Newtonian spectra experiments, so I had these made by the finest craftsman I could find." She smiled contentedly at him as he hefted each one and examined the workmanship with close attention.

"They're beautifully ground," he murmured admiringly. Then he set them down. Flustered, he looked across the table at her. "I don't know what to say."

"You may say 'thank you.' That phrase is always appropriate."

"It's completely inadequate. But thank you."

"That was very well done," she laughed, rising. "And now I'd better go down and take my tea. I promised not to stay too long."

He rose with her. "Yes. We don't want the entire household trooping up here to find you."

She paused at the door, still aware of an unseen, bewildering barrier between them. "May I come and give you a hand from time to time? As I used to do?"

His eyes dropped from her face, and he ran his fingers through his hair uncomfortably. Here was the question he'd been dreading. How was he to answer her? She had just brought him the most thoughtful gift he'd ever received. In response to her generosity, could he say, *No . . . I don't want you here any more*?

Once again he permitted his eyes to sweep over her. The sight charmed his eyes and tore at his insides. From the top of her dusky, carelessly brushed curls to the tips of her tiny black slippers he adored her. To him everything about her was touched with a magical beauty. The way her dark curls picked up glints of light, the way her eyes gleamed when a theoretical concept became suddenly clear to her, the way her spectacles slipped down just a bit on her nose when she became absorbed in reading, the way she rubbed the back of her neck when she grew tired, the way she crossed her legs primly at the ankles when she perched on the stool—everything about her tantalized and tortured him. How could he endure having her beside him for hours every day when it was clear from her sisterly manner that she didn't think of him in any other way?

Simon knew he was an eccentric sort. The second son in a large, boisterous family, he had been from childhood the silent one. Quiet and unobtrusive, he had always remained on the sidelines of the family's activities, unobserved but observing. Silence became a mode of behavior, a screen behind which, in his diffident boyhood, he'd hidden himself. By now, in his manhood, it was an ingrained habit. He could not express aloud his very deepest feelings; putting them into words seemed to make them trivial.

In matters of science, it was different. Words were tools, like mathematics, to clarify the abstract concepts and make them tangible. He could talk for hours about physics, astronomy and the complexities of nature. But about personal things—loneliness, grief, desire, love—

he felt strangely mute. The feelings that haunted his mind and troubled his spirit he could not easily subject to the analytical, practical, trivializing daylight of words. They belonged to the secret shadows of night and silence.

He sometimes thought playfully of subjecting silence to the same scientific scrutiny he gave to light rays. What was the nature of this strange phenomenon, silence, which seemed to envelope him almost against his will? What particles or undulations did it consist of? How could an experimenter refract its rays to dissect its substance? How could it even be defined, when its nature was so very contradictory? Sometimes it expressed inexpressible joy; other times inexpressible terror. It could conceal secrets, yet at times it revealed those secrets with more clarity than words. It could muffle music; bury noise; almost seem, at times, to still the beating pulse of the world . . . yet at other times it could sound as loud as thunder. No, silence, though it was his long-time friend, would not succumb to scientific probing. It was an impenetrable mystery like time, like love, like faith.

Even now, with Pippa looking up at him questioningly, he couldn't order silence to release its grip on him. The only words that came to his mind were those he couldn't say.

She was looking up at him with an eyebrow cocked. "It was a very simple question, Simon. Yet you're very silent."

"*Silence is the best tactic for him who distrusts himself,*" he muttered ruefully under his breath.

"What did you say?"

"Nothing. Just something said by La Rochefoucauld."

But she'd heard what he said. "I don't understand, Simon. Have I done something wrong? Are you angry with me?"

"No, of course not."

"Then *may* I come—?"

"You don't wish to waste your time here now," he

said, his eyes dropping away from her face. "You have other, more pressing matters to which to give your attention."

She studied his face quizzically. "Have I?"

"Haven't you? All those suitors . . .?"

Her brows knit and she bit her underlip in confusion. "There *is* something wrong, isn't there? I thought there might be, when I realized you hadn't written a word to me since I left. *Have* I done something to offend you, Simon?"

"No, I've already said you haven't."

"Then what *is* it? You used to say that my assistance was a 'measureable asset' to your work, remember?"

"I remember. But you've grown up now, and you should be spending your time in more . . . productive ways."

"What ways are those?"

He turned away and began to finger the things on his table. "Ways and means by which young ladies get themselves married," he mumbled. With absentminded neatness, he put his small glass lenses in their slots in a wooden holder, lined his pencils in a row, placed his grinding tools and pots of compound on the shelf behind him. "Isn't that what young ladies are supposed to do?"

"Yes, I suppose they are. But I don't find myself very interested in—"

"You should be interested." He turned to face her again. "You just said yourself that the time is ripe. You're soon to be twenty-three. And William is past thirty now."

Her breath caught in her throat. "William?" She felt herself blush. "What has William to do with this?"

"Don't be missish with me, Pippa. You and he would have been wed by this time if he hadn't been such a fool about that blasted accident."

"*Wed?* William and I? I think, Simon, that you're being shockingly unscientific on this subject . . . and jumping to unwarranted conclusions. Nothing ever passed between William and me."

"No? Then something *should* have passed between you. If you give your attention to the matter this time, I'm convinced something will."

"Are you indeed?" She peeped up at him, a laugh in her eyes. "You amaze me, Simon."

"Do I? Why?"

"I had no idea that you gave any thought to such matters."

"Perhaps you don't know me as well as you think. The fact is that I'm very observant of human behavior when I'm in company. I can tell quite easily when a man and a woman are attracted to each other."

"Can you? How strange, considering how infrequently you go about in society. I, on the other hand, am woefully ignorant in such matters. Are you advising me to start a flirtation with William?"

He looked at her askance, his right eyebrow cocked suspiciously. "Are you trying to make me believe you had no such plan in mind yourself?"

Her cheeks reddened again. "Perhaps I had."

He turned away. "Then there's no more to discuss." He began methodically to clear the torn wrapping, the string and the debris from his worktable, keeping his back to her. His whole attitude bespoke polite dismissal.

"But there's a *great deal* to discuss," Pippa objected, feeling as if she'd been suddenly doused with cold water.

"I can't give you counsel on matters of . . . of flirtation," he muttered, picking up his new prisms and holding them up to the light.

She felt herself stiffen. She was not accustomed to being ignored or dismissed. Simon deserved a sharp set-down for this unaccountable behavior. But before the sharp words which had sprung to her tongue were uttered, she thought better of it. This was *Simon* after all. One didn't expect conventional, drawing-room conduct from Simon Sturtevant. He was unique—a true original—and one had to make allowances for such men. "I was not thinking of the subject of my flirtations when I said we had a great deal to discuss," she said quietly. "I was thinking of you and me."

He threw her a quick look. "You and me?"

"Yes. And this . . . awkwardness between us which keeps you from allowing me to work with you."

He crossed the room to his bookcases and carefully placed his new prisms on a shelf. "I feel no awkwardness—"

"Yes, you do." She crossed the room and came up behind him. "You *must* be aware that you're behaving distantly toward me. I can think of no reason for it, unless . . ."

"Unless?"

"Unless you think I'm too ignorant in matters of science—too untutored in optics—to be of any use to you. Is that it, Simon? But I can at least do your simple calculations for you, can't I? I'm still competent in basic mathematics. Or I can copy your notes . . . or even sweep the floor . . ."

A snort of laughter escaped him. "Yes," he said, turning to face her, "and when there's nothing else to do, I can set you to washing the windows, like the veriest little housemaid."

"Oh, la, sir," Pippa responded with a laugh and a tiny, bobbing curtsey, "I never do windows. We upstairs maids 're much too proud fer that. That's fer the skivvies and the underfootmen, y' see."

"Well, then," he retorted with a grin, "there *is* nothing further to discuss. If you won't do windows, of what use can you be to me?"

"Seriously, Simon, isn't there *some* use you can make of me?"

His grin died. "I thought we'd agreed that you'll be too busy—"

"That's rubbish, and you know it. You can't believe that, even if I were to indulge in a *dozen* flirtations, they would occupy all my time."

He shrugged and went back to his worktable. "How do I know about such things? When you ladies are of the age to engage seriously in courtship rituals, you become very absorbed in matters of clothing and hairdressing and such fripperies, don't you? You must be constantly shopping and fitting your gowns and creaming your faces—"

"I never cream my face." She strode to the table opposite him and faced him squarely. "Have you lost all respect for me, my dear? Don't you think *I* should be the one to decide how to spend my time?"

He ran his fingers through his hair helplessly. "I never meant—"

"Then don't be so curmudgeonly. Take my hand and tell me we may go on as before."

He stared from the hand she'd reached out to him across the table to her face. She was looking at him with that irresistible laugh in her eyes and a sweetness in her smile that made his chest constrict. What else could he do but acquiesce and take her hand? "Very well, my dear. Come up when you have nothing better to do."

She grinned happily, blew him a kiss and was gone. He was alone. But the faint aroma of her hair and skin lingered behind, an exasperating, distracting reminder of his deuced ineptitude. Why had he been unable to handle so simple a situation? "Confound it! Why couldn't I just say *no*?"

Frowning angrily, he kicked his stool across the room. "Oh, *damnation*!" he cursed, hopping about on one foot. He'd struck the stool so forcefully with his boot that he'd felt the impact right through the leather. And what good had it done? The foolish act of violence had not eased his inner turmoil in the least. All it had accomplished was to add to his pain the discomfort of a couple of bruised and aching toes.

Chapter Four

WILLIAM WAS coming to dinner. That news, passed on with a decided air of triumph by Aunt Georgie, was enough to unsettle Pippa's serenity. She found herself uncharacteristically rattled. She shouldn't have paid heed to Simon's remarks on the subject of William. If he had not planted the suggestion in her mind that she and William might yet make a match of it, she might not have found herself reduced to this quivering mass of jelly.

She needed to compose herself, and there was time before dinner to do so—two hours, in fact. Time enough for a leisurely *toilette* and a period of relaxation in peaceful solitude. By the time she came down to dinner, she surmised, she would be quite herself.

But Sybil had other ideas. Agonizingly impatient to divulge her worrisome problem to her best friend, she chose the hour right before dinner (when everyone else in the household was safely preoccupied with dressing) to steal down the corridor to Pippa's room.

Sybil had already donned her dinner gown and dressed her hair. She entered Pippa's room with only the briefest of warning knocks and found to her surprise that Pippa was still in her underclothes. Miss Townley, with two gowns over her arm and a third tossed over her shoulder, was arguing the merits of a fourth with her suddenly indecisive charge. "I don't see anythin' wrong with the puce silk," she was saying. "You've never found fault with it before."

"It makes me look like a dowdy abigail," Pippa muttered as Sybil appeared in the dressing-room doorway. "Here's Sybil. Ask her if you don't agree with me."

Sybil leaned on the doorframe and surveyed the scene. In spite of the brief space of time since their arrival, Pippa and Miss Townley already seemed to have settled in. One trunk and a small bandbox were still unpacked, but everything else had already been stowed neatly away. Sybil could only marvel at her friend's efficiency. The small alcove, which her mother had made into a charming dressing room and decorated in the Grecian mode, was more orderly than her own. The satin-covered *chaise longue* in the corner was free of any items of clothing, while her own was littered with shawls, ribbons, discarded undergarments and rejected hair-ornaments. The polished top of the Sheraton dressing table was clear of the hair-pins, brushes and cream-pots which covered hers. Even the washstand in the corner, which Pippa had used for her ablutions, was already wiped clean. How Pippa managed always to maintain such neat, orderly surroundings in a household where the two upstairs maids were notoriously inept was a mystery to her.

"Well, Sybil," Miss Townley was asking, "do you see anythin' wrong with the puce silk?"

"No, but if Pippa doesn't wish to wear it, I would suggest the Saxe blue. Those epaulets and brass buttons are all the rage this season."

"Are they?" Pippa shook her head dubiously. "But don't you think the gown is *trop éclatant* for a little family dinner?" Receiving only a shrug from Sybil in response, she studied the dresses on Miss Townley's arms and forced herself to make a decision. "I'll wear the lilac muslin, Miss Townley."

Sybil took the lilac dress from Miss Townley's arm. "Why don't you go and ready *yourself* for dinner, Miss Townley? I'll assist Pippa in your place."

Pippa, reading in Sybil's determined expression the end of her hopes for an hour of solitude, tried to make the best of it. "Yes, Miss Townley. You know I don't wish you to play abigail for me. Run along and see to your own needs."

"If you had a proper abigail," Miss Townley said sourly, "I wouldn't have to. As it is, however, who'll do up your buttons?"

"I will," Sybil said promptly, urging Miss Townley to the door.

Ada Townley was fully familiar with Sybil's ways, and she understood clearly why she was being dismissed. Exchanging a look of sympathy with Pippa, she shrugged and went to the door. "Don't chatter on past eight," she warned before departing. "Lady Sturtevant doesn't take kindly to bein' kept waitin' for her dinner."

The lilac muslin had not found its way over Pippa's head before Sybil's long-withheld emotions burst forth. "Dash it, Pippa," she complained as she pulled the dress down over Pippa's shoulders, "I've been waiting all *day* to talk to you. And *weeks* before that, worried to death you wouldn't come. You can't imagine how much I need you, my dear, for I'm in the worst fix of my life."

"You always say that," Pippa pointed out calmly as she adjusted the tight sleeves and snapped the fastenings at her wrists.

"This time it's really true! I'm in the suds as deep as can be, and I shall drown in them if you don't help me."

Pippa looked up, surprised at the frightened crack in her friend's voice. "But you *know* I'll help you. Why are you in such a tizzy? Have I ever failed you before?"

"No . . . but this time . . ." Sybil began to pace about the tiny dressing room. "This time, the situation is quite dreadful."

"Now, now, love, don't despair. We shall find a way, whatever it is. Come, button up my dress while you tell me what you've done this time."

Sybil came up behind her and began to fumble distractedly with the buttons. "I'm almost too ashamed to begin," she muttered.

Pippa turned to stare at her. "Good God, Sybil, you're freezing my blood! Whatever it is cannot be as bad as you're making it seem. Please begin *somewhere*."

Sybil, with a quick glance at her friend's face, began to pace again. "Very well, I'll begin with the sapphire."

"The sapphire? The *Sturtevant* sapphire?" Pippa was becoming more and more alarmed.

"Yes. Do you remember it?"

"Of course I remember it. You wore it at the come-out ball. How could I forget so magnificent a gem."

"But do you remember what I told you about it? Its history—?"

Pippa blinked as a childhood memory flashed into her mind. The incident, having had no special significance at the time, was so completely forgotten for a decade that Pippa was startled by the clarity with which it now returned to her mind. She stared across the little dressing room at her tall, lovely friend whose troubled eyes told her that she was remembering, too . . .

. . . They'd been playing in the upstairs sitting room. She could see in her mind's eye how the morning sun had filtered through the dusty windows those many years ago, how Sybil's reddish curls had tumbled down as the child had practiced standing on her head before the unlit fireplace, and how her own spectacles had slipped down her nose with annoying frequency as she'd tried to read.

She remembered pushing them back into place and attempting to return to her story, but Sybil's antics had distracted her. "How can you manage to remain upside down for so long?" she'd asked her friend, feeling both admiring and envious of the other child's amazing physical dexterity.

"It's easy," Sybil had replied complacently, letting her legs come slowly down before her face, arching her back for a quick somersault and bouncing with almost miraculous smoothness to her feet. "What're you reading?"

"A story called 'The Fish and the Ring,' about a princess who discovers a sapphire ring inside a fish. I'll read it to you if you'll agree to teach me to stand on my head."

"No, I don't want to hear about a fish and a sapphire ring. I know all about sapphires. We Sturtevants have a sapphire, you know. Big as an egg."

Pippa had raised her brows suspiciously. "You needn't spin me whiskers, Sybil. Big as an egg, indeed. I don't know why you tell such rappers."

"It's not a rapper. It's the truth, or may I be struck dead by lightning on this very spot! Ask anyone, if you don't believe me. The Sturtevant sapphire is *famous*."

"Oh, pooh!"

"It's *true*! The first King George awarded it to my great-great-grandfather. It's been in our family for three generations. It is given to the heir on the day of his succession, and then he, in turn, presents it to his wife, either on their wedding night or at the time of the birth of a son."

Pippa had leaned forward, fascinated. "Really? You're not making all this up, are you?"

Sybil had turned away and positioned herself to stand on her head again. "True as I'm standing here," she said, upside down. "Mama has it in her jewel box. She'll have to give it to William, of course, when Papa passes on."

"Big as an *egg*?" Pippa had asked, still suspicious.

"Egad, I have it!" Sybil had cried, falling over in excitement. "I know how to make you believe me." She'd turned over on her stomach and looked up at Pippa with eyes alight. "I'll *show* it to you!"

Pippa, by this time fully familiar with Sybil's mischievous tendencies, had recognized the dangerous look in her friend's eyes. "But you can't," she'd objected. "It's in your mother's jewel box."

Sybil had grinned. "I know where she keeps the key."

Pippa's eyes had widened. "But that's . . . that's *stealing*!"

"Rubbish!" Sybil had scrambled to her feet and made for the door. "It's only borrowing. Mama will never know."

It had been a thrilling morning. Pippa had had to distract the servants by pretending to feel ill, while Sybil had stolen the jewel-box key from her mother's secret drawer in her bedside table. By the time she'd rejoined Pippa in the sitting room, she'd had the jewel in her pocket. Pippa had gasped at the sight of it. While it wasn't quite as large as an egg, it was a breathtaking gem. Clear as a diamond and only slightly tinged with blue, it seemed to give off rays of white light. It was set in an ornate mounting of platinum and hung from a heavy, matching chain. The girls had taken turns wearing it and had had a very good time until they'd heard Lady Sturtevant's voice in the hall downstairs. Then Sybil had decreed it was Pippa's turn to replace the stone while Sybil distracted her mother from coming upstairs. Only her promise to teach Pippa how to stand on her head convinced Pippa to go through with the plot. She'd been terrified during the entire proceeding. Even now, a decade later, she remembered the blessed sense of relief she'd felt after managing to replace the gem and the key without being discovered . . .

". . . You *do* remember, don't you?" The now-grown Sybil was looking at her with a half-smile that was both mocking and troubled.

"Yes, but . . . I don't see what your present difficulty has to do with the sapphire."

"It has *everything* to do with it." She intoned the words in a voice of doom.

Pippa stared at her, her knees suddenly turning to water. "Sybil! You *couldn't* have taken it *again*!"

"I could . . . and I did." She made a helpless gesture with her hands. "I've gone and . . . *lost* it!"

"Lost the *sapphire*? How could you have lost it? Why did you wear it in the first place?"

"I wasn't wearing it. Are you thinking that it dropped from my neck? I don't mean to imply that I lost it on the street or at a ball or some such place. I know where it is. I lost it on a wager."

"A wager? Are you saying you *gambled* it away?"

Sybil merely lowered her head.

"But . . . it wasn't yours to wager."

Sybil's head came up sharply. "Confound it, I'm well aware of that! It's William's now. William . . . of all people! If he should discover . . .!" The girl shuddered at the thought.

Pippa shook her head in confusion. "I don't understand. How did you come to make so costly a wager?"

"I didn't wager on the stone, exactly. I used the sapphire to pay my gambling debts."

"But . . . the sapphire must be worth *thousands*."

Sybil sank down on the chaise. "My *debts* were in the thousands, Pippa. Four thousand, to be exact."

Pippa, aghast, sank down beside her. "Four *thousand*—? Sybil! How is it possible? If you played silver loo day and night for a *year* you couldn't have—"

"It wasn't silver loo," Sybil said, avoiding her friend's eyes. "There's a Mrs. Membry who runs a gaming hell in Tottenham Court Road where the play is . . . rather steep . . ."

"A gaming hell? Where *ladies* play?"

"Some ladies. Not many, I admit. I used to prevail upon Surridge to escort me there."

Pippa didn't know what to make of all this. That Sybil had gone to a gaming hell sounded to her ears like a step into depravity. Who would have been so irresponsible as to take her there? "Surridge?" she asked, racking her brain. "Who's Surridge?"

Sybil's eyebrows rose. "Didn't I write to you about Lord Surridge? I was betrothed to him."

"*Betrothed?* I thought you were betrothed to someone named Birkby."

"That was *months* ago," Sybil said impatiently. The subject of her ex-suitors was, she felt, completely irrelevant.

"Good God, Sybil, you are making my head swim. What happened to Mr. Birkby? He didn't meet with an accident, did he, and pass on?"

"No, of course not. I jilted him."

"But . . . I thought it was Edward Pattison whom you jilted," Pippa muttered, putting a hand to her forehead in bewilderment.

"Yes, but that was *last* year. And none of this has anything at all to do with—"

"I know. I was just confused. But I think I have the matter clear at last. You jilted Sir Edward and then Mr. Birkby, and now you're betrothed to Lord Surridge."

"No, I'm not betrothed to anyone. I . . . er . . . released Surridge last week."

"Good God! A *third* jilt?"

Sybil put up her chin. "Well, you needn't ring a peal over me about it. Egad, Pippa, you sound just like *Mama*! I've had all the scolding about being a jilt that I can stand. We were speaking of the *sapphire*, if you please."

"Yes, you're right. I didn't mean to ring a peal over you. It's just a bit startling to learn all this news so abruptly."

Sybil gave her a rueful grin. "I know. I'm a shocking flirt, am I not? But I really *meant* to be true to Surridge. I fully intended to go through with the nuptials. I liked him quite well, really, until—"

Pippa cast her friend a wary look. "Until—?"

"Until I met Lord Oxbrough. It was then I realized I couldn't settle for Surridge. Not with a sure-card like Basil Oxbrough roaming about on the loose."

"Good heavens, are you now betrothed to *him*?"

Sybil shook her head. "No, blast it. He barely knows who I am. Met him at a rout-party and stood up with him once, but I doubt he even remembers me. I mean to *make* him notice me, however, once this other matter is set right and I can concentrate my mind on other things."

"I see." Pippa grinned at her friend in admiration. "I must say, Sybil, that I find your spirit amazingly resilient. There isn't much that can keep you in low tide, is there?"

"Why should I be in low tide? One doesn't fall into the dismals over affairs that are nothing more than passing fancies."

"Is *that* what you call them? In that case, they aren't worth dwelling on. You're quite right. Let's get back to the subject of your debts. You were saying that you lost the money at Mrs. Membry's, is that correct?"

"Yes. There, you see, a lady can gamble like a gentleman."

Pippa's grin died. "Why did you wish to gamble like a gentleman?"

"Because I hate playing cards with ladies . . . the games are so deucedly dull. We had more fun than that when we were children. We used to wager for hundreds of pounds a rubber, remember?"

"*Pretend*-pounds," Pippa reminded her.

"Dash it all, Pippa, it was better than quibbling over coppers, as the ladies of the *ton* do! Silver loo, faugh! It's a game for *biddies*."

"But perhaps it's better than going to gaming hells and losing fortunes and falling into debt," Pippa said gently.

Sybil glared at Pippa as if ready to do battle, but suddenly her body sagged. She dropped her head in her hands. "Oh, Pippa, you're right. I'm so *ashamed*!"

Pippa slipped a comforting arm round her friend's waist. "I know you are, dearest. Don't despair. If you know where the stone is . . ."

"I know that much." She looked up, her mouth tight. "Mrs. Membry has it. She held most of my vowels, you see, and when she demanded payment, I exchanged the stone for them."

Pippa turned wide eyes on her. "Did you actually steal the sapphire from William's rooms?" she asked, trying not to sound appalled.

"Good heavens, no. I have my share of pluck, but not as much as *that*. Mama still had the stone. William told her to keep it until he becomes leg-shackled. I took it from her jewel box, just as I did when we were children. Then I pried it from its setting (so that it couldn't be easily identified) and gave it to Mrs. Membry as temporary payment of my debts, to hold until I come by the cash to redeem it. But Pippa, I live in daily fear that William will come home one day and announce his betrothal. He'll ask Mama for the gem, and when they find it missing . . . heavens, I can't bear thinking of it. What will William *do* to me?"

Pippa looked down at her hands. "*Is* William about to be . . . betrothed?" she asked, feeling her heart sink in her chest.

"Good Lord, how should I know? He never confides in any of us. The only one of us he might take into his confidence is Simon, and Simon would never repeat a confidence. I suppose we might hear some gossip if William were seriously courting a young lady, but it's possible that we could be kept in ignorance until the last moment. If he should spring such news upon us—tonight, for instance—I should have an attack of the vapors on the spot!"

Pippa thought that perhaps *she* might react in an equally dramatic way if such news would be forthcoming. But she put the thought aside. It was foolish to borrow trouble when trouble was readily available all around her. "Let's not worry about shadow-problems, Sybil. Let's concentrate on those we're certain of. Mrs. Membry, for instance. Did she say she would permit you to redeem the sapphire when you came into possession of the sum of your indebtedness?"

"Yes, she did. I couldn't have parted with the stone under any other circumstances."

"Very well, then, we shall go to redeem it as soon as I've collected the money."

"But Pippa, it's . . ." Sybil's eyes lowered in abject shame. "It's . . . four thousand pounds!"

Pippa nodded thoughtfully. "Yes, I understand. I shall have to see my man of business to acquire such a sum, of course, but he's never asked me to account for my expenditures before, so he may not do so now."

"But I can't permit you to lend me such a sum as that! If you can let me have a thousand, I'm certain that I can win enough—"

"Are you speaking of *gambling*? That's how you fell into this coil in the first place! No, my love. I shall let you have the whole sum. But you must promise me that you'll never again indulge in deep play."

"Oh, Pippa, *gladly*! I shall be happy never to look at a card again, if only I could have the stone back. But four thousand pounds! Are you sure your man of business won't object?"

"If he does, I shall merely look him in the eye and brazen it out. He won't dare to question me if I appear firm and confident."

Sybil, heady with relief, felt the balm of dawning amusement. "I suppose you think that, if you look frowningly at him through those spectacles of yours, you'll set the poor man in a quake."

Pippa couldn't help laughing. "Old Mr. Wishart in a quake? I don't think your brother William, at his *worst*, could put Mr. Wishart in a quake. Mr. Wishart could sit stolidly through a typhoon. But if my behavior is sufficiently self-assured, I don't think he'd dare to question me, do you? It's my very own money, after all, and I may do with it as I wish."

Sybil's smile faded and her eyes misted over. "Oh, Pippa, you're an angel! I don't know what I should have done without you."

"Never mind that. Dry your eyes, love. And button up my dress, if you please. It won't do to go down to dinner half undone."

Chapter Five

PIPPA WAS so preoccupied with Sybil's problems that she forgot her nervousness at the prospect of greeting William. She and Sybil entered the drawing room where the others were already waiting, and she was startled to find William coming right toward her. She barely had time to admire the new touch of grey which had frosted his temples since she'd seen him last (and which made him seem even more strikingly attractive than ever) before he took her hands in his and bent to kiss her cheek with brotherly affection. "You are looking quite grown up," he remarked, a glow lighting his eyes as he studied her.

She wrinkled her nose at him. "I should thank you, William, if that were intended as a compliment. But as I said to Simon, everyone is bound to grow up, so growing up is scarcely a condition to incite admiration."

"But you must know I meant it as a compliment. Simon surely must have told you that not everyone grows up with such impressive augmentation of one's earlier grace and charm."

A snort came from Simon across the room. "Simon hadn't the presence of mind to say any such thing," he remarked drily, picking up two wineglasses from a tray and bringing them to his sister and Pippa. "Not that I don't agree that William is completely right."

"Then I do thank you, William. And you, too, Simon, even if you didn't say it." She accepted the glass of wine from Simon's hand and caught his eye. Simon looked at her meaningfully, as if saying, *There! What did I tell you?*

Lady Sturtevant, despite her pleasure in witnessing this affectionate reunion, urged the assemblage to make for the dining room. "I'm quite ravenous," she said, taking Dolly's arm and leading him to the door, "and we can continue this chatter just as easily over our roast."

William gave Pippa his arm, and Simon brought up the rear with his sister and Miss Townley. The dinner was a most pleasant meal in spite of the excessive garlic with which the chef had seasoned the roast. Lady Sturtevant was in high spirits and made much of Pippa's presence among them. She ordered William to make a welcoming toast, which he did with great presence. Pippa blushed when everyone rose and held up their glasses in her direction. "I'm not royalty, after all," she remarked shyly in response, "but only family. You shouldn't make a fuss."

It was enjoyable to dine in the intimacy of the family. No outsiders were present to gasp when Latcham dropped a platter of vegetables or to inhibit the flow of casual conversation and familial jollity. William, seated at the head of the table, was warm and affable as the host. Lady Sturtevant, at the foot, directed the conversation, first asking Pippa to recount her activities of the past four years and then trying to bring the girl up-to-date on the latest gossip. After relating the details of a number of scrapes which the missing Herbert had perpetrated at Cambridge, she went on to give the new arrival all the news of the London *ton*. With a great deal of helpful embellishment from Sybil and Adolphus, she told Pippa about the wedding of the Regent's sister, Mary, to the Duke of Gloucester and of the scandal, just then unfolding, surrounding Lord Byron's precipitous departure from England. During all this excited chatter, William merely interjected a number of caustic comments, while Simon was content merely to devote himself to an absentminded but steady ingestion of food.

When dinner was over, the men declared themselves unwilling to remain behind without the ladies, and they all repaired to the drawing room. Sybil wanted Pippa to accompany her on the piano while she sang, Lady Sturtevant tried to organize a game of cards, and Adolphus attempted to separate Pippa from the others so that he could continue the conversation he'd begun earlier that day. William, however, intervened. "Where are you taking Pippa?" he demanded of his youngest brother.

"Only to the window. I want to talk to her."

"Not now, Dolly," his mother said in reproof. "We want her with us."

"To play the piano," Sybil added firmly.

"To play *cards*," Lady Sturtevant corrected, equally firm.

"And what about you, Simon?" William asked sardonically. "Don't you want Pippa for some purpose, like the others?"

Simon shrugged and got to his feet. "Only to bid her goodnight. I'm for bed."

"Well, you'll *all* have to wait, I'm afraid," William declared. "I must have a few moments of private conversation with the lady myself."

"I *say*!" Dolly objected vociferously. "I asked first!"

"Sorry, old man," William said coolly, "but I'm afraid my wishes must take precedence over yours."

Dolly cast himself upon the sofa, his expression petulant. "Don't see why," he mumbled.

"Because, you mooncalf, I'm the head of the family,

and you're the tail." William crossed to Pippa and offered her his arm. "Age has its privileges, you see," he added over his shoulder. Then he smiled down at Pippa. "May I have a moment of your time, my dear?"

Pippa, embarrassed to distraction by this demand for her company, glanced round the room. Simon, bowing his goodnight over his mother's hand, turned and gave her one of his intent looks before making for the door. Everyone else in the room seemed to accept without question that William's demands came first. Pippa therefore gave William a smile and a nod, stood up and took the proffered arm. As William led her out of the room behind Simon, her heart beat within her chest with a discernibly heightened rhythm. Could Simon have been correct in his surmises? *Was* William about to attempt to rekindle the flame that had cooled?

She had not long to wait for her answer. William led her down the hall to his study, motioned her to a chair and immediately launched into the subject on his mind. "I don't for a moment wish you to believe that I'm not glad to see you back with us, Pippa," he began, leaning upon his desk.

"That, my dear William, has an ominous sound," she responded, a touch of self-mockery in her smile.

"Ominous? Why?"

"Because I had no reason to believe, until you said those words, that you *weren't* glad to see me."

"Oh, I see. Well, I didn't say them to alarm you but only to assure you of my pleasure—and that of all of us—at your presence here. But—"

"Yes," she sighed, "I suspected there was a 'but' on the way."

"I'm afraid there is. I wish to make it clear, my dear, that I don't wish a recurrence of the difficulties we encountered during your last stay."

Pippa was bemused. "Difficulties?" She had to make a mental adjustment to follow him, for the conversation was not taking the course she'd expected. "What difficulties?"

"Don't play the innocent with me, Pippa. You know

very well. You've always encouraged Sybil—and Herbert and Dolly as well—in all sorts of frippery nonsense. My father, absorbed in politics as he was, didn't take notice of all the ways in which you aided and abetted the younger Sturtevants—helping them to indulge themselves in whims and caprices and mischief. But I shall be watching more closely—"

"I don't know what you're talking about, William. How do I aid and abet—?"

"You know quite well how. You encourage all of them in their foolish idiosyncracies."

"Idiosyncracies? I would rather call them *singularities*. Aren't you glad that your sister and brothers are not in the common mold?"

William fixed her with a speculative stare. "No, I'm not glad. I don't care for wildness and eccentricity. There is much to be said for common sense and conformity—two very underrated qualities. But I don't wish to enter into a discussion of my siblings' peculiarities, only to ask that you don't use your influence with them to counter mine."

"Counter yours? I don't know what you mean."

"I'm thinking primarily of money matters. I don't wish you to provide anyone of my family with funds for any reason whatever."

Pippa could only gape at him. "Is *that* what you brought me here to talk about? *Money* matters?" She drew herself up proudly. "I don't think I like your tone, William. If you're thinking of the time I tried to pay a trumpery milliner's bill for Sybil, I'd like to remind you that I did not succeed. You took that opportunity away from me yourself."

"I wasn't thinking of that incident in particular. And don't try to pretend that was the only time you provided someone in the family with financial assistance."

"It seems to me, William, that you're being rather high-handed. Every one of you has always been exceedingly generous to me. Why should you object if I try in some measure to return some of that generosity now and then?"

"Because, my dear, I'm trying to instill in my self-indulgent family some semblance of discipline and order. I cannot have them running to you behind my back for your largesse so that they can procure for themselves the trifles and gimcrackery that I've refused them."

Pippa felt herself confronted by a most awkward impasse. He was asking her not to provide finances for any of his siblings after she'd already committed herself to buying a horse for Adolphus and to providing a large sum of money to Sybil. "I don't wish to undermine your efforts, William," she said with the utmost sincerity. "I have the greatest respect for your desire to discipline your charges, even if I don't agree with your attachment to the virtues of conformity." Her voice was steady, but she kept her eyes fixed uneasily on the hands folded in her lap.

"Then you'll give me your word?"

She twisted her fingers. "My *word*? To do what?"

"To do *nothing*!" I want your word that you'll not provide anyone in the family, including Mama, with so much as one copper ha'penny."

She lifted her head, pushed her spectacles up on her nose and looked him in the eye. "I can't make such a promise, William. Please don't ask it of me."

"Why can't you? It seems a simple enough request. I'm not an ogre, am I? I provide my family with everything they need, and more. Why can you not promise to leave all financial decisions to me?"

She put a hand to her forehead in considerable dismay. "I have every intention of doing just that. But I can't promise *never* to behave generously to my friends. That is asking too much of me. There may be some circumstances, unforeseen at this moment, which would require—"

"There are *no* circumstances which would require your bounty!" he snapped.

"Perhaps not *require* it, exactly, but which I would find appropriate—"

"*I* would not find *any* such circumstances appropriate!"

Her spirit quailed at the anger in his voice. She'd antagonized him already, and not one day had passed since her arrival. If she weren't so close to tears, she would find the situation laughable. To think she'd imagined, when he'd asked for a private word with her, that he intended to engage in a renewed flirtation! What a *fool* she was. "I can't make the promise you wish of me," she said, her voice becoming decidedly unsteady. "I can't permit you to exercise so strict a control over my freedom of action."

His nostrils flared. "And what of *my* freedom? What of my right to conduct my family's affairs as I see fit?"

"I shall try not to behave in any way contrary to your wishes. That is all I can promise you."

"That is *not enough*! I demand your word that you will act in accordance with the rules I've outlined. And if you refuse—"

She put up her chin. "If I refuse, what then? Will you put me out on the street?"

He gave her a bitter smile. "No, I can scarcely do that, can I? My mother and sister would scratch my eyes out."

She studied him curiously. What sort of man was this? Why was he so resentful of her position of independence? "But you would like to, I think. If it weren't for the rest of the family, you *would* put me out, wouldn't you?"

"No, I would not. I don't know what sort of monster you think I am, but I assure you that I have other, less drastic means to get my way in this."

"Have you, indeed? I wonder what they are."

"If you buy the horse Dolly is trying to foist on you, you'll soon learn." He ignored her gasp of surprise and walked angrily to the door. He threw it open and stood aside, indicating clearly that she was free to take her leave.

She rose from the chair, stiffbacked and proud. "The

horse would be for *me*, not Dolly," she said quietly as she walked past him in the doorway. "I hope you don't object to my purchasing a horse for *myself*."

He grasped her arm. "There are three horses already in the stable suitable for you," he muttered furiously. "Don't cross me in this, Pippa! I'm not a man to be easily outmatched."

"I am not *trying* to outmatch you."

"Then tell Dolly you will not buy that animal!"

"You are bruising my arm, Lord Sturtevant," she said, staring at him coldly.

He flushed and dropped his hold. "I'm . . . sorry."

"So am I." She was too angry at his high-handedness to think clearly, but she knew she didn't wish to exacerbate this rift between them. She gave him a long look and drew a breath. "You can be assured that I shall give your wishes in the matter of the horse my most careful consideration."

He did not respond. Their eyes held for a moment, and then he gave her a small bow in acknowledgement of her tiny concession to his demands.

She dropped a formal curtsey in return. "Goodnight, my lord."

His face showed a mixture of confusion and chagrin. "Goodnight, ma'am," he muttered. And he shut the study door with a thwack.

Chapter Six

PIPPA DIDN'T sleep at all well. When she finally quit her bed the next morning, she discovered (by counting the chimes of the hall clock) that it was only six. Not a sound issued from the hallways or the kitchen downstairs. (The servants, aware of the Sturtevant penchant for sleeping late, did not trouble to rouse themselves before half-past seven.) With a sigh, she tried to find ways to busy herself until the rest of the household was astir. She dressed; she unpacked the last trunk and tucked the contents into the appropriate drawers and chests; she attempted without success to interest herself in a book she found on the mantelpiece; and she paced about the room. After all this, she heard the clock strike seven. Only seven.

She sighed again and went to the window. The sight of the dewy grass which carpeted the tiny rear garden cheered her. It glistened in the morning sunlight as if dotted with gems. A brisk September breeze rustled through the one large oak tree, causing the just-reddening leaves to wave at her happily. It was going to be a beautiful day. If only she could keep her mind from reviewing the altercation with William, she would be quite content. But her mind would not obey, and the realization that she'd fallen out with him before having had the chance to develop some sort of mutual understanding was depressing.

A tap at the door roused her. Miss Townley, dressed in a wrapper and slippers, stood in the hallway bearing a heavily laden breakfast tray. "I knew no one would be about as yet, so I went down and fixed you a morsel to eat," she whispered.

"A morsel? I should rather call it a feast. You're a ministering angel, Miss Townley. Come in and eat it with me," Pippa urged.

"No, thanks. I've already had my coffee. I'd best take myself off to dress. I hate to be caught in my nightgown after seven, even if everyone else in this household doesn't dress 'til afternoon."

She padded off down the hall. Pippa looked down at the tray in her hands with a touch of dismay. There were three covered dishes in addition to toast, a jam-pot, a full teapot and a plate of hot biscuits. She could never consume it all in one morning. Wasn't there anyone in the house who might be awake and willing to share it with her? Sybil? Aunt Georgie? Not likely.

Then she was struck with an inspiration. There was *one* person certain to be awake—and he was not likely to have given a thought to breakfast. With a smile she made her way up the stairs to Simon's study.

As she suspected, he was already at his work. When he responded to her knock, she could tell from his abstracted expression and a glimpse of the worktable behind him that he'd been busily engaged in drawing those strange-looking diagrams into the open notebooks which were spread over the entire surface of the table. It seemed to her that he wished she hadn't come. She backed off at once. "I don't mean to disturb you, Simon," she mumbled awkwardly. "I only thought you might be hungry and that we might share . . ."

He seemed to engage in a momentary inner struggle, but after a short pause his warm grin appeared. "The smell of that toast is tantalizing," he said. "Come in."

He cleared a corner of the table, took the tray from her and set it down. After he placed the second stool cater-cornered to his own, the two of them sat down and, exchanging smiles, set upon the food with relish. Under the covers they found coddled eggs, two thick slices of fried ham and a dish of soused herring. "I can't remember when I've been offered a more sumptuous breakfast," Simon remarked, pouring a cup of tea for his guest.

"That's because you so rarely come down to breakfast. As Aunt Georgie points out at every opportunity, you take a perverse delight in neglecting your health."

"Contrary to what Mama thinks, a large breakfast is not essential to good health, you know."

"Perhaps not," Pippa retorted, offering him a biscuit, "but it can be very satisfying. You're enjoying yourself right now, aren't you? Admit it."

"Enormously," he confessed. He munched the bun with obvious satisfaction and swallowed it with large swigs of hot tea. "If I were offered a breakfast like this every morning—especially if served by so charming a waitress—I could easily learn to become a glutton."

This unusual gallantry warmed her. It more than made up for his earlier hesitation in admitting her when she'd first appeared at his door. "Then I'll bring you breakfast every day," she offered with magnanimous good cheer.

His smile immediately faded. "You certainly will *not*!" he exclaimed in what was clearly a voice of alarm. Then, catching her look of hurt surprise, he made a quick recovery. "What is this desire on your part to play the servant?" he asked in a tone of light raillery. "Yesterday you offered to sweep my floor and now you want to bring me breakfast."

She laughed, deliberately overlooking his first reaction. "I only wish to make a contribution to scientific development," she said, her tone equally frivolous.

"If you wish to advance the cause of science," he retorted, "don't tempt me again with such a feast. A large breakfast makes one too sluggish to work."

She studied him closely. "But that's not your real reason, is it? Something about my presence troubles you. What *is* it, Simon?"

His eyes fell. "Nothing. Is it so surprising that I don't wish to impose on your time and efforts? Besides, you shouldn't let Mama worry you about my health. I'm as strong as the proverbial ox. And Emma usually brings me tea during the morning, so I am sufficiently well fed."

"Very well, Simon, I shan't press you." She threw him a teasing glint. "If you find Emma as charming a waitress as I—"

Simon snorted. Emma, in addition to being past fifty, was hard of hearing, possessed a bulbous nose decorated with a large wart, and walked with a flat-footed clumsiness. One could find several favorable adjectives with which to describe her, but *charm* was not among them. "I'll *have* to find her charming," he grinned, "for if I permitted *you* to wait on me, you can well imagine what rages I'd have to endure from Mama and William."

"Nonsense. Aunt Georgie would probably cheer. And as for William . . ." She paused.

Simon reached for a slice of ham. "William would give me a well-deserved dressing down."

Pippa, suddenly serious, shook her head. "He wouldn't care a rap. You see, Simon, you were quite wrong about William's intentions toward me."

The movement of his ham-laden fork toward his mouth ceased in mid-air. "Was I?"

"Quite wrong. Do you know what he wanted of me last night? My promise not to supply anyone in the family with funds."

"Mmmm." He put down his fork and looked at her thoughtfully. "I don't see what that has to do with his intentions," he said after a moment.

"A great deal. The interview ended with a spirited argument, during which it became quite clear that your elder brother doesn't like me at all."

"Rubbish! He just doesn't like to be crossed. Why did you argue with him? You *shouldn't* be supplying any of us with funds."

"If I want to . . . to lend someone a sum of money . . . or to buy someone a present, I don't see what business it is of his," Pippa said, her voice taking on the belligerence of the night before.

"I'm sure William wouldn't object to your buying a few modest gifts. But as to your becoming the family moneylender, I quite agree with him that such a role is inappropriate for you. It's *his* place to deal with the family finances, not yours. If I were in his place, I, too, would resent any attempt of yours to usurp my position."

"Usurp his position?" She looked at Simon in astonishment. "I could not—*would* not—ever try to usurp him!"

"Then there wasn't any real need for a quarrel between you, was there?"

Pippa didn't respond. The concentration of his gaze made her fidget on her stool. She couldn't tell him that she'd promised to provide Sybil with a large and necessary sum of money. Yet it seemed clear, from the intensely questioning look in his eyes, that Simon could read in her face that she'd withheld some important details from him. Perhaps she shouldn't have brought up the subject at all.

Nevertheless she was glad she'd done it. Simon had made her see that William was not so much at fault as he'd seemed. William, fearful that she would try to undermine his position of authority over his financial management, had treated her high-handedly. But she, guilty over her commitment to Sybil, had been equally stubborn. The argument had been caused by them both, not by William alone. Simon had made her see that she needn't nurse her feelings of resentment. In fact, it was clear that she should attempt to make it up with

William. Through the matter of the horse, perhaps . . .

She glanced up at Simon. "Would it be wrong of me to buy a horse that Dolly is urging on me?" she asked. "Since William has asked me not to do it, I mean."

"Of course it would. Why *should* you buy a horse for Dolly?"

"It would not be for Dolly. It would be for me."

He gave her a shrewd look and then began to collect the dishes and pile them neatly on the tray. "Would it?"

"Yes. Strickly speaking, I would own the horse."

"But Dolly would ride him."

"Yes. What's wrong with that?"

Simon shrugged. "I can't advise you, Pippa. No one, not even William, has the right to tell you how you may spend your own money. If you really want the horse—"

"The truth is that I'm considering the purchase to please Dolly. I doubt that I'll be able to ride a horse called Salvaje. But if I purchase the animal, I shall certainly antagonize William, won't I? And if I don't, then *Dolly* will be crushed."

"Poor, rich little Pippa," Simon said with his sudden grin. "You *are* on the horns of a dilemma."

"Yes, but laughing at me doesn't help," she said with a touch of reproach.

"You'll work it all out, my dear," he said, turning to his notebooks. "I have confidence in your ability to deal with all this."

Pippa, feeling herself dismissed, sighed, picked up the tray and went to the door. "That's just what Mama said to me before she sailed. I only wish I had that confidence in myself."

Later that day, Pippa paid a visit to her man of business and, after withstanding his disapproving cluckings and glowering stares, left his office with a thick roll of bank notes stuffed into her reticule. She had not yet made a decision about the purchase of Dolly's horse, but there was no question in her mind that Sybil must be extricated from her difficulties. Whatever William might think of her actions (though she counted on the expectation that he never would learn of them), she didn't see how she could refrain from coming to the aid of her distracted friend.

The very next afternoon, she and Sybil (telling Lady Sturtevant that they were off on a shopping expedition) made for the domicile of Mrs. Membry. The carriage rode over the crowded, cobbled streets for what seemed to Pippa to be an inordinately long distance, and when they rolled to a stop in Tottenham Court Road, she looked out of the window and surveyed her surroundings with considerable trepidation.

From the outside, the stylish town house gave no evidence of being a gaming hell. And the butler who admitted them (after Sybil had grasped Pippa's hand and dragged her firmly up the steps to the front door) seemed to Pippa to be perfectly respectable. Even the sitting room to which the butler led them was pleasantly innocuous. Pippa sat down on the edge of the sofa and tried to relax. She could see nothing here about which to feel afraid.

But when Mrs. Membry herself finally made an appearance, all of Pippa's uneasiness returned in full measure. At first she couldn't put her finger on just what it was about the woman that disquieted her. Mrs. Membry had an ample, motherly figure and soft, fly-away hair which she attempted to keep in place by the use of a great number of ornate and mismatched combs. She had evidently been roused from her bed by their call and had hastily donned a loose, gaudy Chinese kimono, but even her attire was comfortably unthreatening. It was her eyes that made Pippa quake. Never had she seen in a pair of eyes such an expression of pure, naked avarice.

"I'm sorry to 'ave kept you waitin', m' dears," Mrs. Membry said with the high-pitched, artificial warmth of a professional hostess, "but, y' see, I never go to bed before dawn. There's always a client or two 'oo won't quit the game 'til I compel 'em to go . . . and then there's the countin' an' the closin' up. Before you know it, the sun's up, so I 'ave to catch up on my beauty sleep durin' the day. May I send Phelps for a drop o' negus for us all? I myself never start m' day without a swig. It's the lemon-juice wot's in it, more than the wine, I'm fair certain, that gives one a lift."

"No, thank you, Mrs. Membry," Sybil said impatiently. "We don't intend to stay more than a moment. This is my friend, Lady Philippa Wyckfield, and she—as you can see—doesn't feel comfortable sitting about in a gaming house, even at two in the afternoon. I've come to redeem my sapphire, ma'am, so if you'll just get it for me, we can give you the money, take ourselves off, and you can go back to your pillows."

Mrs. Membry's eyebrows rose. "Redeem your *sapphire*, Miss Sturtevant, dearie? You ain't sayin' as you've come by four thousand pounds of the ready?"

"That's just what I'm saying," Sybil declared, removing the roll of bank notes which she'd been clutching in her muff and waving it aloft.

"Well, I never expected—!" Mrs. Membry narrowed her eyes and looked from Sybil to Pippa and back. "Your luck 'as surely taken a change for the better . . . 'r else your friend—'er ladyship, there—is mighty plump in the pocket."

"Neither my luck nor the plumpness of her ladyship's pocket is of any concern of yours," Sybil retorted icily. "Just get the sapphire and let us go."

"Wish I could oblige, Miss Sturtevant, I truly do. But I sold the sapphire long since."

"*Sold* it?" Sybil turned quite pale, and she and Pippa exchanged shocked glances. "How could you have sold it?"

"I thought you said she would save it until you had the money to redeem it," Pippa muttered to her friend in an undervoice.

"Yes, so I did." Her eyes glinting fire, Sybil jumped up and rounded on Mrs. Membry in a flash. "How *dared* you do such a thing? I *told* you I would have the blunt in a few weeks. You promised you would keep the stone for me!"

Mrs. Membry leaned back in her chair and shrugged.

"You gamesters always says you'll 'ave the blunt in a few weeks. 'Ow wuz I to know you meant it? A stone like that ain't no good to me layin' about in my safe. An' if I wore it, no one'd b'lieve it wuz real. They'd just take it fer paste, like most o' my trinkits. So when I got a good offer fer it, I took it."

"But you had no *right*—!"

" 'Oo says? You gave me the stone, an' I gave you yer vowels. Everything as proper an' right as rain."

"What about your *word*, you pawky hag?" Sybil cried in fury.

"Wut am I, a bleedin' *pawnbroker*?" Mrs. Membry demanded, getting to her feet in offense and waving her arms belligerently. The thin veneer of polite hospitality she'd affected slipped completely away. "I 'ave an establishmint t' run 'ere, y' know. A business establishmint wut requires *cash*. All you arrogant swells'd like nothin' better than t' pay off yer debts with yer bracelits an' yer watch-fobs an' yer family silver, but wut am I supposed t' do wi' all that, eh? I'd be swimmin' in *wares* if I let you all pay yer debts that way. I make it a rule t' take on'y those items I kin turn into cash wi' no trouble."

"Then why did you tell me you'd keep it for me?"

" 'Cause you *axed* me to, that's why! 'Ow was I t' know you'd find the blunt so easy?"

"Do you mean to say," Pippa asked, horrified, "that you intended to sell the stone from the *first*?"

"Wut else?" She hitched her kimono tighter at her waist and stalked to the door. "I ain't in business fer my 'ealth."

"Just a moment," Pippa said with quiet dignity, rising to her feet. "I think that, before you go, you'd best give us the name of the purchaser."

Mrs. Membry turned and looked Pippa over impudently. "Oh, y' think so, do ye? An' wut if I don't wish t' reveal it?"

"You deceitful mawworm," Sybil said between clenched teeth as she stepped forward threateningly, "you'll tell us or—"

Pippa put a restraining hand on Sybil's arm. "Will one of these bank notes loosen your tongue, ma'am?" she asked calmly.

Mrs. Membry's pursed mouth relaxed into a sly smile. "It might at that, m' lady," she said, crossing to Sybil and pulling a bill from the roll that Sybil still clutched in her hand. "The purchaser wuz Lady Oxbrough."

"Oh, good God!" Sybil, as if she'd been dealt a blow, dropped down into the nearest chair. "That's Basil's *mother*!" she exclaimed, appalled.

Even Pippa had heard of the influential Lady Oxbrough, a leader of London society and a lady of unimpeachable breeding. "Is *she* one of your . . . clients, Mrs. Membry?" she asked, surprised.

Mrs. Membry pocketed her banknote. "No, but 'er son is. When I showed 'im the stone, he suggestid I take it t' show 'er. Lady Oxbrough 'as a real likin' fer sapphires, y' see."

"I think I'm going to die!" Sybil muttered dramatically.

Pippa, not wishing her friend to disclose anything to Mrs. Membry which might be indiscreet, pressed a warning hand on Sybil's shoulder. But Mrs. Membry was shrewd enough to guess why Sybil was so upset. "You 'ave yer eye on Oxbrough, is that it? Well, y' needn't think I've done you in. Never said a word t' Lady Oxbrough, nor to 'is lordship neither, about 'ow I came by the sapphire. I ain't one t' flap my tongue fer no good purpose."

"Do you expect me to be *grateful* for your silence?" Sybil snapped. "How can I keep my identity and the identity of the stone a secret if I have to go to her to buy it back?"

"Hush, Sybil. There's no point in discussing this with Mrs. Membry," Pippa said in a cautionary undertone. Then urging Sybil to her feet by giving her a significant prod on the shoulder, she turned to Mrs. Membry. "I suppose, ma'am, that you required a larger sum from Lady Oxbrough for the sapphire than the amount of Miss Sturtevant's indebtedness."

"I'm entitled to a bit o' profit fer my trouble, ain't I?" Mrs. Membry retorted defensively.

"I don't think you're entitled to anything, ma'am, but I have neither the time nor the inclination to discuss the matter with you. Come, Sybil. We must be on our way." And she took her friend's arm, pulled her from the chair and started for the door.

"Are ye sure, Lady Philippa, that you don't care fer gamin'?" Mrs. Membry asked, suddenly sweet again. She followed them into the hallway. "I'd be real pleased t' welcome you to my tables and t' extend any amount o' credit that you'd require."

"Thank you, ma'am," Pippa said coldly, leading a depressed, spiritless Sybil to the outer door, "but I don't think you'll be seeing *either* of us on these premises again."

Mrs. Membry gave a self-assured and infuriating leer. "I won't take those words as final, dearie. There's many and many wut 'ave told me the same thing wut came back to these premises within a fortnight."

Sybil wheeled around. "Is that so?" she demanded, not so dejected that she could permit this last insult to go unchallenged. With a final show of animation, she shook off Pippa's hold on her arm. "Damnation, if I were you, Mrs. Membry, I shouldn't hold my breath waiting for *us* to return."

But Pippa took hold of her arm again and propelled her from the house. Without giving her friend the opportunity to say another word, she hustled her into the waiting carriage, gave the driver a sign and jumped aboard. She didn't wish to remain in Mrs. Membry's vicinity for one moment longer. Even the air, she felt, was subject to contamination. The sooner they could draw breaths somewhere else the better.

Chapter Seven

"LADY OXBROUGH, of all people," Sybil wailed, throwing herself against the velvet-covered seat of the carriage and putting a trembling hand to her forehead. "I shall *die*!"

Pippa, accustomed to Sybil's taste for hyperbole, patted her friend's arm calmly. "Yes, love, so you shall one day, as we all shall do. But not today, please. We have too much to do. We may as well call on Lady Oxbrough at once. When she learns the true origin of the sapphire, she will understand that its rightful place is with the Sturtevants and will willingly sell it back to us."

"*Call* on Lady *Oxbrough*? Are you mad? If I show my face in her drawing room asking for the sapphire, she'll immediately realize that I'd lost the stone by deep gaming, and she'll be bound to warn her son away from me."

"But, Sybil, since you and Basil Oxbrough are barely

acquainted, I don't see that it would be so tragic a loss. Surely the recovery of the sapphire is more important than the vague possibility that your acquaintance with Oxbrough will lead to a romance."

"But my heart is *set* on Oxbrough! There *must* be a way to buy back the sapphire without Lady Oxbrough learning my identity. Let's go home. I must have time to think."

Pippa suspected that Sybil's "thinking" would involve her more deeply in this already-troublesome coil. It would turn out just like their childhood adventures: Sybil would concoct some mischievous scheme, draw Pippa into it, and before it was over, Pippa would find herself mired in difficulty while Sybil would make a gleeful escape.

She was soon to be proved right. That very night, Sybil (dressed only in a nightgown, her feet bare and a single candle held, Lady-Macbeth-like, in her hand) slipped into Pippa's bedroom after everyone had retired. "Pippa?" she whispered into the dimness of the room. "Wake up! I have a plan."

"Mmmmph. What—?" Pippa shook herself awake and sat up groggily, trying to shake away the dream-shadows which still clogged her mind. "A . . . *plan*, you say?"

"Yes, to buy back the sapphire. I told you I would think of something."

"I knew you would," Pippa said drily, now fully awake and bracing herself for what was to come.

"It's a quite simple plan, really," Sybil said, placing the candle on the bedside table and perching herself cosily on the bed beside her friend. "You are to call on Lady Oxbrough tomorrow, but without me."

"Without you? Why?"

"I can wait outside in the carriage, if you like. Just down the street, of course, so that no one at Oxbrough House will see the crest. Don't stare at me in that wide-eyed way, love. I promise it will be very easy."

"Easy!" Pippa made a face at her friend, reached out to the bedside table for her spectacles and put them on.

She'd believed, since childhood, that if she could *see* more clearly, she could *think* more clearly. "I don't understand what you hope to gain—"

"I hope to gain anonymity. You've not met Lady Oxbrough since our come-out, right? And then it was only the briefest of introductions. She won't remember you after four years. You will not give your name nor volunteer any information about yourself or me. You'll just say that you represent the rightful owner of the sapphire and offer to buy it back."

"Sybil, that's nonsensical. She won't believe I represent the rightful owner, if I don't *identify* the owner—or even myself!"

"She may, if you offer her a profit over what she paid to Mrs. Membry."

"She may or may not. She may prefer the stone to the profit. But even if she does agree to sell it to me, how can you be sure she won't *guess* my identity . . . and from that, yours?"

"How can she guess? You haven't been in town for years."

"Nevertheless, I *was* presented to her once. And I've been recognized by a number of people since my return, in spite of having been away for years. What if she remembers me, too?"

"It's not at all likely. However, you must be sure." Her eyes glittered in the candle-glow. There was nothing that so animated Sybil's face as plotting some bit of chicanery. "Of course!" she exclaimed, inspired. "You'll wear a veil!"

Pippa gave a hoot of laughter. "A *veil*!" The image of herself confronting Lady Oxbrough draped in veilings like a Sultana was amusing but too ridiculous to contemplate seriously. "With a veil, my love, *you* could confront her as easily as I. Why don't *you* put on a veil and go to her yourself?"

But even as she spoke she knew it was no use. Once Sybil made up her mind there was little hope of changing it. Three days later, her bonnet and face shrouded with a double thickness of veiling, Pippa descended wearily from the carriage, waved a nervous adieu to a grinning Sybil and walked down the street to Oxbrough House.

Lady Oxbrough, who had just ordered her own carriage to be driven round to take her to her Wednesday afternoon card party, was tempted to tell the butler to inform her visitor that she was not at home; she had no inclination to be late for her game of whist. But the butler had said the lady gave no name, and her curiosity was piqued. "No name?" she remarked to the butler. "How strange. What does she look like, Crippins? Have you seen her before?"

"I cannot say, my lady. She is wearing a veil."

"You don't mean it. A *veil*? I must say, we do seem to have the ingredients of a mystery here. Send the person to the library, Crippins. I'll join her there. And tell the coachman to walk the horses if I'm not out in a quarter of an hour."

Lady Oxbrough completed her toilette, put on her hat, threw her pelisse over her arm and strode purposefully into the library. The veiled creature rose from her chair. "L-Lady Oxbrough?" she asked, sounding mysteriously timid.

"Yes, I'm Lady Oxbrough. And I must say that you have the advantage of me, ma'am, for I don't know *how* to address you. If this is some sort of prank, I'll tell you at once that I don't like it. You are making me late for my game, and unless there's a good reason for this . . . er . . . masquerade, you will certainly face my wrath."

Pippa, her spectacles shrouded by veiling, could barely see her hostess's face. She could discern that she was facing a large, matronly woman in a purple gown and matching turban, but the woman's expression was not at all clear. "This is no prank, your ladyship," she said as bravely as she could, "but a matter of business. If you can spare me a few moments, I shall try to be brief."

"Business, eh?" Lady Oxbrough studied her visitor curiously. Judging from the voice and figure, it was apparent that she was facing a young woman, and one of obvious breeding and taste. "I must say, you employ very strange methods of conducting business. However, you've made me curious. Sit down, sit down, and tell me what this is all about."

She motioned the visitor to the sofa and took an adjacent chair. The young woman folded her hands in her lap and began. "I've been given to understand, your ladyship, that you have recently purchased a sapphire—"

Lady Oxbrough seemed to start. "How did you come to know that? I haven't mentioned it to a soul."

"It doesn't matter where I learned of it. What is important is that the . . . er . . . person from whom you bought it had no right to sell it. She was holding it on trust, you see, for . . . for the lady I represent. It is a treasured family heirloom, and she . . . the family . . . has asked me to buy it back. I'm prepared to pay you a considerable sum in addition to the amount you paid for the gem, of course—"

Lady Oxbrough held up her hand to stop Pippa's flow of words. She leaned forward and smiled with satisfaction at the veiled face before her. "Do you take me for a fool, my dear? Do you think I don't know who you are?"

Pippa stiffened. "You couldn't—! Besides, it doesn't matter who I am. I am only acting as agent—"

"Oh, for heaven's sake, girl, take off that ridiculous veil. You're the Wyckfield chit, or I don't know a guinea from a groat."

Pippa could only gasp. "How—?" Her hand flew to her veil to feel for its position, fearful that it had somehow blown aside. But it was perfectly in place. Then how had Lady Oxbrough guessed?

Lady Oxbrough gave a snort of laughter which made clear to Pippa that her gasp of surprise had given Lady Oxbrough all the assurance she needed to conclude that her guess was correct. Pippa was not handling matters at all well. Sybil would be justified in thinking her a complete bungler. Well, she would not capitulate at the first assault. She would try to hold out. She put up her chin. "I don't know whom you are speaking of, your ladyship."

"Don't you? I must say, my dear Lady Philippa, you'll gain nothing by continuing this silly pretense. I knew from the first that I'd got hold of the Sturtevant sapphire. I'm not surprised that someone has come to recover it, but I rather expected it would be William."

Pippa sighed in defeat. "I wish it *had* been William," she muttered under her breath. "But how did you know *my* identity, ma'am?" she asked, putting up her veil and peering interestedly but with some embarrassment at Lady Oxbrough's face.

"You're not as tall as that madcap Sturtevant girl, that's how. I'd heard that Lady Philippa had returned to the Sturtevant *ménage*, you know. It's one of those *on-dits* I'm not likely to miss. So the mystery was quite easy for me to unravel."

"I see. Well, I didn't have much hope for this scheme from the first. Though I must admit to some surprise that you identified the *stone*. It isn't even in its setting."

Lady Oxbrough leaned back and smiled in self-satisfaction. "That is because you don't know me, my dear. I *collect* gems, you see. I must say that we collectors are an obsessive lot. We try to learn everything we can about the pieces in our collections, and we are envious to the point of murder of anyone who possesses a specimen which we covet. I've wished for the Sturtevant sapphire since I first saw Georgina wearing it twenty-five years ago. When that creature—Mrs. Membry, was it?—came to me with it, I could scarcely believe my luck. I would have paid her three times what she asked. That dunderheaded woman had no notion of the value of what she was peddling."

"But doesn't it trouble you, ma'am, to realize that you've taken advantage of a situation to obtain what does not truly belong to you?"

Lady Oxbrough threw Pippa a look of scorn. "Not at all, dear child, not at all. Everything was quite legal. I didn't *steal* the gem, did I?"

Pippa stared at the self-satisfied matron sitting opposite her, her heart sinking in her chest like a stone in water. "Then you're saying that you won't sell back the gem to its rightful owners?"

"That's right, my girl. *I'm* the rightful owner now. Possession is eleven points in the law, and lawyers tell us there are but twelve." She rose as if to conclude the interview.

"But you know in your heart—"

"Nonsense. We're speaking of a *gem*, not a *lover*! I feel no guilt whatsoever. I must say, you may as well save your breath, child. I don't intend to sell it, and that's that."

"Not even if I . . . I offered you *more* than its value?" Pippa asked desperately. "*Four* times what you paid for it?"

Lady Oxbrough lifted her brows in surprise. "If the Sturtevants can offer as much as *that* for the bauble, why did they let it go merely to pay off some gambling debts?"

"The gem fell into Mrs. Membry's hands through . . . through a series of most grievous mischances—"

"Ha! I see it all quite clearly. The gem fell into Mrs. Membry's hands because that shatterbrained Sybil Sturtevant *gambled* it away. That's it, isn't it?"

"However it came about," Pippa interrupted firmly, "Mrs. Membry was supposed to hold the gem in temporary safe-keeping. She was *never* given permission to dispose of it. That was the agreement. She behaved quite dishonorably. Please, Lady Oxbrough, you would not wish to take advantage of Mrs. Membry's dishonorable dealings, would you?"

"Wouldn't I?" Lady Oxbrough chuckled with delight. "I relish every dishonorable detail. We collectors love to acquire our treasures through these murky dealings, I must say. It adds to the zest of collecting."

Pippa eyed the elderly woman in astonishment. She'd never before met anyone so gleefully avaricious. "But how can you take pleasure in wearing it when you will know that in acquiring it for yourself you've given so much pain to others?"

"My dear child, you *are* sweet. Very sweet . . . and very naive, I must say. I don't *wear* my gems. That would be such vulgar display. I merely *acquire* them."

"Acquire them? But to what purpose?" Pippa asked, bewildered.

"For the pleasure of the acquisition. I acquire my gems, set each one in its own compartment in a section of a specially constructed jewel cabinet and take them out and look at them whenever I'm so inclined. And, if I grow tired of a particular specimen, or discover it has a flaw, I trade with another collector or sell it. That, in a nutshell, describes the entire art of collecting, I must say."

"But that sounds as if you have a great many—"

"Hundreds. I'd be delighted to show them to you some day. I have a diamond that is said to have belonged to the Borgias, a giant ruby worth a king's ransom, and a piece of jade whose color is so pure that Birdwell and Kerr (the famous jewelers, you know) have been quite unable to find me a matching piece. And a dozen other specimens which would delight your eye."

"If you have so many, your ladyship, can you not consider parting with one mere sapphire?"

Lady Oxbrough laughed, shook her head and chucked Pippa beneath her chin. "You're a lovely creature, my dear, I must say. Lovely. I wonder if my son has yet had a glimpse of you."

"You are not answering me, ma'am," Pippa said with a touch of asperity. Lady Oxbrough, with her air of self-satisfaction and her tendency to pepper her conversation with "I-must-say", was not easy to like. "Surely one stone more or less cannot—"

"My dear child, if you had the soul of a collector, you wouldn't bother to ask. Believe me, there's nothing you can say to pry the sapphire from my collection. But I fear I cannot stay to chat any longer. I am shockingly tardy for my Wednesday afternoon whist, an appointment which I keep with unfailing regularity. Do forgive me, my dear. I must say that I've enjoyed our little visit. Good day, Lady Philippa. Do come back again. I would be very pleased to show you my collection."

Pippa left Oxbrough House in a state of shock. Neither she nor Sybil had anticipated complete failure. She was at a loss as to how to proceed. With her spirits plummeting, she climbed into the carriage and ruefully related to Sybil what had occurred. Sybil, after a short explosion of temper to relieve her frustration, grew thoughtful and asked Pippa to repeat the tale. "Tell me everything Lady Oxbrough said," the girl demanded. "Don't leave out a word."

"May I not even leave out 'I must say' with which she introduces every sentence?" Pippa asked drily.

But Sybil would not be distracted from her purpose. Pippa had to repeat the conversation as closely as she remembered it, not once but three times. By that time they'd arrived home, and Sybil dropped the subject. She behaved perfectly normally during the rest of the day and evening. Pippa, if she didn't know better, would have sworn that nothing at all was troubling Sybil's mind.

But late that night, after Pippa had fallen asleep, Sybil came to her room again, candle and all. "Wake up, Pippa," she whispered, shaking her friend ruthlessly. "I think I have it."

"Have't?" poor Pippa mumbled groggily.

"Wake up, I say! I've thought of a *plan*. I know exactly what we must do to get back the sapphire.

"Talk abou' it in th' mornin'," Pippa mumbled, turning her face into the pillows and trying desperately to cling to a rapidly disintegrating dream.

Sybil shook her determinedly. "Don't you want to hear it? Wake *up*, you slug!"

Pippa reluctantly lifted her head. "Very well," she said thickly, pulling herself erect and forcing her eyes open. "What's the plan this time?"

"Now, love, don't make a fuss. I've thought and

thought, and this is the only way to accomplish it."

Pippa was now fully awake and filled with trepidation. "Oh, dear. I'm not at all certain I want to hear this. What *is* this only possible way?"

Sybil smiled her familiar, mischievous smile. Even in the candlelight Pippa could see the gleam of excitement which the prospect of a new adventure inevitably brought to her friend's eyes. "Promise you won't cry out?"

"Cry out? Good heavens, this is going to be worse than I thought! All right, you bobbing block, tell me at once. Without roundaboutation, if you please. What is your plan?"

"It's really completely foolproof. Lady Oxbrough said that possession is eleven points in the law, right?"

"Yes . . ."

"So *we* are going to take possession of it."

"Are you completely mad? How can we possibly do that except by . . . Good *God*! *Sybil!* You *can't* mean—?"

Sybil chuckled. "Exactly! We're going to *steal* it."

Chapter Eight

FOR THE next few days, Pippa felt sick with apprehension. In her view Sybil's plan was monstrous. But Sybil wouldn't listen to a word of opposition, declaring that unless Pippa could invent a superior strategy, they had no choice. This was just the sort of *contretemps* in which Sybil was constantly mired and was the very reason why Pippa had been reluctant to return to the Sturtevant household. She was too old, too timid and too sensible to enjoy this sort of scrape. When she'd been a child, she'd been enchanted by Sybil's untrammeled sense of adventure, but now that she was grown she found that the strains and tensions far outweighed the pleasures of such exploits.

Sybil's plan, this time, was by far the most outrageous she'd ever concocted. The two of them were to call on Lady Oxbrough when they were certain she would not be at home—on a Wednesday afternoon when (as her ladyship had remarked to Pippa) she invariably attended her Wednesday afternoon whist game. Then, as soon as they were admitted, Pippa would fall down in a swoon. The servants would all cluster round (for Sybil would scream and make a grand commotion), and as soon as their attention was rivetted on the prostrate Pippa, Sybil would steal upstairs, ransack her ladyship's bedroom, find the jewel, leave the bank notes in its place, return downstairs, revive her friend and the two would make for the carriage. It was, as Sybil insisted repeatedly, "as easy as wetting with water."

Nothing that Pippa said in objection weakened Sybil's determination. When Pippa pointed out that Lady Oxbrough would be certain to guess the identities of the young women who stole the gem, Sybil shrugged and said it couldn't be helped. When Pippa reminded her that Lady Oxbrough would then surely warn her son to avoid the madcap Miss Sturtevant, Sybil winced but remained adamant. When Pippa warned that her ladyship might come to their door with a magistrate, Sybil retorted that they could not be accused of stealing, since they would have *paid* for the gem. "But, Sybil," Pippa had argued in despair, "buying and selling require agreement on *both* sides. If Lady Oxbrough won't agree to sell, the fact that you leave the money in place of the jewel is not enough to constitute a valid purchase. I don't believe it is at all legal—"

"Oh, pooh!" Sybil riposted airily. "You sound like a lawyer. If it should ever come to a legal case, I will argue that Mrs. Membry had no legal right to sell it to Lady Oxbrough in the first place. So there."

Sybil insisted that her conscience was completely clear. The gem would be paid for and would be in the Sturtevant's possession. Eleven-twelfths of the law, by Lady Oxbrough's own calculation. She was therefore satisfied that there was little Lady Oxbrough could do to get the stone back. Her plan, she declared firmly, was almost completely foolproof.

Pippa tried in every way she could think of to dissuade her friend without success. She toyed briefly with the idea of refusing to go along with Sybil on this wild escapade, but she knew that Sybil would not forgive her for what she would certainly call cowardice if Pippa failed her at such a crucial juncture. As the fateful Wednesday approached, her stomach grew more and more knotted with tension.

If it had not been for this looming imperilment, Pippa would have found her life quite enjoyable. Her relationship with all the Sturtevant males was markedly improving. To her surprise, William came and took her for a drive in his phaeton. His attitude was pleasant and conciliating; he did not once refer to the subject of their earlier disagreement. They conversed about politics, books and the theater with amicable awareness of their similarities of views, and Pippa found herself drawn to him again. He even offered to escort her and Sybil to the theater the following Tuesday evening. If Pippa's conscience hadn't been stricken by the awareness of the plot brewing behind his back, she would have felt quite dizzy with delight.

Her association with Simon, too, was improving. Simon had received a most flattering letter from the famous scientist, Thomas Young, praising his efforts in his analyses of light waves and requesting that Simon prepare a paper to present to the Royal Society. Simon, excited by the honor and the prospect of discussing his ideas with the most learned men of the kingdom, readily accepted Pippa's offer of assistance. Every morning, Pippa joined him in his laboratory, helping him set up equipment, taking notes, and listening to him expound on the mysteries of the nature of light and the various avenues of inquiry which he and the other scientists were following to try to solve them. It was truly a fascinating field of inquiry: if light was composed of minute particles, as Newton had claimed, then how would one explain the characteristics of reflection and refraction? And if light was composed of waves, as Huygens had claimed (and as Dr. Young had proved in his recent demonstration of the "interference effect"), how did the waves of light travel through the nothingness of space? Simon was convinced that Young's wave theory was basically sound, even if there were many unanswered questions. His own contribution—the slow, painstaking measurements of the varying wave-lengths in the different colored rays of the spectrum—might bring science one step closer to the answers.

Simon's excitement in his work was contagious, and Pippa would have been happy to spend her days working at his side, but Sybil would have none of it. As soon as she arose (usually at noon) and dressed, she came up to the laboratory and dragged Pippa away. There was little that Pippa could do to prevent Sybil's interruptions, for as soon as Sybil appeared in the doorway, Simon pokered up and ordered her to go. "I won't have you burying yourself up here," he repeated daily. "Four hours a day is more than enough." And he would pull off the apron she wore to protect her gown and push her out the door.

Brief as it was, the few hours spent in meaningful work were the most satisfying part of her day. Simon might be stiff and awkward when she arrived in the morning, stubborn and glum when he dismissed her at noon, but in between—when he explained what he was doing, or praised her ability at calculation, or shared with her, eyes shining, a new discovery he'd made—the feeling between them was warm and close.

Even her relationship with Dolly—which she feared would grow strained if she refused to buy the horse—proved to be less troublesome than she'd expected, for he quite suddenly ceased to press her about the matter. By some astutely casual questioning, she discovered that he'd had a violent quarrel with the friend who owned Salvaje. "Doodle Ludell and I are not, for the time being, on speaking terms," he told her glumly. Since Dolly was too angry to do business with Mr. Ludell, Pippa was relieved of the strain of having to make a decision. If only Dolly would remain estranged from his friend long enough for Pippa to conclude the matter of the sapphire, she'd then be able to concentrate on the problem of the horse.

But the matter of the sapphire was so overwhelming that she could take no real pleasure from these other occurrences. As the fateful Wednesday drew close she found herself unable to think of anything else. By the time Tuesday rolled round, she was almost beside herself. Others in the family couldn't help noticing that something was amiss. Aunt Georgie, watching with concern as Pippa poked aimlessly at the food on her breakfast plate, inquired if she were certain that she felt "quite the thing." A short while later, Simon asked the same question after she'd made a mull of a perfectly simple set of calculations. She'd blushed and mocked herself with a hearty show of merriment, but he peered at her with a wrinkled brow nonetheless.

Finally (and most disturbing of all her absentmindedness that day), she completely forgot that this was the evening that she and Sybil were to go to the theater with William. If Sybil hadn't come to her room to ask what she intended to wear, she would not have been prepared when he called for them. As it was, she made herself ready on time, but she found herself unable to enjoy the evening. She was too nervous to concentrate on the play or even to respond to William's conversational initiatives with any depth or charm. Sybil, however, was bubbling with excitement, flirted outrageously with the many young men who called at their box during the intermissions, and chattered away so incessantly that Pippa's reticence was not noticeable.

If William was disturbed by Pippa's preoccupation, he said nothing about it. He delivered them to the door at the end of the evening, kissed both their hands and drove off in apparent good spirits. But Pippa felt certain that he'd been as bored with her absentminded monosyllables as with Sybil's chatter. In her advancing relationship with William, she was sure that this evening she'd taken a backward step.

The following afternoon, despite Pippa's repeated misgivings, arguments, protestations and urgings for cancellation or at least postponement, Sybil pushed Pippa into the carriage, and the two miscreants set out on their deplorable mission. Although they knew that Lady Oxbrough would immediately guess the identities of the culprits as soon as she discovered that the sapphire had been pilfered, Sybil had insisted that the two of them wear veils. "In that way, her ladyship won't be *absolutely* certain who it was," she'd explained optimistically. "The servants won't be able to describe us to her."

It was the veil on Sybil's bonnet that caused the first disaster. Its double thickness clouded her vision, but in her eagerness to execute her scheme, she ignored the impairment. Impatiently running past the more cautious Pippa, she dashed up the steps of Oxbrough House, and, misjudging her footing, tripped on the top step and twisted her ankle. "Oh, *damnation*!" she cried out in pain.

"Good heavens, Sybil, are you hurt?" Pippa asked, running up to her.

Sybil winced in agony. "Hang it all, I think I've sprained my ankle."

Pippa knew she should have felt the consternation appropriate to such a situation, but she felt instead a breath of relief. "Then lean on me. We'll go home at once and call a doctor."

"Go *home*?" Sybil threw her friend a look of disdain, in spite of her obvious discomfort. "Before we accomplish our mission? I should say not!"

"But . . . we can't go ahead with this scheme if you're incapacitated."

"Yes, we can. This is all to the good. We don't have to *pretend* an injury—we have a real one. *I* shall take your place as the swooning one, and *you* shall go upstairs for the sapphire." And before Pippa could protest, she knocked loudly at the door.

"But, Sybil, you can't expect *me* to do the stealing!" Pippa objected in alarm.

"Hush! Do you want someone to hear? You *must* do it, Pippa. I can't climb the stairs to the bedroom in this condition. I can't move quickly enough to—"

The opening of the door silenced her. The butler

stood in the doorway, his impassive expression giving way to stupefaction at the sight of two veiled ladies on his doorstep, one leaning heavily on the other. "My word!" he exclaimed. "What—?"

Sybil gave an anguished groan and lifted a limp hand to her forehead.

"My friend has . . . er . . . tripped on your doorstep," Pippa explained awkwardly.

"On *our doorstep*?" Crippins, the butler, peered at them suspiciously.

"Yes, you looby," Sybil muttered between groans. "We've come to . . . to see her ladyship."

"Her ladyship is not at home."

"Oh, good God!" Sybil, a consummate actress, winced in convincing annoyance. "Are you telling me we've come all this way—and I've painfully injured myself—for nothing?"

"I'm terribly sorry, ma'am," Crippins responded uncertainly.

"*Sorry*! It does no good to my injury to hear *that*." And with another agonized groan, she fell heavily against Pippa, giving her a meaningful pinch as she did so.

"I fear my friend is badly hurt," Pippa said, gamely attempting to play her new part.

"I think my ankle is *broken*!" Sybil added with tremulous theatricality.

"Oh, dear!" The butler wrung his hands, a victim of unaccustomed indecision.

"Well, don't stand there like a cod's head!" Sybil fumed. "Can't you see that I'm about to swoon? Let us in!"

"Swoon? Now, ma'am, you don't want to do that!" Crippins, giving a sigh of surrender, shook himself into action. "Here, Miss. Give me your arm, and let me help you to the sitting room. It's just down the hall."

With Sybil leaning on him with all her weight and screaming with pain at every step, they made their way to the first doorway, Pippa following behind with her heart beating in terror. As Sybil had predicted, the hallway began to fill with servants. Three housemaids and a pair of footmen seemed to materialize out of nowhere and followed them into the staid, ornately furnished sitting room. As soon as Sybil caught sight of them, she uttered a pitiable groan, released her hold on the butler's arm, wavered slightly and sank to the floor. One of the maids gasped loudly and another cried out in alarm. "Good heavens!" Crippins mumbled and knelt down beside the fallen girl.

"Per'aps ye should rub 'er wrists," one of the footmen said.

"Splash 'er wi' water," cried the excitable maid.

"Brandy," offered the other footman.

"*Sal volatile*," Sybil whispered, allowing her eyelids to flutter.

Crippins leaned over her. "What is it you said, ma'am?"

"Where's Pi—my friend?" Sybil asked in a tiny voice, her eyes closed.

"Here I am, love," Pippa said, kneeling beside the butler.

"*Sal volatile!* I'm so . . . dizzy . . ."

Pippa looked across at Crippins. "She needs some aromatic spirits. Oh, dear, I haven't brought my vinaigrette."

"Her ladyship must have *sal volatile* in her dressing room," a maid suggested.

"Well, then, Alice, don't stand about gawking," the butler ordered, patting Sybil's hand helplessly. "Run up and get it!"

The maid, Alice, started toward the door. Pippa, who according to plan should have gone with her, knelt frozen to the spot. Sybil, fluttering her eyelids, took in the situation at a glance. "Go with her, my dearest," she said in a sickly voice, at the same time poking Pippa surreptitiously but viciously to underline her words. "You may be able to help her find it."

"Yes . . . of course." Pippa got to her feet and, with

trembling knees, followed the maid from the room.

"Shouldn't we put the lady on the sofa?" one of the footmen asked.

Crippins agreed. The last look Pippa was able to take of the sitting room showed the butler and the two footmen attempting to lift her friend from the floor while the two remaining maids fluttered about in sympathetic agitation. Sybil's screams followed Pippa and the maid down the hall, and they sounded so wrenchingly sincere that Pippa knew her friend was really in pain. She felt a wave of admiration for Sybil. The girl was suffering actual torment yet she was putting on a performance worthy of Mrs. Siddons. Pippa had no doubt at all that her friend would manage to hold the servants' attention for as long as it would take Pippa to return.

The sounds of Sybil's screams and the servants' distressed voices faded as Pippa and the maidservant climbed up a wide staircase to the upper floor. "This way, Miss," the girl said and led Pippa to her mistress's bedroom. "The dressin' room's through 'ere."

As they passed through the bedroom, Pippa peered through her veils, straining to get a close look at the furnishings. Was there, among all these wardrobes, cupboards, tables, commodes, stands and other appurtenances with which the room seemed to be cluttered, a chest or cabinet which might appropriately house a collection of jewels? And wouldn't it be locked? How long would it take her to find the cabinet? And then, how would she open it? Sybil had said nothing to answer those questions. Pippa's legs shook with fear at the prospect of what was facing her.

But the maid had already disappeared into the dressing room, and Pippa was forced to follow. She leaned on the jamb of the dressing-room door to steady her legs, while Alice looked at one after another of several vials and bottles she took from the shelves which lined the walls surrounding Lady Oxbrough's dressing table. After what seemed like ages, she chose something and turned. "Have you found it at last?" Pippa asked faintly.

"Yes, Miss, I think so. Is this what yer friend wants?" The maid held out a stoppered jar.

Pippa took it, lifted the stopper and sniffed. "Yes, that's *sal volatile* or something close enough," she murmured, suddenly wondering in desperation how to convince the maid to permit her to remain behind.

The maid smiled triumphantly. "I *knowed* 'er ladyship'd have it. She 'as all *sorts* of medicines an' ointments an' things. See? Shelves and shelves of 'em."

Pippa nodded, brightening. "So I see. I'll look through these shelves to see if there's anything else we can use. But perhaps you'd better run downstairs with this, Alice. Your name is Alice, isn't it?"

"Yes, Miss. I'll run right down, if yer certain you can find yer way on yer own."

"Of course I can. Don't worry about *me*. Just hurry, please. Hurry!"

The maid bobbed and ran swiftly from the room. Pippa breathed a sigh of relief and threw back her veil. At least now she could *see*. She returned to the bedroom and let her eyes roam over the room. It was the sort of room she expected Lady Oxbrough to live in—the furniture dark, massive and ornate, and the many surfaces covered with the bibelots and *objets d'art* one expects an avid collector to accumulate. On each of her night tables were several candlesticks, no two alike. They were made of silver, bronze, brass, crystal, and even some materials Pippa couldn't identify. One was made of porcelain and ormolu and shaped to represent a boy looking at a butterfly perched on his finger. On a large wardrobe stood a collection of vases of assorted shapes and sizes, all covered with elaborate designs. On the top of an elegant Sheraton commode had been placed a number of enameled bowls, a gold-framed miniature and a figure of a Chinese man carved in white jade on a stand made of what appeared to be blue marble. A chest of drawers against the far wall held a large ormolu clock and two matching urns which were magnificently faced with Grecian figures sculptured of ivory. And between the windows, on a long, low writing table flanked by two *torchères* of carved ebony, was a glass-doored display case veneered in tortoiseshell, divided into small, square sections all lined in black velvet and containing—good *God!—the jewels! Right out in the open!*

Pippa could scarcely believe her eyes. She ran across the room to the writing table and, with fingers that shook, clumsily pulled open the delicate glass doors. It was not hard to find the sapphire, for Lady Oxbrough had placed it quite near the center of her collection. Only the jade she'd spoken of, an enormous ruby and a diamond of breathtaking clarity seemed to hold places of greater importance. Pippa removed the sapphire gently from its niche and closed the glass doors. Now all she had to do was to place the bank notes on the table and leave.

The bank notes! she thought with a gasp. They were still in Sybil's reticule! *Downstairs!* They had forgotten to transfer them to Pippa's keeping when they'd reversed roles!

Pippa sank down on the nearest chair, dropped her head in her arms on the table and groaned aloud. What was she to do now? She would not—*No, Sybil, I will not!* she muttered aloud—take the gem without paying for it. She had not been comfortable about leaving only four thousand pounds in the first place. Lady Oxbrough had undoubtedly paid five and had said it was worth three times that. Pippa had wanted to leave the full value of the stone for Lady Oxbrough to find, but Sybil wouldn't hear of it. She would not agree to a penny more than the four thousand pounds she'd pledged. Now, however, Pippa didn't even have *that*. She certainly couldn't go down to the sitting room, take Sybil's reticule while the eyes of five servants watched, and return to Lady Oxbrough's bedroom. It was too ridiculous.

But it was just as ridiculous to put the gem back in the display case and go down to Sybil empty-handed, especially after having gone this far. Sybil would never forgive her. There had to be another alternative.

She lifted her head and looked about her, desperately searching for some sort of solution. Her eye fell on another object on the writing table, on which, in her excitement at finding the jewel collection, had escaped her notice—an inkstand. It was a rather breathtaking piece, with a malachite base, three wells, and a fluted malachite column rising a full foot above the base and topped with a gilded figure of the god Mercury. The inkstand immediately suggested an idea: a note. She could write a note—a promissory note which she could leave in place of the money.

With trembling haste she pulled open the drawer of the table, which not surprisingly revealed a cache of paper and pens. She carefully placed the jewel on the table before her, drew out a sheet of paper, readied a pen and began to write: *Dear Lady Oxbrough: This document certifies that I, the undersigned, will deliver into your hands by evening tomorrow, the twentieth day of September, 1816, the sum of fifteen thousand pounds to replace the full value of the sapphire which I have removed from your—*

A sound behind her made her jump. The door opened, and a masculine voice said, "I say, Mama, what's going on downstairs?"

Pippa, with a horrified intake of breath, wheeled about in her chair so abruptly that her spectacles fell from her nose. Through a blur she could discern the vague outlines of a man's form clothed in a red dressing gown.

"Good Lord!" the apparition gasped in furious bewilderment. "Who the devil are *you*? And what, may I ask, are you doing in *my mother's bedroom*?"

Chapter Nine

PIPPA WISHED wildly that she would faint away. Of course, she'd never in her life fainted—her constitution was too sturdy—but then, she'd never in her life been caught stealing, either. It would be wonderful to faint and thus to be removed from this scene of humiliation. By the time she'd have been brought round, someone else would have made all the necessary explanations, and she'd be permitted to go home to find solace for her shame in the privacy of her room. But fortune was, as usual, not with her.

"Well, speak up!" the man standing before her demanded.

"M-My spectacles . . ." Pippa said weakly, feeling about on her lap. "I think they've fallen somewhere . . ."

"You don't need spectacles to *speak*, young lady. Who are you?"

"I can't *think* without them," she muttered, getting down on her knees on the floor and feeling about blindly. "They must be here somewh—"

The fellow, seeing the glasses on the floor, knelt down beside her, picked them up, lifted her chin and placed them on her nose. "There, is that better?" he asked, keeping hold of her chin.

Pippa peered at him interestedly. *This must be Basil Oxbrough*, she reasoned, for she had not heard that Lady Oxbrough had any other sons. She could see why Sybil was taken with him. Lord Oxbrough had the swarthy good looks that ladies always found appealing. His hair and eyes were strikingly dark, and his chin attractively cleft. Pippa could see, from his stocky, athletic frame to the modish styling of his hair, that the fellow was a member of the sporting set that called themselves Corinthians. If the touch of heaviness in his jowls and the slight puffiness of his cheeks gave a premonitory hint that his muscular body would one day go to fat, it was a detail that Sybil had probably not noticed. Except for that, Oxbrough seemed just the sort of fellow Pippa would have expected Sybil to admire.

He, meanwhile, studied her with equal interest. "My, my," he muttered appreciatively, "I seem to have snared a prize. Behind those owlish spectacles, I see a creature of rare beauty. Who are you, my girl? You'd better tell me, for I must say I don't intend to let you go until you do."

"Yes, but I don't think we need remain here on the floor, do we? My knees are beginning to ache, and the angle at which you're holding my chin is giving me a crick in my neck."

The gentleman gave a haw-hawing laugh and released his hold. "You're a cool card I must say! Here, let me help you up."

He rose, gave her a hand and pulled her to her feet. "Thank you, I must say," she muttered drily as she brushed her skirts. His little mannerism of speech, being so much like his mother's, amused her. "I take it you're Lord Oxbrough."

"That's right, ma'am." He gave her a flourish of a

bow, as full of sarcasm as it was of propriety. "I would have liked to say at this juncture that I'm delighted to make your acquaintance, but I must remind you that I haven't yet *made* your acquaintance. *Your* name, ma'am?"

She looked up at him measuringly while her mind raced about trying to find a way out of this coil. Now everything was in a muddle. The sapphire was lying on the writing table beside the almost-completed note—evidence which Lord Oxbrough had not yet noticed but which he was bound to discover at any moment. And when he did, he would understand everything. He might very well send for a magistrate and have her carted away in irons! And Sybil, meanwhile, must be beside herself in suspense, wondering what was going on upstairs. This entire escapade was about to end in complete disaster unless she found a way out. If only she could pocket the gem and the note before Oxbrough discovered them, perhaps she could fabricate some excuse for being there and make her escape.

She clasped her hands behind her back and moved surreptitiously closer to the desk, keeping her back to it and trying to maneuver herself between the desk and Oxbrough. "My name?" she echoed archly. "Must you know my name? There is such a . . . a delicious air of mystery about not knowing, don't you agree?"

He smiled at her indulgently. "You're a charmer, my dear, I must say. And under other circumstances, I might enjoy unraveling a mystery, but I'm not comfortable with mysteries in my mother's bedroom. So, charmer or not, you must give me your name and the reason you're here."

"If I'm a charmer, my lord," she said, edging closer to the desk, "let me demonstrate my tricks. If you close your eyes and count to ten, I can make myself disappear." She inched her fingers along the desk's surface until she felt the paper. Knowing she couldn't pocket it without his seeing it, she pulled it to the edge of the table behind her and let it fall to the floor.

He, meanwhile, grinned at her sally. "Sorry, I can't

permit you to charm me as much as that," he said, taking a step toward her.

"No, I didn't really think you could." Her fingers had now reached the gem. Keeping a smile fixed on her lips and her eyes on his face, she carefully curled her fingers round the stone. But just as she had the sapphire safely clutched in her palm, Lord Oxbrough made an abrupt movement. Lunging toward her with unexpected suddenness, he reached behind her and clapped his hand on hers, pinning her down with vise-like strength. "All right, girl, you may as well let it go."

He was close enough to hear the pounding of her heart as he exerted a painful pressure on her fingers. He slowly increased the pressure until she gasped. "Very . . . well, my lord, take it." She let the gem drop into his hand. "There," she said with forced calm. "Now, let me go."

He gave a triumphant chortle. "Haw, haw! Not as cool as you were before, are you, eh? Don't much like being manhandled, I see. Not that I blame you, I must say." He released her and stepped away. "Now, let's see what we—" He looked down at what he'd captured. "Egad! Mama's sapphire!"

"It's not 'Mama's sapphire,' " Pippa muttered in chagrin, rubbing her bruised hand. "She acquired it by a fluke. And at the expense of . . . of someone else."

He looked up at her, arrested. "At the expense of whom? The Sturtevants?" A light of recognition lit his eyes. "Oh, *now* I know who you are! Mama told me that someone had come to buy the stone." His lips stretched into a leering smile, and he leaned over and fingered her veil. "A lady in a veil. Mama said that she turned out to be a beauty. Even told me that I ought to make it my business to seek her out. What *was* the name she mentioned . . . ? Wickham? Wycliff? *Wyckfield!* That's it! You're Philippa Wyckfield."

Pippa pulled the veil from his hold, put up her chin and attempted to march past him, saying nothing.

Oxbrough caught her by the arm. "No, I shan't let you go just yet." His eyes roamed over her with a brazen freedom and a gleam of decided approval. "What were you attempting to do, you madcap? Did you really intend to *steal* the bauble?"

"Not exactly," Pippa said, reddening. "I was going to . . . to pay for it."

"A likely tale, I must say! Do you take me for a flat?"

She tried to tug free of his grasp. "I don't take you for anything at all. You may believe what you like. But I must ask you to release my arm. Either call the magistrates or let me go."

"I *should* call the magistrates, shouldn't I?" Oxbrough mused, enjoying himself hugely. "But I won't. I admire you too much to turn you in."

"*Admire* me? Whatever for?"

"For your courage and your spirit of adventure. I must say, my dear, that I myself would have quailed at performing such a feat. You are quite admirable. Coming up here brazen as you please, removing the gem with all the aplomb of a seasoned burglar, and then facing your captor with such singular *sang-froid*—"

"You are mistaken, my lord." Pippa didn't know why, but she had an unshakable urge to bring the man to a more sensible evaluation of the situation. "There's nothing at all admirable in what I did. It was dishonest and furtive, and I quailed at it from the first. For you to see anything admirable in such behavior is ridiculous."

Lord Oxbrough, his eyes still gleaming with fascination, shook his head. "There's no need for false modesty with me, Lady Philippa. I'm quite won over. I must say, I've always had a penchant for madcap females, and you seem to bring it off with more finesse than I've ever before witnessed. You clothe your wildness with such a remarkably matter-of-fact veneer that you become a true original."

Pippa, her nerves already taut with the strain of the afternoon's events, found Lord Oxbrough's fulsome compliments irritating in the extreme. "Rubbish!" she snapped impatiently. "The plan to steal the sapphire wasn't even mine. But, my lord, if you are sincere in your decision not to call the authorities or have me sent to Newgate prison, please release my arm and let me go."

"Very well, my dear, whatever you wish. You are free to go."

Pippa looked up at him suspiciously, but she found him beaming at her with perfect sincerity. She turned quickly to the door before he should change his mind.

"Ma'am—?" he asked as she put her hand on the knob.

She winced. *What now*? she thought as she looked back at him. "Yes—?"

"Don't you want the sapphire?"

She blinked in surprise. "Of *course* I want it." she said, frowning at him doubtfully. "But you haven't the authority to sell it to me, have you?"

"No, I'm afraid I haven't. However, I have a great deal of influence with my mother. Perhaps I could persuade her . . ."

"Oh, Lord Oxbrough, *would* you?" Pippa dropped her hold on the door knob and came back to him. "Persuading her to sell the gem would be the best solution for our . . . my problem!" she exclaimed, hope leaping up into her breast.

"Yes, I thought it might be. Of course, it would take a tremendous effort on my part to convince Mama to part with the stone. She's an avid collector, I must say . . . almost fanatic in her enthusiasm for acquiring jewels and art objects and such."

Pippa became suddenly wary. "Yes, I'm sure it will be difficult—"

"I shall succeed in the end, of course, but it will be a very great effort. I don't think I care to embark on it, unless—"

"Yes, my lord? Unless—?"

"Unless I could look forward to some sort of recompense for my pains."

"Recompense? What sort of recompense? Are you asking for a commission of some sort?" She fixed him with a measuring look. "A percentage of the selling price, perhaps?"

His eyebrows rose. "What I cynical little creature you

are, my dear, behind that innocent facade! I must say, you seem to have a number of facets to your character, and all of them surprising. But to answer your question, no, I am not asking for a commission. Do you take me for one of those damned cent-per-cent fellows?"

"Then what sort of recompense *do* you want?"

"Can't you guess?"

"No, I can't. I haven't the foggiest idea—"

He smiled down at her and took her hand. "Only your promise that you'll ride out with me on Friday . . . and twice next week."

She stared at him in astonishment. "Ride out with you?"

"Yes. In my phaeton, you know. You *do* ride out with gentlemen now and then, don't you? A lovely creature like you must have any number of callers."

"But I don't understand, my lord. What sort of recompense is *that*?"

"The very best sort, I assure you. You needn't take so naive an attitude with me, my dear. The pose is unsuited to a jewel thief. You must realize that my object is to pursue you."

"You can't be serious, sir! I can't 'ride out' with you. Syb—I mean, I'm not what you think me. Not at all!"

"Why don't you let me be the judge of that?"

Pippa's hand flew to her mouth. There seemed to be no end to the obstacles which blocked the path to the sapphire. Now it was Lord Oxbrough's dawning interest in her. How could she encourage him when Sybil had expressed such a decided preference for him? Yet if she failed to encourage him, he might well refuse to speak to his mother about the stone. She sighed and looked up at him worriedly. "You're deluding yourself, Lord Oxbrough. There is really nothing of the madcap about me. This sort of escapade is not at all my style. Please believe this: if you took me riding, you'd find me colorless and dull."

He hooted. "I very much doubt that, I must say. But, ma'am, if you want the sapphire, we shall both have to chance it, shan't we?"

In vexation, Pippa wheeled about and headed for the

door. But before departing, she looked back at Lord Oxbrough in defeat. "Very well, my lord. Friday, at one. But you will have the stone with you, I trust."

He smiled in self-satisfied triumph. "I shall try, Lady Philippa, I shall try. That is all I can promise at the moment."

With that she had to be content. She left without another word. Hurrying downstairs, she realized that she could have been in worse case—she could have been leaving the premises in chains.

In the sitting room, Sybil was propped up on the sofa, a mound of pillows behind her back and a large pile supporting her foot. The butler was hovering over her, a glass of brandy in his hand. The maid, Alice, was kneeling at her side, offering her a whiff of the *sal volatile* every few seconds. Another maid was waving a fan over her. The third was watching from the sidelines, but the footmen had evidently been sent about their business. Sybil, uttering a bleating moan with every other breath, was a sight worthy of a place on the stage. Her left arm was raised over her head, the wrist resting gracefully on her forehead. Her right arm hung down to the floor in pathetic listlessness. Her face was still mysteriously veiled (the fact that she'd managed to keep it covered during all this time—in spite of the butler's offer of brandy and Alice's ministrations with the salts—was, in itself, an admirable feat), but her red hair had slipped from its fastenings and was spread luxuriously over the pillows. Pippa didn't know how her friend had arranged herself so expertly in a pose that expressed both gracefulness and restrained agony. *There* was the girl Lord Oxbrough would appreciate, if only he'd had the sense to come down and look at her.

But Pippa was too impatient to quit the premises to hang about indulging her mind in might-have-beens. She lowered her veil and squared her shoulders. "My dear," she said firmly from the doorway, "if you're feeling a bit better, I think we should *definitely* start for home."

"Oh?" Sybil's head came up abruptly, cocked at a questioning angle.

Pippa made a slight, negative shake of her head. "At once!" she said with emphasis.

She could almost see Sybil's look of chagrin through the veil. "Yes," Sybil mumbled, obviously crushed, and lifted herself to a sitting position. "I think I can . . . manage it . . ."

With the help of the maids and the butler, she got to her feet and crossed the room to Pippa.

Pippa took hold of her arm. "I think we can maneuver well enough on our own now, thank you," she said to the butler.

"Yes," Sybil said faintly, "I'm so much better for having had a rest. Thank you all most sincerely for your kindness."

The butler waved the maids away. "It was nothing, ma'am. Are you sure you don't wish to wait for her ladyship's return?"

"No, I think it best if my friend takes to her bed and puts herself under the care of her doctor," Pippa said, starting to assist the limping Sybil to the door. "But I, too, wish to give you and the staff my thanks."

"Yes, ma'am, but . . ." The butler's earlier misgivings came back in full measure. "Don't you wish to leave your names?"

"That won't be necessary," Pippa responded, pulling Sybil almost ruthlessly out the door.

"What happened?" Sybil demanded as soon as the door was closed behind them.

"What happened was that your ridiculous scheme failed," Pippa said irritably. "If you don't mind, Sybil, I'd rather not speak of it now. Let's just get home."

"But you *must* speak of it! Everything seemed to be going so *perfectly*. How could it *fail*?"

"Quite simply, *I must say*. I was *caught*."

Chapter Ten

LADY OXBROUGH, having lost all three rubbers of whist, came home in a vile temper. The news that her son had gone out for the evening, leaving her to dine alone, did nothing to elevate her spirits. And when she went up to her bedroom and discovered that her sapphire had disappeared, she flew into a towering rage.

She sent for the servants, lined them up and subjected them to a violent scene. One of them, she was certain, was the culprit, and she threatened them with every sort of retribution from instant dismissal to incarceration in the darkest hole of Newgate unless a confession was made and the jewel returned. It was only when her diatribe ceased that the butler was able to tell her of the visit of the two veiled ladies—with Alice adding the detail that one of them had come upstairs with her and had remained behind for a long while after Alice had returned to the sitting room.

Lady Oxbrough realized at once that it had been

Philippa Wyckfield and the Sturtevant chit. She apologized to the staff (covering her embarrassment by promising each of them a guinea's rise in their annual wage as amends for her hasty accusation) and dismissed them. Then she sat down on her bed to try to decide what to do. She had not the slightest qualm about calling down the law on the heads of those two miscreant young women, but there was a problem. Her dealings with Mrs. Membry had been of so disreputable a nature that she had not a shred of proof of the purchase—not a bill-of-sale, a warrant, a voucher or a receipt of any kind.

It was then that her eye fell on a sheet of paper on the floor under her writing table. She picked it up and scanned it quickly. Her eyebrows lifted in astonishment, and she read it again, slowly and carefully. After a moment she laughed aloud. She *had* them now! The foolish Wyckfield chit had written almost a full confession: "*. . . the sum of fifteen thousand pounds to replace the full value of the sapphire which I have removed from your—*"

But why hadn't she finished? Had she heard someone in the corridor? Had she become frightened, snatched up the gem and run off? Well, no matter. Lady Oxbrough had in her hands quite enough to incriminate the little thieves. She would have the gem back in her possession any time she wished. There was no hurry. First she would wait to see if the very magnanimous sum of fifteen thousand pounds would truly be delivered by tomorrow. Only then would she decide what sort of punishment she would inflict on the pair. Meanwhile, she found her spirits very much improved.

She might have been a great deal less sanguine had she known that the object of the controversy—the sapphire itself—was at this moment reposing in a bureau drawer right across the hallway, under a pile of her son's shirts!

Pippa refused to tell Sybil anything about the occurrences in Lady Oxbrough's bedroom. "All is not lost," she assured her friend, "but until I know the outcome, I don't wish to discuss the matter."

"Do you mean to say there is still hope?" Sybil asked from her place on the *chaise longue* in her bedroom. Miss Townley had just finished examining her swollen ankle and had gone to fetch Simon, giving Sybil her first opportunity since they'd come home to speak to Pippa in private. "Why won't you tell me the whole tale?"

"Because I don't wish to raise your hopes for nothing. The matter is not yet closed, but I have only the flimsiest of reasons to expect anything to change. If and when the matter is successfully concluded, I shall tell you all."

"But can't you even tell me who it was who caught you?"

"No, for that would only lead to a dozen other questions, and I'm too tired to answer them."

"Really, Pippa, you can be very irritating at times. At least tell me how you escaped."

"By the exercise of charm, will, and animal cunning," Pippa said in flippant dismissal. "And if you don't stop asking me questions, I shall leave you to bear Simon's handling of your ankle all alone. You'll have no one but Miss Townley to hold your hand and smooth your fevered brow—"

"All right, all right! You win. I shan't ask you another thing. But do you promise to tell me everything as soon as you can?"

"Yes. You have my word."

"And do you think I needn't despair about getting the sapphire back?"

Pippa frowned, sat down on the edge of the chaise and took Sybil's hand in hers. "I don't know, my love. Perhaps you needn't despair, but if I were you I wouldn't permit myself to hope, either. The chances of—"

But the door opened at that moment, and Simon, carrying a bottle of liniment and a roll of bandages came striding in. Miss Townley followed with his box of medical supplies—ointments, potions, swabs, scissors, forceps, scalpels, sutures and other instruments and devices he'd collected over the years to deal with medical emergencies. He'd told Miss Townley he didn't think he'd need any of them, but she'd carried them along just in case.

Simon, as usual, asked no questions about how his sister's ankle had come to this pass, but as he, with Miss Townley's assistance, bound Sybil's ankle tightly, he cast one of his intent looks at his sister's strained face and Pippa's flushed one. When his doctorly task was completed and he'd packed up his things, he observed drily that he hoped they hadn't concocted any hair-brained schemes for the next few days. "Sybil ought to keep off her feet for a week at least," he said. "It's only a sprain and doesn't require a doctor's care, but it does require rest."

"What makes you think we *were* concocting any hair-brained schemes, you clunch?" Sybil asked, her feelings of gratitude warring in her breast with her feelings of guilt and making her sound belligerent.

"Do you think I can't read the signs? Pippa's flushed and highly wrought, and you're pale, disheveled and way up on your high ropes. You're up to *something*. You needn't tell me what it is, but I suggest that you both postpone your pursuit of it until Pippa has rested and returned to her usual calm and you're able to walk." He picked up his belongings and strode back to the door. "Of course, since what I said is mere ordinary horse sense, I don't suppose you'll heed a word of it."

Pippa would have liked very much to heed Simon's words, but circumstances required that she abandon every shred of 'horse sense' (and indeed, every natural instinct which warned her that she was getting deeper and deeper into trouble) and pursue the goal to the end. She was thankful only for the fact that Sybil, conveniently confined to her bed, would not be able to keep her eye on Pippa's doings. Pippa would therefore be able to make preparations for her appointment with Lord Oxbrough without having to endure Sybil's questions and no-doubt-violent objections.

But Pippa permitted herself to hope that, should

Lord Oxbrough have the sapphire with him on Friday, she'd be able to pay him, thank him, dismiss him and put the whole business behind her. To that end, she took herself to the city on Thursday afternoon to pay another call on her man of business, Mr. Wishart. When she informed him that she needed an additional sum of money, he raised his eyebrows, but when he learned that the amount she was requesting was twelve thousand pounds, his usual taciturnity deserted him, and he demanded an explanation. "If ye're makin' an investment, lass, wi'out discussin' it wi' me," he said furiously, his Scottish burr becoming more pronounced with his elevated spleen, "ye'll best hire yersel' anither man!"

Pippa leaned across the desk and patted his hand. "Of course I'm not, Mr. Wishart. I would never do such a thing."

"Then wha' need have ye fer so great a sum, eh? Dissipation? Gamblin'?"

Pippa merely gave him a serene smile. "I assure you that I live as modestly as I ever did. You're a dear man to worry over me, but there's not the least need."

Mr. Wishart, who'd known her since she was a child of ten when her mother had put all the child's inherited wealth in his care, had no doubt of her sincerity, but the sum was too large to make him easy in his mind. "Harken t' me, lass. Twelve thousand pounds canna be called pin money. 'Tis no that I dinna trust yer gude sense, but I'd be mislippen if I dinna offer my advice—"

"I know that, Mr. Wishart. But this is something personal. For a friend, you see."

He peered at her from under his thick, white-tinged eyebrows. "A friend in trouble?"

"Yes. I couldn't refuse to help, could I?"

"Hummph. Twelve thousand pounds, added to the five thousand ye pocketed t'other day, makes a grand sum to be givin' away. I trust this'll be the end on't."

"I expect so," Pippa said in cheerful reassurance.

Mr. Wishart shrugged, returning to his usual cluckings and mutterings as he wrote out the draft on her bank. But before she departed, he couldn't resist a last word. "We've a sayin' in the north, ye ken, t' which ye should pay some heed: *Money makes nae so many friends as foes.*"

The words rang in her head all day. Sybil had asked for four thousand pounds originally. Now Pippa was proposing to spend almost four times that amount to redeem the jewel. Would so great a sum cause Sybil to feel too greatly indebted? Would it affect their friendship? Was Pippa making a mistake in taking her friend's problem on herself this way?

She hoped not. There was nothing else she could think of to do; the sapphire *had* to be returned under any circumstances. And she intended never to tell Sybil the exact amount of the transaction. If Sybil didn't know how large the amount was, she wouldn't feel so greatly indebted, and the friendship would not be strained. Mr. Wishart's Scottish maxim was only a generalization; it didn't have to be true in *this* case. And the extra two thousand pounds she'd taken—if she *did* use any of it to purchase a certain horse—was really for her own use. No, she concluded, money was not the problem. She would put Mr. Wishart's words out of her mind.

But the problem of the sapphire would not be dismissed. It nagged at her like an infected tooth. There was only one activity that promised any relief—her work in Simon's hideaway. She climbed up the narrow stairs to his workroom and found, to her surprise, that Simon was in an unusually cheerful mood. "It's tomorrow, you know," he explained in answer to her query about the cause of his high spirits.

"Tomorrow? *What's* tomorrow?"

"The meeting of the Royal Society. My *speech*."

Pippa's face lit up. "You've *finished* it! Simon, how wonderful! May I hear it?"

He grinned at her, unable to contain his feelings of elation. Nevertheless, he shook his head. "No, you don't want to listen to it now. It's much too long and tedious." He ran his fingers through his hair in a gesture of unmistakable embarrassment. "But if you'd care to come with me tomorrow evening," he added, a touch of shyness in his manner, "you can sit in the gallery and listen."

"Oh, Simon, *may* I? I would like it above all things." She was touched to the core by the invitation. It was plain that he'd found it difficult to ask her but wished deeply for her to accept.

"Yes, of course you may, if you're certain you won't find it too dull a way to pass the time."

"*Dull?* It will be the most exciting evening imaginable! What time shall I be ready?"

"Eight, I think." He put a hand through his tousled hair again. "But, Pippa, do you think . . . ?"

"Yes?" She looked at him curiously.

"Do you think you might come up to my rooms a bit earlier? To . . . er . . . look me over?"

"Look you over? Whatever for?"

"Just to check my apparel. To make certain that my waistcoat isn't too gaudy or that my coat isn't the wrong color for my breeches. I've never thought much about dress, you know. Never bother about such details. I don't have the knack of looking fashionable. I'd ask Mama, but her taste is a bit too lively for the purpose, I'm afraid. One ought to look properly restrained when appearing before the Royal Society, wouldn't you say?"

Pippa smiled at him fondly. The meeting of the Royal Society was an important occasion in his life, and he was touchingly excited by it. "You'll look impressive in whatever you wear. It's what you *say* that will matter, not how you're dressed. But I'd be honored to 'look you over' if you wish it."

"Thank you. Seven-thirty, then, so there'll be time for me to make any changes you might suggest."

"Of course. Seven-thirty on the dot." But she suddenly grew thoughtful. "Speaking of Aunt Georgie, Simon, why aren't you asking her to come along? And the rest of the family, for that matter. Sybil is indisposed, of course, but William and—"

"None of them would wish to come. They haven't the least idea of what I've been doing, you see, and an evening of listening to long speeches concerning the nature of light waves would be, to them, a crashing bore."

Pippa couldn't argue. In all the time since she'd arrived, she'd never once seen anyone in the family show the slightest interest in Simon's work. They probably wouldn't even understand how great an honor it was to be invited to present a paper before the most learned society in England. "Very well, then, it shall be just you and I. But I intend to give them a full account of your triumph after we return. They'll be sorry when they learn what they've missed."

"What gammon," Simon said with a laugh. "Who said anything about a triumph? I'll consider myself fortunate if I don't stumble over my tongue or put half the assemblage to sleep. If you've agreed to come because you're expecting a triumph, my girl, you'd better stay at home."

She drew herself up in mock offense. "It's too late to renege now, Simon Sturtevant. Once you've asked a lady to accompany you for the evening, you can *not* withdraw. Whatever my expectations, you are stuck with me." With that, she ruffled his hair affectionately and walked with bouncing good spirits to the door. "I shall be going with you, will you or nill you. So there."

He caught her hand. "Thank you, Pippa," he said, his eyes on hers with that intent look of his.

For a reason she couldn't fathom, the look made her heart jump in her breast. "There's no need to thank me, Simon," she murmured.

"Yes, there is. You can't . . . you don't know what it means to me."

Something in his voice—and something in her response to it—was vaguely upsetting, but her mind brushed it aside. "I think I do," she said with cheerful objectivity. "The speech is an important event in your life. You need to have *someone* in the family present to share the experience with you. Isn't that it?"

He gave her a long, enigmatic look. "Perhaps." He dropped his hold on her hand and turned away. "Whatever the reason, I'm very glad you'll be with me."

"So am I, Simon," she said softly, wondering why she felt like crying. "Very glad indeed."

Chapter Eleven

HER FIRST thought the next morning, when she threw open the draperies and was greeted by the bright autumn sunshine, was of Simon's good fortune to have so fine a day for his great event. But the press of other matters soon drove thoughts of Simon from her mind.

She spent the morning at Sybil's bedside, trying to cheer the depressed girl. There was nothing that Sybil hated so much as inactivity. Sybil's state of mind reminded Pippa that it would do Sybil no good to learn that she, Pippa, had an assignation with Lord Oxbrough that afternoon. As soon as she left Sybil's room, Pippa found Latcham and instructed him not to announce Lord Oxbrough's arrival to anyone but her; she wanted Sybil to get no word of the tryst until the sapphire was safely in hand.

When Oxbrough appeared on the doorstep promptly

at one, Pippa was hatted, gloved and ready, the bank notes wadded into her reticule.

"I must say," Oxbrough exclaimed effusively at his first sight of her, "you look even more enchanting than when I last saw you." And indeed she did, for her green walking-dress of brocaded jaconet, with its immaculate white tucker and lace-edged collar and cuffs, emphasized the slim curves of her figure, and the straw-colored chip hat perched atop her dark curls gave her face a delightful piquancy.

"When you last saw me, my lord," Pippa quipped, taking his arm and ushering him from the house before he could be seen, "I was on the floor of your mother's bedroom searching blindly for my spectacles. I can imagine how enchanting *that* was. It is therefore not surprising that my appearance now is improved."

"But you *were* enchanting then, my dear, you have my word." He handed her up into his high-perch, open carriage with a flourish. "I'm still reeling from the effect of that first impression of you."

Pippa raised an eyebrow. "Reeling, indeed! I hope, Lord Oxbrough, that you don't intend to spend any more time uttering senseless effusions. Especially since you know that my purpose in riding out with you is nothing more than a matter of business."

He climbed up beside her and picked up the reins. "I don't know any such thing," he said with a complacency that set her teeth on edge. "As for me, I don't intend to discuss business at all. I intend to enjoy the ride, and I must say, my dear Lady Philippa, that my spirit shall be sorely crushed if you touch on any subject other than the clemency of the weather, the splendor of the autumn scenery or the charm of your driver."

"I don't wish to crush your spirit, sir, but the weather is of all subjects the greatest bore, the splendor of the scenery is not at all apparent in this crowded, narrow street, and my driver's charm is not a fit subject for discussion—neither by you nor by me. Therefore, unless you wish to spend the hour I have set aside for this meeting in absolute silence, I suggest that you agree to discuss our business."

He gave an appreciative, haw-hawing laugh. "You *are* a delicious creature. How can I resist you? What is it you wish to discuss?"

"You know well enough. The sapphire. Have you—?"

"You needn't worry about it, my dear. I have it safe."

A wave of relief flowed over her. "Oh, Lord Oxbrough, have you *really*? However did you manage it? I was almost certain that her ladyship would never give it up! I'm *so* grateful to you. You make me ashamed of having been so short with you a moment ago."

"I didn't mind. I must say that I find you delightful in *all* your moods. That bodes well for our marriage, don't you agree?"

"What?" The glow of relief that had brightened her face faded at once. She turned to him, dumbfounded. *"Marriage?"*

"Yes, my dear. I made up my mind to it the moment I placed those spectacles on your adorable little nose. 'Basil,' I said to myself, 'that's the chit you've been waiting for all these years.' And I must say, everything about you that I've since discovered only supports my initial impression that we're ideally suited."

"Ideally *suited*? Are you mad? We hardly *know* one ano—"

"Pippa!" The shout came from somewhere down the street behind them.

"Is someone calling you?" Oxbrough asked, seeming not at all perturbed at having his marriage proposal interrupted.

She turned to see Adolphus dashing down the street after the carriage, pulling a chubby, red-faced young fellow along behind him. "Oh, it's Dolly," she muttered, not sure whether she was relieved or chagrined at this intrusion.

Oxbrough reined his horses to a stop, and Dolly came running up. "What a bit of luck!" he exclaimed breathlessly. "We were just speaking of you. Pippa, I want you to meet my friend, Donald Ludell, whom everyone calls Doodle. Doodle, this is Lady Philippa Wyckfield."

Mr. Ludell, breathing hard from being hauled pell-mell down the street, made an awkward bow. "Pleasure, ma'am," he managed, his ears beet-red.

"How do you do, Mr. Ludell?" Pippa smiled, nodded and proceeded to make the two young men known to Lord Oxbrough.

No sooner had the gentlemen exchanged bows when Dolly broached the subject that had sent him careening down the street after the carriage. "It's Doodle who owns the horse I told you of," he said, clapping Mr. Ludell on the shoulder proudly.

"Yes, I remember," Pippa said. "I'm happy to see that you and Mr. Ludell are again on speaking terms."

"Oh, we always make up our differences in short order. Doodle don't hold grudges, and I don't neither. Right, Doodle?"

The red-faced Mr. Ludell nodded enthusiastically. "Right."

"So you see, we can proceed with buying his horse. You know, Pippa, Doodle's stables ain't but a hop-and-a-jump from here. We can go round and see Salvaje right now."

"But, Dolly, I'm . . . er . . . occupied with Lord Oxbrough at the moment, as you can see—"

"That's all right. I'm sure Lord Oxbrough would be interested in seeing the horse. He knows horse-flesh, if his pair there is any indication. Fine-looking greys they are, your lordship."

"Thank you, Mr. Sturtevant. They are the sweetest goers in my stables," Oxbrough said in the tone of camaraderie that one horse-lover takes with another. "Silken mouths, both of 'em."

"Thought so," Dolly agreed knowingly.

"Yes, but we don't have time for it now," Pippa put in uneasily. "I've given Aunt Georgie my word to return by half-past two."

"But, Pippa," Dolly muttered, stepping close to the

carriage and pulling himself up on a spoke of the wheel so that he could whisper in her ear, "Doodle's had another offer. He needs the blunt, you see, and can't hold Salvaje for me indefinitely. I've bargained him down to eight hundred guineas—he'd easily get a thousand, you know—so we oughtn't to wait much longer."

Pippa glanced sidelong at Lord Oxbrough, patiently waiting for her to conclude her conversation. Of all times for Dolly to press her about the horse, this was the worst. She had to turn Lord Oxbrough from his foolish proposal of marriage back to the subject of the sapphire without offending him, and she had less than three-quarters of an hour in which to do it. Therefore she had to get rid of Dolly immediately. "Oh, very well, Dolly," she whispered hastily, "tell your friend Doodle that I'll buy the animal."

"Pippa! You don't mean it! You'll buy him *sight unseen*?" Dolly almost fell from his perch in delight.

"Yes, yes, only *do* take yourself and your friend off at once. I'm discussing a most important matter with Lord Oxbrough, and I must conclude it within the hour."

"Pippa, you're a brick! You won't be sorry, I promise." He jumped down and gave his friend a triumphant wink and a poke on the arm. "Say your good-byes, Doodle," he ordered. "Pippa and Lord Oxbrough have to go."

The amenities of farewell were exchanged, and the carriage rolled off down the street. Pippa leaned back with a sigh, wondering if her hasty decision in regard to Salvaje would come back to haunt her.

Lord Oxbrough chuckled. "Are you involved in some sort of madcap scheme with young Adolphus, too?" he asked.

"I am not involved in madcap schemes with *anyone*, my lord. I don't know why you persist in thinking of me in that light."

He grinned down at her fondly. "You're not going to pretend that the whispers, the winks and the secret exchanges between you and that fellow were merely to settle the time for him to come home to tea, are you?"

"No, I'm not. But neither was it madcap scheming. This is just why I'm convinced we would never suit, my lord. I am not at all the sort of person you insist on believing me to be."

"Well, we need not settle the matter of a betrothal at once. There is time for us to become better acquainted. I must say, I'm quite willing to court you for a while."

"But I'm *not* willing. Please, my lord, let's conclude our business. I have fifteen thousand pounds right here in my reticule. Take it, give me the stone and let us have done."

"Now, now, my dear, don't be impatient. You shall have the sapphire in due time, and it won't cost you a groat."

She stared at him in bewilderment. "What do you mean? Surely your mother didn't agree to part with the stone without getting the full value, did she? She must have wanted to get what she *paid* for it, at the very least."

"My arrangements with my mother are *my* little secret, my dear, and are not to concern you at all. Only the arrangements between ourselves—between you and me—should concern you. I intend to give you the gem as a gift."

"You *are* mad! I couldn't accept so costly a gift from a . . . a gentleman, especially one who is almost a stranger to me."

"But I shan't be a stranger for long, shall I? Not after I've been a suitor for a time, I must say. So you see, you have nothing about which to worry your mind. On the day that we become betrothed, the sapphire will be yours." Then, turning away to cluck at the horses, he added in a tone that would brook no argument, "But, my dear, *not one day sooner*."

Chapter Twelve

PIPPA TOLD herself that she was the sort who could keep her head. Therefore she didn't permit Lord Oxbrough's threatening pronouncement to throw her into a taking. She simply refused to discuss the matter of a betrothal any further. "Please take me home," she said quietly. She was seething with fury, however. She would very much have enjoyed telling him what a cur she thought he was, but she held her tongue. She didn't want to do anything she would later regret. She uttered not another word until he deposited her on her doorstep, bowed over her hand and left. Before she took any further action at all with regard to Lord Oxbrough, she needed time to think.

But she was not given any time for thinking. As soon as she stepped over the threshold, she was greeted by an agitated Latcham. "Lady Sturtevant has been asking for you, Lady Philippa," he said in an urgent whisper. "Something's happened that's thrown her into a veritably tizzy. If you'd be so good as to go upstairs, you'll find her in her bedroom."

Pippa winced. *Good heavens*, she thought in alarm, *what now*? But aloud she merely said, "Yes, Latcham, I'll go up at once. Just give my hat and gloves to Miss Townley, will you, please?"

The butler hurried off with her things (after dropping one of her gloves, picking it up and dropping the other one), and Pippa ran up the stairs. She found Lady Sturtevant pacing about her bedroom in a state of near-hysteria. Nearby, standing stiffly before the fireplace and watching their mistress with tense faces, were the two upstairs maids, Emma and Noreen. Noreen, the younger of the pair, was launched in a long-winded and breathless monologue. The girl was known for being a chatterbox who punctuated her flood of words with high-pitched and irrelevant giggles, but there were no giggles issuing from her throat now. "It's just as I tol' ye, ma'am," she was saying. "We never even know'd there *was* a sa-fire in yer jewel box. I dusted th' box time an' again, but I'd never take it on meself t' open it. Never! Would I, Emma?"

"Eh?" asked the hard-of-hearing Emma. "What's that ye said?"

"I said I wouldn't open it," the anguished Noreen repeated.

"Open what?"

"That jewel box there."

"Oh. No, ma'am, she wouldn't never open it, not unless ye'd ask 'er to," Emma said, nodding her head so vigorously that her three chins quivered.

Pippa stepped over the threshold, bracing herself for the worst. "What is it, Aunt Georgie? Has something happened?"

"Oh, Pippa, my love! You're just the person I've been wishing to see. Come in, and close the door behind you. I'm quite beside myself, and these two feather-brains are giving me no help at all. The Sturtevant sapphire is *gone*! I don't know how it can have happened, but it's completely *vanished*."

Pippa's conscience smote her a painful blow. What had she and Sybil wrought? And what would be the end of it? "But, Aunt Georgie, surely you don't think Emma and Noreen had anything to do with it," she said, appalled.

Lady Sturtevant made one of her wide, extravagant gestures. "I don't know *what* I think! I don't think they'd steal anything, but perhaps they upset the jewel case while dusting or some such thing, and then the stone was accidentally swept aside."

"But, m' lady, I didn't *never* overturn the jewel box," Noreen said, starting to snivel. "I *swear* I didn't."

"Why're ye bawlin'?" Emma asked, blinking in confusion. She put a protective arm about the younger maid. "Wut's 'er ladyship sayin' to ye?"

"She has no need to cry," Lady Sturtevant muttered in disgust. "I am not accusing her of anything. You've both been with me too long for—"

"Eh?" Emma leaned forward nervously. "Wut's that? Did ye say we do wrong?"

"I said you've been with me *too long* to —"

"Too *long*?" Poor, bewildered Emma looked at Noreen in horror. "Is she sayin' that she's givin' us the *sack*?"

"Oh, hush," Noreen hissed. "She's on'y sayin' she don't think we pinched it."

"I should 'ope not," Emma declared, her large bosom heaving in agitation.

Lady Sturtevant made an exaggerated gesture of complete helplessness. "Do you *hear* this, Pippa? It's been like this for a quarter-hour. Questioning them is like talking to a pair of *eels*! One never knows which way the conversation will turn next."

" 'Tain't our fault," Noreen said with a tearful pout. "We don' know wut ye wish us t' *say*! We don't know nothin' about no sa-fire. Wouldn't know a sa-fire if we wuz to find one in our porridge."

Pippa could bear no more. "Let them go, Aunt

Georgie. I don't believe that they know anything about it."

Lady Sturtevant sank down upon her bed in despair, giving the maids a wave of dismissal with one limp hand. When they'd left the room, she looked up at Pippa with anguished eyes. "I don't know why I sent for them in the first place," she mumbled in self-disgust. "They didn't steal it, and they couldn't have lost it by dropping the jewel case. The *setting's* still there! My head is in such a whirl, I don't know what I'm *doing*! It's been stolen, all right, but how or by whom I can *not* imagine. I don't know what to do or how to go about searching for the culprit. I know you think I run a slapdash sort of household, dearest, where such things are *likely* to happen, but—"

"I don't think anything of the sort," Pippa said firmly, sitting down beside her Aunt Georgie and putting a supportive arm about her.

Lady Sturtevant let herself sag against Pippa's shoulder. "Oh, Pippa, what shall I do? Latcham is a clumsy oaf, and the footmen are unreliable, but I can't believe that they would *steal*. And Miss Townley, of course, is quite beyond reproach. I can think of *no one* in the house who would do such a thing."

"No one in the house would," Pippa murmured reassuringly, wondering what on earth she could say without incriminating Sybil.

"How can I face William?" the older woman moaned. "How can I *tell* him? *He* certainly believes I run a slapdash household. He's bound to accuse me of carelessness. But it *wasn't* carelessness, I assure you. I've never taken the sapphire out of the drawer! *Never!* Not once in all these years have I ever worn it! Why, oh why, if thieves had to rob my jewel box, did they take the *one thing* I dread to lose?"

"But, Aunt Georgie, surely you know that William will understand. If you explain to him that the gem has been stolen, he can scarcely blame *you*—"

"Yes, he can. He'll say he's always warned me that I

surround myself with a staff of idlers, cheats and incompetents, that I run the house with deplorable inefficiency, and that it's a wonder I haven't been robbed of every valuable I own."

"He won't say anything of the sort. But if you'll take my advice you won't say anything to him just yet."

"Shouldn't I?" She looked at Pippa dubiously. "Why not?"

"Well, the stone may yet turn up. Perhaps it's only been misplaced, you know. These things always happen with jewelry. One is sure that the bauble is gone forever, and one day it turns up between the pillows or under the folds of a coverlet."

"Yes, I know what you mean. I found a diamond drop that had been missing for months caught in the lace collar of a gown. But the sapphire hasn't been worn."

"Nonetheless, I suggest that you wait."

"But how long can I put off—?"

"Who knows? Certainly a fortnight or so. William will not be asking for it very soon, will he?"

"No, I suppose not. But I shan't be able to look him in the eye, knowing that I'm keeping so dreadful a secret."

"Nonsense. Just put the whole matter out of your mind for a time. I have a feeling that the sapphire will turn up very soon."

Lady Sturtevant turned to her in some relief. "Do you *really*, Pippa? Oh, I *hope* you're right. You're so sensible that I trust your judgment implicitly." She threw her arms about the girl in a fond embrace. "You're such a joy to have near one, my love. I bless the day you first came to us to stay. I only wish—" All at once her face stiffened, and her arms dropped from Pippa's shoulders. "Oh, good God! I just remembered!"

"What is it?" Pippa asked, her heart jumping in fright.

"He's coming to *tea*!"

"Who?"

"*William*, of course."

Pippa didn't know whether to laugh at Aunt Georgie or strangle her. "Well, what's so alarming about that?"

"I couldn't possibly face him . . . not today. *You* go down to him, Pippa. Just say that I have the headache . . . and that I send my love. I *do* have the headache, you know. My nerves are quite shattered. You don't mind serving the tea, do you, dearest? Just this once?"

"Of course I don't mind. Just lie down here quietly for a few hours and rest. Try not to think of anything but pleasant matters, and you'll be feeling yourself by dinner time."

Pippa walked downstairs slowly, trying desperately to think of a solution. She had to get the sapphire back—that much was certain. But it was also certain that she had no intention of becoming betrothed to Lord Oxbrough to accomplish it. Somehow she had to convince Oxbrough to change his mind. The trouble was she hadn't the slightest idea of how to go about it.

William was already waiting in the sitting room when she arrived. In spite of the disturbed state of her mind, she was glad to see him. Standing at the window, lit by the rays of the late afternoon sun, he looked particularly handsome. His dark blue, exquisitely cut coat, the starched whiteness of his neckcloth and collar, the clipped neatness of his hair all combined to create a picture of a gentleman of self-possessed perfection—and a most welcome contrast to the disheveled confusion of the atmosphere of the house. Without thinking, she held out her hand to him, exclaiming, "William, you are a sight for sore eyes!"

His face lit in pleased surprise, for she was not usually so openly affectionate in her manner to him. "Pippa, my dear," he said, crossing to her and taking her hand, "I wanted to say the very same thing to you."

With her hand in his, they stood unmoving in the center of the room, smiling warmly at each other. Neither wished to be the first to break the spell. But after a few moments, Pippa lowered her eyes, blushed and withdrew her hand. "Your mother sends her love, but she asked to be excused. She has the headache. We can take our tea upstairs with Sybil, if you like."

"I'd rather have it here, with only you, if you don't mind," he said bluntly. "I haven't had a moment alone with you—except for a couple of brief rides in my carriage—since that first day of your arrival, when I was foolish enough to spend the time quarreling with you. I've been meaning to apologize for that."

"So have I, William. I was at fault, too. It was never my wish to flout your authority in this house."

"I know that. I fear I'm sometimes rather pompous about asserting my authority."

"I wouldn't call you pompous," Pippa murmured, keeping her eyes resolutely lowered. She was suddenly, disturbingly aware of his closeness and the warmth in his voice. "Not pompous at all."

He lifted her chin with one finger, forcing her to meet his eyes. "Pippa?"

"Yes, William?" Her voice was calm, but her pulse was racing alarmingly.

"I've wanted, for a very long time, to tell you . . ."

"Yes?"

He stared at her for an endless, breathless moment. "You're so very lovely . . ." On a sudden impulse, he lowered his head and pressed his lips gently on hers.

At that moment, the sitting room door was flung open, and Adolphus, in a state of high excitement, dashed over the threshold. "Pippa, it's done! I've brought—! Oh, my stars!"

William let her go at once and moved swiftly away. "Yes, Dolly? You were saying—?"

The poor boy looked from one to the other in acute embarrassment. "I'm m-most dreadfully sorry," he mumbled, backing to the door. "I didn't m-mean . . ."

"That's quite all right," William assured him calmly. "What is it you wanted to say?"

Dolly colored to the ears. "Nothing. Nothing at all. I'll tell Pippa later."

William's mood changed abruptly. His brows

snapped together in sharp suspicion. "Tell her now!" he ordered curtly. "You needn't mind me."

Pippa, disturbed as she was by the infuriating interruption, was nevertheless dismayed by William's tone. "If Dolly wishes to speak to me in private, William, I don't think you should—"

"Shouldn't I?" His face was taut with anger and disappointment. "This is about that damned horse, isn't it? Do you take me for a fool?"

"It ain't about a horse," Dolly denied bravely. "It's about a . . . a . . ."

But Pippa held up a restraining hand. "Whatever the subject, William, it's between Dolly and me. I don't think you have the right—"

"Very well, ma'am!" William snapped. "I'll go and leave you to your 'private business.' But if I learn that you've bought that blasted animal in spite of my explicit orders to the contrary, you'll hear a great deal more of this from me!" He strode across the room and out the door, slamming it furiously behind him.

Pippa, shaken, sank down on the sofa with a groan.

Dolly watched her miserably. "I'm sorry, Pippa. I didn't know he was here. Latcham didn't mention—"

"Naturally," Pippa muttered with bitter sarcasm. "Latcham can always be counted on not to give information. That's one of the things that keeps the house running with its usual smoothness."

Dolly had never heard her speak like that. "I'm dreadfully sorry, Pippa. Dash it all, I've made a mull of it," he muttered, deeply troubled.

Pippa was immediately smitten with remorse. "No, you haven't, Dolly. This has nothing to do with you. I shouldn't have spoken so nastily."

"Will William make matters difficult for you when he learns what I've done?"

Pippa got up and looked at the boy questioningly. "You've bought Salvaje, then?"

"Yes. And I . . . I've put him in the stable."

Pippa sighed and took a turn about the room. "Then William will surely see him, won't he?"

"Well . . . not at once. Robbins won't say anything about it. I've seen to that. But the next time William decides to visit the stables, he'll be bound to—"

"Then I suppose we'd better get him out of there. Find us another stable, Dolly, that I can rent." She walked slowly to the door. "And do it soon, my dear. I cannot face another scene with William over this. Not right now."

"Pippa?" Dolly came up beside her, his brow wrinkled in apprehension. "Have I done something dreadful? Are you in very great trouble with William because of me?"

"It's not because of you, Dolly." She tried to reassure him with a weak smile and a pat on the cheek. "If anything dreadful was done, it was more my doing than yours. Don't worry about it."

His expression did not clear. "Pippa, you're not . . .?"

"Not what?"

"Not in *love* with William, are you?"

Pippa gave a small, discouraged little shrug. "I only wish I knew," she muttered and went wearily from the room.

Her head swimming with emotions, she shut the door of her room and lay down on her bed. Dolly's question echoed in her mind. *Was* she in love with William? When he'd bent his head and kissed her, she'd believed that the answer was just about to come. But there hadn't been time. Dolly's unfortunate interruption had separated them too soon. The moment before Dolly's entrance, Pippa had felt almost blissful. But William's subsequent behavior had not been at all to her liking. His temper had been too short, his reaction too swift and ill-considered. He seemed to her too fixed on his own judgments; he couldn't allow any explanations, deviations or differences. If he were less rigid, perhaps Dolly would have gone to *him* for the horse instead of to her, and the quarrel would have never come about. William was a stubborn, opinionated man. Yet, in those moments when he'd been tender, she'd been decidedly attracted to him.

Much more attracted, she had to admit, than she'd been toward Lord Oxbrough. She couldn't imagine what Sybil could see in *that* fellow. Pippa burrowed her face in her pillow with a deep sigh. What was she to do about *him*? The situation of the sapphire was indeed a muddle, and she could think of no way out.

Her whirling thoughts were interrupted, a short while later, when Miss Townley tapped at the door to ask if she needed help to dress for dinner, adding that she needn't make a fuss because Lady Sturtevant had decided to remain closeted in her room. Only she, Adolphus and Miss Townley herself were expected to present themselves at the table tonight. "In that case, Miss Townley," Pippa said, "I'll forego dinner and go to bed myself. Will you mind not having my company tonight? I feel weary to the bone this evening."

Miss Townley said she thought it would do the girl good to retire early. "You've been lookin' too peaked to please me," she said, promptly undoing Pippa's buttons and helping her into her nightdress. Before Pippa knew it, she was tucked under the covers and settled for the night.

She shut her eyes, but her mind was still unsettled and her spirit depressed. Her many problems circled round her brain in a meaningless parade, but the repetitive examination of them did nothing to jog her mind into finding a single solution. Above and beyond the specific problems that nudged at her consciousness, something else—something troublesome, a nameless and formless shadow—seemed to hover over her. It was as if she'd lost something important but had forgotten what it was.

Eventually, she fell into an uneasy doze and dreamt that she was in a dank, evil-looking cave full of rocks and slimy pools. In the distance she could see the cave's opening, where a figure, silhouetted by the daylight beyond, stood beckoning to her. She tried desperately to reach the figure—was it Sybil?—but each time she climbed over a rock or waded through a pool, others appeared to block her passage. Who was it beckoning? Sybil? No . . . it was a man, familiarly tall, with a head of tousled hair and slim of waist and hip. Was it Simon?

Good God! *Simon!* She sat up in bed with a start, her heart beating in alarm. She was supposed to go with Simon to the Royal Society this evening! She'd forgotten all about it! How *could* she—?

She leaped out of bed, fumbled for the tinder box and with trembling hands attempted to light a candle. She succeeded only after the third try, and, putting on her spectacles, she stumbled barefooted across the room and held the candle up to the clock on the mantel. It was half-past nine.

Foolishly, half-hysterically, she dashed from the room, ignoring her nightdress and bare feet, and ran up the stairs to the third floor. She burst into the laboratory, but it was empty. So too were Simon's rooms beyond. He was gone.

Dismayed to numbness by her own thoughtlessness, she wandered aimlessly back to the laboratory and placed her candle on the worktable. She climbed up on a stool, leaned her elbows on the table, propped up her chin with her hands and looked helplessly about. There were reminders of him all around her. His equipment had been neatly and carefully stored away and his notebooks stacked against the wall. His pencils were lined up in readiness for the next day's work. His lenses were polished and filed away in their appropriate slots in a wooden holder he'd built for them. Not a spot, a smudge, a particle of ground glass, a shred of torn paper disturbed the surface of the cleared table. Here in this garret-like room, over a house full of confusion and disarray, was discipline, symmetry, order.

There was not a sign that Simon had been at all disturbed by her defection. Everything was in its normal place. No glass prism had been flung against a wall, no neckcloth had been ripped from his throat and tossed upon his bed, no chair had been kicked aside in anger or disgust. Yet she could hear, as clearly as if he stood there behind her saying them, the words he'd said to her the day before: *You can't . . . you don't know what it means to me to have you come.*

She shut her eyes in pain. "Oh, Simon," she whispered brokenly to the empty room, "I'm sorry. I'm so . . . very s-sorry . . ." And a tear slipped from under the shut lid, ran down her cheek and fell with a tiny plopping sound upon the table, forming in its asymmetrical wetness the only stain on the pristine surface.

Chapter Thirteen

SOMEWHERE DOWN below a clock struck two. Pippa, sitting huddled against the wall on the top step of Simon's staircase, woke with a start. Where was he? The Royal Society meeting could not possibly have lasted beyond midnight. She shivered in the early morning chill and wondered if she should run downstairs and put on a robe; it was neither practical nor seemly to greet Simon in only a nightdress.

But from a long way off she heard a sound. She couldn't be certain at this distance, but it could have been the front door. Then a most surprising commotion followed. It was *singing*! Simon, apparently unconcerned about disturbing the household, was noisily climbing the stairs and singing a song in thick, almost unrecognizable accents. She could barely make out the words:

"Should I desire t' be a lover,
Sing fie and fiddle-dum-dee,
Should I desire t' be a lover,
Three mugs of brew an' I recover,
Sing ho, no diff'rence, no diff'rence to me,
No dim-dam-diff'rence to me.

"Should brown-eyed girls prove they're untrue 'uns,
Sing fie and fiddle-dum-dee,
Should brown-eyed girls prove they're untrue 'uns,
I'll change at once to girls wi' blue 'uns,
Sing ho, no diff'rence, no diff'rence to me,
No dim-dam-diff'rence to me."

The song was growing louder, and before Pippa could recover from her astonishment, Simon lurched onto the landing below her, giving her her first glimpse of him. He made a shocking apparition in the dim light of her candle. His beaver was pushed back from his forehead at a precarious angle, revealing a mass of disheveled red hair. His coat and waistcoat were unbuttoned, and underneath she could see a crushed and untied neckcloth and a rumpled shirt half undone. The knees of his breeches were soiled, as if he'd stumbled in the street.

He swayed unsteadily on his legs as he round the turn, and he seemed about to fall. But he grasped the newel-post, laughed whoozily and resumed his song, singing to the post as if it were a wench:

"I'll love ye less, I'll love ye greater,
Sing fie and fiddle-dum-dee,
I'll love ye less, I'll love ye greater,
I'll be your now but not your later,
Sing ho, no diff'rence, no diff'rence to me,
No dim-dam-diff'rence—"

"Simon?" Pippa called down diffidently.

"Who's there?" he asked with a start, blinking up at the candlelight above him.

She held up the candle to get a better look at him. "I think you're *foxed*!" she gasped.

"Oh. 'S you," he said cheerfully, lifting his hat and making an exaggerated but unsteady bow. "No need t' work t'day, so y' can go. Holiday, y' see. I'm cele . . . le . . . lebrating."

"So I see. I've never before heard you singing tavern songs. You must have stopped at several of them."

"Yes, 'ndeed. Four, I think."

"Then you must have been a success tonight."

"Success?"

"Yes. At the Royal Society. You *did* make your speech, didn't you?"

"Oh, yes. Made m' speech."

"And did it go well?"

"I s'pose. Lots of ap . . . applause an' handshaking. Dr. Young was pleased."

"I'm so glad." She put the candle down and got to her feet. "It *was* a triumph, then."

He stared up at her for a moment, the whoozy cheerfulness fading from his face. Then he clapped his beaver back on his head and began to sing again.

"Some kiss wi' tears and some wi' laughter,
Sing fie and fiddle-dum-dee,
Some kiss wi' tears and some wi' laughter,
I kiss 'em all and leave right after,
Sing ho—"

He ceased abruptly. "You're not wearin' shoes," he remarked and began to climb the stairs. But half-way up he stumbled, turned and precipitously sat down. His hat fell off and rolled down the stairs to the landing.

"Sing ho, no diff'rence, no diff'rence to me, No dim-dam-diff'rence—" he sang to it in farewell.

She descended the few steps separating them and sat down beside him. "I'm so sorry I missed it, Simon," she apologized softly.

"*No dim-dam-diff'rence to me,*" he sang again.

"It makes a difference to me, my dear," she insisted, putting a hand gently on his arm.

He shrugged it off. "If it had really made a difference," he said with sudden, almost-sober precision, "you'd have been there with me."

"It must seem that way to you, but—"

"*Seem* that way?" He shifted on the stair so that he could look her squarely in the face. "*Seem*, ma'am? It doesn't *seem*. It *is*."

Her eyes fell guiltily from the coldness in his. "Simon, you don't understand. I really *meant* to—"

"Of course you did. You just forgot."

She could only nod dumbly.

He snorted. "Don't look s' downcast 'bout it, m' dear. *Everyone* forgets Simon. He's a most pe . . . culiar physical phenom . . . enomenon—an almost invisible man."

She lifted her head sharply. "Come now, Simon, this isn't like you. I know I was grossly at fault, but you needn't exaggerate the impor—"

"Exaggerate? Do you think I ex . . . *aggerate*?" He rose to his feet, shaking his head to dissipate his dizziness. "I assure you 's quite true. I sh' be presented to th' Royal S'ciety, not 's a physicist but 's a *freak*. Simon Sturtevant, th' Disappearin' Man! Gentleman of th' S'ciety, le' me describe to you this rare pheno . . . menon. This creature standing b'fore you, normal in all apparent respects, 's in reality one of nature's wonders. He's able to *disappear*. Yes, gentlemen, y' may well gasp. When th' rest of the creatures in his habitat have need of 'im—when his help is required in a medical 'mergency, f'r example, or an extra man's wanted f'r dinner—he materializes in th' physical substan . . . tiality you see now. But when the need 's over, he ev . . . aporates, dema . . . terializes, dissolves into *tiny* particles and becomes invisible."

"Oh, Simon, *please*—"

"Aha, good sir, y' don' *like* this peculiar creature? Of what use t' the world 's such a phenomenon as a disappearin' man, y' ask? Tha's only because you haven't given th' matter suffi . . . cient thought. Think, my good sir, of th' practical advan . . . tages to society: a creature who appears *only when convenient*! We don' have t' worry 'bout housing 'im, feeding 'im, providing 'im wi' sources of recreation. Just snap our fingers at times when 'is presence 's convenient and then simply permit 'im t dis . . . s . . . s . . . sintegrate."

Pippa was half enjoying and half disliking this strange performance. "Simon, you *can't* believe that I—"

"But, gentlemen," he went on, ignoring her, "this creature is, 's far as we know, the only one of its kind. He alone cannot make a signi . . . ficant mark on society, no, no. Unless he can be bred in large numbers, I admit tha' his usefulness 's limited. Th' problem of breeding 'im, however, appears t' be insoluble. 'E doesn't remain in 'is visible state *long enough t' inspire mating*!"

Pippa couldn't help laughing, but she had no intention of encouraging him in his besotted dramatizing. "Now, Simon," she said, rising and taking hold of his arm, "that's quite enough. You've made your point. But I've said I'm sorry. What else can I—?"

"*Damn* it," he snapped, suddenly angry and grasping her arms, "you can look at me sometimes as if I were really *there*!"

She stared up at him, aghast. Was he implying that she was as guilty of ignoring him as the rest of the family? "Surely you don't mean that *I'm* guilty of—?"

"You're th' worst of th' lot! You see me every day an' never even notice that—" He stopped short and peered at her closely. He'd been too cast away to see her clearly before. But now, despite her spectacles and the flickering light of the waning candle's flame (guttering fitfully in the socket of the candlestick she'd left on the top step), he could discern the gleam of pain in her eyes. They were wide open and dark with hurt and shock. Her lips, slightly apart, were trembling, and her arms hung unresistant and limp in his grasp. Had he, in his own pain and anger, lashed out at her in cruel retribution?

He felt dizzy and sick. Though his resentment at her having failed him still stuck in his craw like a poisoned arrow, he hadn't intended to strike back at her. He hadn't intended to say anything about it at all. *Damnation,* he thought, *why had Silent Simon suddenly talked so much?* The hurt in her face was worse than anything; he wanted only to wipe it away. "Oh, confound it, Pippa," he mumbled in self-disgust, "I shouldn't have said—"

But his head was muddled. This unexpected scene, combining as it did his dizziness from too much drink and her tantalizing closeness, was too much for him. His hands slid up to her shoulders, and with the strangest sensation—as if he were keeping himself from drowning—he pulled her into a desperate embrace, burying his face in her neck with a groan.

Pippa was, at first, too surprised to protest. This was Simon, her beloved friend, whom she'd badly hurt. She wished only to soothe him, to make up to him for having forgotten him. Feeling nothing but tenderness and regret, she slipped one arm about his waist, lifted her other hand and gently smoothed his hair.

But Simon instinctively had prepared himself for a quite different reaction. He'd expected a stiffening, a rejection, an angry rebuff. In utter stupefaction, he lifted his head and gazed down at her. She was looking up at him with almost a smile. To her, the embrace had meant that he'd forgiven her, nothing more. She was, of all things, *serene*! He wanted to shake her. "Blast you, woman," he muttered through clenched teeth, "won't you ever *see*?" And almost viciously he pulled her to him again, causing her spectacles to fall from her nose, tightened his hold and kissed her in a way that could not be misinterpreted.

Pippa could neither move nor breathe. Even her mind seemed to be shocked into immobility. *Simon! What—?* it began to ask, and then it froze. She was aware only of feelings—strange and unexpected shivers and flushes, the pounding of her heart, the agonizing pressure of his arms across her back, the pulse that began to quiver at the base of her throat. Only after a long while did her brain begin to function. It reminded her of where she was, that it was well past two in the morning, that she was clad only in a nightdress, and that what Simon was doing was, to say the least, decidedly improper. She gave a stifled cry, pushed with all her might away from him and said in a horrified whisper, "Simon, get *hold* of yourself!"

Still angry, he flung her from him and turned away. She tottered, out of balance, down one step and fell back against the wall. The sound made Simon wheel about again. "*Pippa*! You're not . . . hurt . . .?"

"No."

They stared at each other, breathless and appalled. Neither had ever before indulged in so melodramatic a scene. Neither could guess the extent of the damage the last few moments had inflicted on their friendship. Pippa's breath came in quick little gasps. Her thoughts, too, as disturbed as her breathing, were racing about in her head in wild little spurts, as if her mind, like her body, was trying to find some sort of equilibrium. "My glasses . . ." she murmured helplessly.

They both knelt down to feel for them. Simon spotted them and gently, apologetically, placed them on her nose. Her vision thus clarified, her mind began to function. It immediately asked to understand the significance of the scene they'd just played. Had Simon enacted a drunken melodrama, or was the performance a true expression of his feelings? Her eyes flew to his face for a clue. *Good heavens,* she asked herself, *is it true that I've never looked at him carefully before?*

Simon winced under her silent gaze. "Dash it all," he muttered uncomfortably, getting to his feet, "don't look at me like that. I'm *drunk*, that's all. I didn't mean to—"

"Yes, of course," Pippa said quickly, dropping her eyes from his face and sitting back on her heels.

She didn't believe him; he could see that at once. He could hardly bear the strain between them. He hated himself for the weakness that had allowed him to reveal himself to her. "I *am* drunk, y' know," he insisted. "Soused. Sozzled. Completely cast away. By tomorrow, I won't remember anything that's passed."

She flicked a quick glance at him. "Won't you?"

"Not a thing. Look at me, Pippa! Have you ever seen anyone more, as they say, 'well to live'?" To prove his point, he stretched one leg to the upper stair, struck a pose of exaggerated clumsiness and began to sing again in loud, boozy abandon:

"I've learned of love from twenty lasses,
Sing fie and fiddle-dum-deeeeee—!"

She smiled and put her hands up to her ears. "I believe you, I believe you!" she assured him, getting up. "You're soused, you didn't mean any harm, and you'll have forgotten this entire incident by tomorrow. So hush, you gudgeon, and go up to bed before you wake the whole house with your foolishness. Goodnight, Simon."

He gave her a crocked salute, handed her down the remains of her candle and began a meandering stagger toward his room. She didn't watch him go but pattered silently on her bare feet to the landing below and down the hallway to her room. But before she shut her door, she stood on the threshold listening as he, from his far-off bedchamber, sang loudly on.

"I've learned of love from twenty lasses
That soon or late the fancy passes,
Sing ho, no diff'rence, no diff'rence to MEEEE!
No dim-dam-diff'rence to me."

Chapter Fourteen

SHE DID NOT permit herself, that night, to mull over the scene. She simply shut her eyes and willed sleep to come. Sleep, she realized, would be more helpful than troubled speculation. If she began to ponder all the problems that day had dealt her, she would not get a wink. The sapphire, the horse, Oxbrough, William . . . and now Simon. It was all too much to contemplate. Better to get to sleep, and let the problems take care of themselves.

She slept until ten and would have remained abed even longer had not Miss Townley barged in. "Are you sick?" her old friend demanded suspiciously. "I've never known you to sleep away an entire mornin'. I know the day is rainy and depressin', but that's no reason to sleep away a perfectly good Saturday. Ain't you goin' up to work with Simon today?"

Thus were her problems thrust right upon her at the moment of waking. What *was* she going to do about working with Simon? Would it be awkward? Would it be better to avoid the whole situation by quitting her activities in the laboratory completely? Or would Simon be even more hurt by such evasionary tactics?

She didn't know what to do. She hadn't given any thought to last night's incident. Perhaps she should have, for she had no clear idea of the significance of Simon's behavior. What had he been trying to tell her: merely that he was inwardly furious at her neglect? Or was he saying a great deal more?

Miss Townley, with her usual speedy efficiency, was hurrying Pippa into her clothes, not permitting the girl a moment for calm reflection. "If there's anythin' I can't abide," she muttered as she whipped about the room, pulling out a muslin morning dress from the wardrobe, buffing Pippa's shoes, stowing away her nightdress and putting a brush to the girl's hair, all in the space of a few moments, "it's wastin' away the mornin'. The first part of the day is the most productive time. I always say that folks who sleep late have a bit of the degenerate—Good heavens, girl, what's *this*?"

"What?" Pippa asked, still sleepy despite having performed her ablutions and having been almost completely dressed.

"This bruise on your arm! When did you hurt yourself? And how?"

Pippa looked down at the black-and-blue smudge on her upper arm. That was where Simon had grasped her a few hours before. She felt her color rise at once. A flash of recollection brought the scene to her consciousness with the shock of reality. She could feel the painful grip of his hands on her arms, the jolt of surprise when he'd taken her into that angry, impassioned embrace. She remembered every sensation, every shiver of her flesh, every beat of the blood in her veins. He, of course, would remember nothing. Perhaps all he'd felt had been the anger. Perhaps—her breath caught in her throat with a start—the passion had been *hers*!

"Well, how did it happen?" Miss Townley demanded again.

"I haven't the slightest notion," Pippa answered absently and slipped her arms into her dress, her mind now preoccupied with a new concern.

All during breakfast and her morning visit to Sybil, Pippa struggled with the question of her work with Simon, but she could come to no conclusion. In spite of her indecision, at a little past eleven she found herself making her way to the third floor. It was as if her feet intended to take her there whether her mind wanted to or not.

She met Emma on the top of the narrow stairs. The housemaid was carrying a breakfast tray which had obviously not been touched. "Is anything amiss?" Pippa asked.

"Eh?"

"The tray. Didn't he take his breakfast?"

"Not 'im. Still in bed. First time ever I've known 'im to stay in bed. Won't even let me in!" she muttered, shaking her head.

"Here, give it to me. Let me see what I can do."

She went through the empty laboratory to his bedroom and tapped on the door.

"Go away, Emma," came his voice, thick with weariness. "For God's sake let me be."

"It's not Emma. I've brought your breakfast. May I come in?"

"No. Go away, Pippa, please. I don't want breakfast. Breakfast is the last thing in the world I want."

"Nevertheless it will do you good. Do let me in."

"No! Go away. I'm not dressed."

"Then pull the covers over you. See here, Simon, I won't brook a refusal. I'm coming in, so pull up your covers. I shall count to three."

"Don't you understand? I've the most devilish headache. I can't see anyone. Go away, like a good girl."

"One—!" she counted firmly.

"I warn you, ma'am—"

"Two—!"

"—I'm completely naked!"

"Three!" She pushed open the door and marched in.

Before she even looked in the direction of the bed, she placed the tray on his bedside table, went to the window and threw open the draperies, lightening the room with the grey light of an overcast sky. Then she turned and boldly looked at him.

He had evidently removed his coat and shoes before falling into bed, but that was all. He still wore everything else he'd worn the night before. His shirt was open and dreadfully rumpled, his breeches looked even dirtier in the daylight than they'd seemed the night before, and his unshaven face and bloodshot eyes gave him the look of an habitual souse. But he was not naked. "Liar," she said, sticking her tongue out at him.

"Trespasser," he said in quick rejoinder, and then winced. He put a shaking hand on his matted, dark-red hair and groaned. He hadn't lied about his headache.

"I've trespassed only for your own good," she said calmly, plumping up a discarded pillow and inserting it behind his back. "A cup of tea and a bit of toast is bound to make you feel better."

"The only thing that'll make me feel better," he muttered, "is death."

"Serves you right." She poured a cup of the still-steaming brew, sat down at the edge of the bed and handed it to him. "Four taverns, indeed! That would probably be too much even for a chronic tippler. But a novice—!"

"Did I go to four taverns?"

"So you said." She looked at him suspiciously. "Don't you remember?"

"Not much."

"I see. But you *do* remember the Royal Society and your speech, don't you?"

"Oh, yes. That much is quite clear."

She looked down at her folded hands and clenched them nervously. "Then you also remember that I failed to go with you. That's why I had to see you this morning, Simon. I want to tell you how *very sorry* I am that—"

His face hardened. "You've already told me. It's not

necessary to tell me so again."

Her head came up sharply. "Then you *do* remember what happened after!" she accused.

"I remember that you waited up for me and gave me an apology. That's all."

"Is it? Don't you remember your monologue about Simon the Invisible? Or . . . anything else?"

"No, I'm afraid I don't." He sipped his tea with gingerly disgust. "Was I very revolting?"

"No. You were . . . interesting. You said, among other things, that I look at you every day but never *see* you."

"Did I?" He kept his eyes resolutely on his cup. "That's just the sort of fustian one might expect from a maudlin souse."

"Oh, I don't know about that, Simon. There may be some truth in it. *In vino veritas*, you know."

He gave her a look of wry amusement. "In *wine* there may be truth, my dear, but I drank only ale."

"So you don't believe what you said? That I don't really see you?"

"I believe that everything that happened last night is best forgotten."

"I don't think I *can* forget it, Simon," she said in a low voice, her eyes back down on her hands.

He put the cup on the table and hitched himself over on his side so that she couldn't see his face. "You'll forget it whether you think so now or not. I expect that you'll be too busy to keep such nonsense on your mind."

"Busy? Why?" Her face brightened. "Have you some new experiments you wish me to help you with?"

"No, of course not. I meant with your suitors. Household gossip has it that you have two already. And who knows how many more lurk over the horizon. They should keep you busy enough."

"Now that *is* fustian. Who on earth said I had two suitors?"

He turned to look at her over his shoulder. "It's common knowledge among the staff. Lord Oxbrough and

William have been distinctly identified. You're not going to deny it, are you?"

"I don't suppose you'll believe me if I do." She peered at him curiously. "Are you thinking, Simon, that that's why I didn't keep our appointment last night? Because I was too busy with my 'suitors'?"

He threw himself back against the pillows in disgust and shut his eyes. "Damnation, Pippa, I don't want to talk about last night! My head feels as if it's swollen to twice its size, my mouth seems lined with fur, and my stomach is bouncing around inside me like a demented balloon. Let me be."

She rose. "Very well, my dear. I'll go. But I hope that, when you're feeling better, you'll overcome your reticence and talk with me about this."

She went to the door feeling oddly let down. He'd erected a thick wall between them again, and she hadn't been able to make a breach. Before leaving, she took a look back. He had lifted himself up on one elbow and was watching her. When their eyes met, her stomach did a peculiar flip-flop inside her. Something strange was happening to her in response to him . . . and it would require some serious thinking. "G-Good day, Simon," she said.

"Pippa?"

She paused.

"About helping me with my experiments . . ."

"Yes?"

"I've decided that I'm going to move out, you see . . ."

"Move *out*?" She could only gape at him.

"Yes. Take my own rooms. Somewhere close to Dr. Young. He suggested last night that we could accomplish more working together than going our separate ways as we've been doing. So you see—"

"You won't be needing my help any more."

"No."

"I see." She was aware that every muscle in her body had stiffened. "Very well, Simon. Wh-whatever you wish." She gave him a brisk nod and went quickly out the door. There was no reason to linger. She knew a dismissal when she heard one.

She walked hurriedly down the stairs and back to her room. She shut her door, sank down upon her bed and stared out ahead of her. She was stunned. Something had happened to her of great significance, and she didn't even know what it was. Only her feelings seemed to know that she'd been dealt a blow. Her mind was utterly calm and logical. Simon had dismissed her, true, but it was only to be expected. She'd offended him the night before by forgetting their appointment—an appointment that had been very important to him. He was merely getting back at her. It was all perfectly understandable. Then why was she feeling so confused, so empty, so absolutely devastated?

Her mind might be calm and logical, but somehow she couldn't think. She felt tired, sluggish and unable to function. She ought to get up. She had a dozen things to do. But she continued to sit on the edge of the bed, staring out at absolutely nothing and feeling exactly as misplaced and lost as if she'd just discovered that the world beneath her feet had been completely cut away.

William had not spent a comfortable night either. He was angry at himself for having lost his temper with Pippa again, and he'd lain awake for hours berating himself. Perhaps the girl had been right; perhaps he *had* been overbearing in intruding on her privacy. Surely she was entitled to speak to Dolly without *his* intrusive supervision.

The truth was that he was quite taken with Pippa. Every time she looked up at him with those wide, wise eyes behind her owlish spectacles, he felt a constriction in his chest. She was a most appealing little chit to whom it would be very pleasant to be wed. His mother had hinted a number of times that Pippa would make an ideal wife. If only he could be sure that she was not, beneath her serene, rational, contained exterior, an impulsive shatterbrain like Sybil.

He'd arisen early that morning but had waited impatiently until noon before calling at his mother's house. It wouldn't do to seem too eager. But when Latcham told him that Pippa was closeted in her room, he was reluctant to disturb her. Containing his impatience, he went to his study to pass the time working on the household accounts until she came down.

He was interrupted by a tap at the door. It was the groom, Robbins, who requested a word with him. "Sorry t' disturb ye, m' lord, but Mr. Adolphus ain't anywhere about, y' see."

"You're not disturbing me, Robbins. What is it?"

"It's the new stallion, m' lord. Salvaje. I know Mr. Adolphus said not to bother you about 'im, but—"

William's eyes narrowed. "That's all right. Go on."

"Well, y' see, 'e's a bit wild. Kicked so loud on 'is stall all night that th' other animals 're gettin' nervous."

William began to tap on the desk with the fingers of one hand. "A new stallion, eh? I haven't yet seen him, Robbins. What's he like?"

"Oh, 'e's a big Spanish beauty an' no mistake. Fine specimen. Pure Barb breed. But too spirited by 'alf. Needs a bit o' trainin', y' know, afore 'e'll be useful I wuz thinkin' that per'aps we could move 'im t' the country fer a while. Ol' Tompson, on the estate, e'd know just how to 'andle 'im."

William was seething. So . . . Dolly had gotten his way with Pippa after all! He stared at Robbins speculatively for a moment. "Would you say, Robbins, that the animal—what did you say his name was? Salvaje?—was in any way suitable for a lady?"

Robbins blinked in surprise. "A *lady*, m' lord? Wouldn't want *you* t' ride 'im as 'e is now."

"After training, then. Would he be suitable?"

Robbins shrugged. "Can't say. I've seen these wild creatures turn calm as lambs sometimes. But this'n is *huge*. Miss Sybil's tall, but if ye're askin' me, I'd say Salvaje'd do better fer a man."

"I see. Thank you, Robbins. Don't do anything about moving Salvaje just yet. Let me think about it."

But after Robbins left, William didn't spend a

moment thinking about it. In a fury, he shouted for Latcham. "Where's Dolly?" he demanded as soon as the butler made an appearance.

"I don't know, my lord. He went out right after breakfast."

"Will he be taking luncheon at home?"

"He didn't say."

William gnashed his teeth in frustration. "Then get me Lady Philippa. At once! I'll see her in the library."

He crossed the hall in angry strides and paced round the library in a rage. How dared that addlepated female fly in the face of his direct order? She was every bit as irresponsible as Sybil—perhaps worse. Whatever tenderness he'd felt for her earlier was gone. He wanted nothing so much as to wring her neck!

Pippa, on her part, did not feel up to an interview with William. She had been through quite enough that morning. But Latcham made it clear that his lordship had been adamant, so, reluctantly, she presented herself at the library door. "You sent for me, William?"

"Yes. Come in and shut the door, will you?" Tightlipped and forbidding, he motioned her to a chair. "I shall get right to the point. How much blunt did you give Dolly for that horse?"

Pippa sighed. "Are you going to persist in pursuing this subject, William? I really don't wish to discuss it."

"No doubt. But we shall discuss it nevertheless. I won't have you doling out large sums of money to satisfy the whims of my charges. *How much*, ma'am?"

She put a hand to her forehead, which was beginning to ache alarmingly. "Have you seen Salvaje, then?"

"No, not yet. But Robbins has described him to me. I would guess, from that description, that my brother's little whim has cost you in the neighborhood of a thousand pounds."

"No, William, you are quite wrong. In the first place, it was not so high a price. And in the second place, it was not Dolly's whim but mine. I've told you more than once that the horse is for me."

"And I've told *you* that you needn't buy a horse. There are several in the stables suitable—"

"But you can't insist that I use your horses if I want one of my own!"

William glared at her. "Let's make an end of that lie! You can't ride Salvaje, and you know it."

"I don't know anything of the sort!" She put up her chin and glared back at him. "And I don't like to be called a liar, either."

"Then don't spout falsehoods," he shot back. "You never intended to ride that horse. You bought him only because Dolly urged him on you. Why, if my guess is correct, you've never even *seen* the animal."

"I didn't have to see him. If Dolly can ride him, I can."

"Dolly is seventeen and horse-mad. He'd ride *anything*. Admit it, ma'am. You didn't purchase that horse for your own use."

"I won't admit anything of the sort. I truly don't see what business it is of yours."

"Isn't it my business? Do you think I can permit my brother's self-indulgence to cost you, my mother's guest, a *thousand pounds*? I shall reimburse you, of course, this very afternoon, and I shall then be the owner of a horse I neither need nor want. So it becomes very much my business, doesn't it?"

Pippa jumped up from her chair. "It does not! You shall *not* reimburse me! Not *one cent*! *I* bought the horse, and I shall keep him."

"Over my dead body, ma'am. Do you think I would permit you to pay for a horse you will never make use of?"

"I *shall* make use of him. This very afternoon!"

He sneered. "Will you, indeed? I'd very much like to see it."

"Then come and watch me."

His eyebrows rose in supercilious amusement. "You'll never even mount him, I suspect, once you've taken a look at him."

"You underestimate me, sir. I shall put on my riding dress at once. You're quite welcome to accompany me to the park."

He bowed in acquiescence. "My pleasure, ma'am. I'll tell Robbins to bring the animal round. Shall we say half an hour?"

Chapter Fifteen

SYBIL HAD been confined to her room for more than three days. Forced to remain in her bedroom from last Wednesday evening to this Saturday morning, she felt she'd endured the equivalent of a prison sentence. In spite of the fact that her ankle was still tender from her injury, she determined to go downstairs to find some company. Leaning heavily on Noreen's shoulder, she painfully and awkwardly maneuvered her way down the stairs and down the hall to the drawing room. But not one member of the household was in evidence. "Where is everybody?" she asked plaintively.

Noreen shrugged. "Lady Philippa's gone ridin'," she offered. "I 'elped her to put on 'er ridin' costume myself. An' Lady Sturtevant still 'as the headache, so she's stayin' in 'er room. Shall I get Miss Townley fer you, Miss Sybil? She's upstairs in the sewin' room, mendin' sheets."

"No, thank you, Noreen. Just help me into the easy

chair near the fire. Someone's bound to come along soon."

Someone did. Adolphus, full of news about the stable he'd found to rent, poked his head into the drawing room looking for Pippa. When he saw that she wasn't there, he tried immediately to withdraw. His sister did not find his lack of interest in *her* presence to be very flattering. "Dash it all, Dolly, *I'm* here," she complained. "I'm out of my bedchamber at last, yet you, you witling, say nothing at all in greeting."

"Sorry, Sybil. I *am* glad to see that you're better, of course. But I must find Pippa. I've something to tell her."

"Noreen says she's gone riding."

"Oh? In the town carriage?"

"No. Noreen said she'd worn her riding dress."

Dolly came into the room, his brow knit. "That's strange. I haven't seen Pippa ride a horse since she arrived. Why would she decide to do so today? The weather's a bit nasty for riding, isn't it? And . . . what horse did she take?"

"I've no idea. Why are you so concerned, Dolly. Is something amiss?"

Dolly shrugged, but he was vaguely troubled. He called Latcham and inquired about Pippa's whereabouts. Latcham answered just as Sybil had—that Lady Philippa had gone riding.

"Did she go alone?" Dolly persisted.

"No, sir. His lordship was with her."

Dolly felt a decided shock of alarm. "His lordship? Do you mean *William*?"

"Yes, Mr. Adolphus. Lord Sturtevant left the house with her."

"Good God! He didn't . . . they didn't go to the *stables*, did they?"

Latcham shook his head. "His lordship had the new horse sent round to the park."

Dolly turned quite pale. "The *new* horse? You must be mistaken! William doesn't *know* about the new horse."

"I think he does, Mr. Adolphus. He ordered Robbins to saddle the *new* horse. He said so quite specifically. Even called him by name. Something Spanish, I think it was."

"Not . . . *Salvaje*?"

"Yes, sir, that was the name."

Dolly moaned. "However did he learn—?" he muttered to himself. Then a new thought occured to him. "Did you say he ordered Salvaje *saddled*? Don't tell me William intends to *ride* him?"

"Oh, I don't think so, sir. Lord Sturtevant wasn't even wearing riding dress," Latcham said soothingly. "Only Lady Philippa appeared to be outfitted for riding."

Dolly stared at the butler, his alarm growing steadily more desperate. "Good Lord! Are you saying that Pippa—?"

Sybil, who had been listening to the exchange with interest, could not understand Dolly's perturbation. "Why are you so concerned, Dolly? Pippa knows how to sit a horse."

Dolly cast her a wild-eyed look. "Not *this* horse. She'll *kill* herself."

"Confound it, Dolly, what are you talking about? Do you know something about this horse that Pippa doesn't?"

"Yes, I do. I'm the one who persuaded her to buy him. As far as I know, she hasn't even *seen* him yet."

"Dolly Sturtevant, are you saying that you cozzened Pippa into buying an animal unsuitable for her to ride?"

"Well, I was going to have him properly *trained* before . . .! Dash it all, Sybil, I can't stand here babbling! I'd better go after them. Perhaps I can catch them up before—"

"Wait just a minute," Sybil snapped, pulling herself from her chair. "I'm coming with you. You will not leave me here in complete ignorance of everything that's going—"

"I beg your pardon," came a voice from the doorway. "Is Lady Philippa at home? There was no one at the door when I knocked, so—"

Latcham and Dolly turned to the stranger in the doorway in bewilderment, but Sybil gasped loudly. "Lord *Oxbrough*!"

Latcham shook himself into action. "I do apologize, your lordship. I can't imagine where the footmen have gone. Lady Philippa is not at home. If you'll follow me, I'll show you back to the door."

"That's all right, Latcham," Sybil cut in. "You needn't show him out. I'm acquainted with Lord Oxbrough. You may leave us." She paused while Latcham bowed himself out and then looked at the visitor curiously. "Did you say you've come to see Pippa, my lord? I didn't know you and my friend were acquainted."

"Oh, we're very well acquainted, I assure you. I hoped to prevail upon her to ride out with me today."

Sybil's eyebrows rose. "Really? *Very* well acquainted? What a sly boots Pippa is, to be sure."

Dolly, shuffling about impatiently near the doorway, was waiting for an opportunity to make his escape. Since the conversation between his sister and the visitor threatened to become lengthy, he decided to be rude and cut in. "I hope you will both excuse me. I must go after Pippa at once."

Oxbrough raised his quizzing glass and stared through it at the young man. "Go after her? Please don't think me encroaching, my boy, but may I ask why?"

"My brother," Sybil said with a touch of disparagement, "is afraid she's about to ride a horse that's too . . . too . . . too what, Dolly?"

Dolly threw her a look of rebuke. "Too spirited for her," he said, annoyed that his sister had found it necessary to reveal so much to a stranger. "And if you keep me standing here, I may be too late."

"Too late for what?" Oxbrough asked interestedly.

"Too late to keep her from a terrible accident."

"You don't say," Oxbrough marvelled. "The horse

is as spirited as that, eh? Likely to toss her, do you think?"

"I think it extremely likely," Dolly responded curtly.

"My, my. Impetuous little creature, I must say, our Lady Philippa." He shook his head in grudging admiration of her. "Always up to some madcap scheme. Well, my boy, my carriage is just outside the door. Would you like me to drive you to her?"

This was the first helpful suggestion Dolly had heard. "Would you, sir?" he asked gratefully. "That would save me a considerable amount of time."

"I'd be delighted. Let's be off at once. Good day, Miss Sturtevant."

"You may keep your good days to yourself, my lord," Sybil said firmly as she hobbled toward them, "and give me your arm. I am going with you!"

Pippa and William drove in his curricle to Hyde Park. When they reached the bridle path, they found that Robbins had not yet arrived with Salvaje. They sat waiting in the carriage, neither of them of a mind to stand about in the chill wind. The day was still damp and overcast, and not one rider was in evidence on the path. "No one is foolish enough to ride in this weather," William muttered.

I wouldn't be so foolish either, if you hadn't pushed me into this, Pippa said to him in her mind. But outwardly she maintained an icy silence and stared out at the heavy sky.

William watched her from the corner of his eye. In her voluminously skirted blue-velvet riding habit and the perky little plumed hat that sat at a cocky angle on her head, she looked almost fragile. She was perched on the edge of the coach seat, her body tilted slightly forward and the folds of her skirt falling over her thighs in graceful swirls. One hand rested on the window-frame of the curricle, and the other lay in her lap, the fingers clenched. Her position, her costume, and even the incongruous spectacles perched on her nose all seemed to underline her delicacy. His tender feelings toward her reasserted themselves, and he began to feel misgivings about his part in this affair. Perhaps he'd pressed the matter too far.

What she'd done was completely reprehensible, but he hadn't intended to make her suffer for it unduly. He had no wish to force her to ride a horse too mettlesome for her. Well, he would not, in the end, let her go through with it. He'd let her frighten herself a little—with her first sight of the animal she would surely back down—and then, as soon as she confessed her fault and agreed to accept repayment, he would forgive her. He was not a monster, after all.

After a few moments they both spied Robbins' approach from the Public Road. He was leading the horse that had caused this drawn-out and difficult dispute. At her first sight of him, Pippa had to press a gloved hand to her mouth to keep from crying out. The stallion was *enormous*. Both she and William stared at the beast in amazement. They had both expected a large, powerful animal, but not one quite so awesome as *this*.

Robbins led him to the path and walked him round in a circle. Whinnying and rearing his head, Salvaje pranced onto the bridle path with the arrogance of royalty. Pippa could see at once why Dolly had wanted him. The animal was quite beautiful. But even a fool could tell he wasn't broken to the bridle. Pippa's heart sank to her shoes.

William, however, had all he could do to hide his grin. Salvaje was formidable. He could detect, in Pippa's stiff posture, that she was terrified by the horse's size and obvious power. She would never mount him. He, William, had won his point.

But Pippa surprised him. "Will you hand me down, sir? Robbins is waiting." She was, outwardly at least, completely calm.

He held his tongue, climbed out of the carriage and helped her down. She walked with brave, firm steps to the horse's side. "What a beautiful fellow you are, Salvaje," she murmured, patting his nose. The horse reared up and, in spite of herself, she took a backward step. "There, there," she said, reaching for his throatlatch to hold the head still, "don't shy away from me. I won't hurt you."

Robbins came up beside her. "Ye ain't goin' t' ride 'im, are ye, m' lady? I saddled 'em like Lord Sturtevant asked me to, but I din't reckon on you bein' the one. I wouldn't advise it, ma'am. Salvaje, 'ere, is a bit wild, y' see. 'E ain't ready fer—"

"I'll just take a short ride, Robbins," Pippa said, hoping her terror didn't show in her voice. "I want to . . . to get the feel of him. Will you help me up, please?"

"Come now, Pippa, this is the outside of enough," William put in. "You know as well as I that you can't ride that demon."

"Perhaps I can't," Pippa said with determination, "but I intend to try. Come now, Robbins, I'm waiting."

Robbins, reluctant to oblige, looked to William for guidance. His lordship shook his head. "Pippa, I cannot permit—"

"You're not my guardian, William. I don't need your permission." She felt very much the fool to proceed with these histrionics. There was no question that she was heading for a catastrophe if she persisted. But William had called her a liar, and a flush of stiff-necked pride made her unwilling to back down. "We've come here for the express purpose of demonstrating that this is my horse and that I intend to make full and frequent use of him. Unless you are willing to concede that point, let me go ahead with the demonstration."

William flushed in frustration. How had he let matters get so far out of hand? If he conceded the point, she would give up this foolish venture and be safe. But he would gain nothing. She and Dolly would have won. *Confound it*, he told himself, *if she can proceed with this game, so can I*. She would give up in the end. She wouldn't ride that horse. She was not such a fool as that. Once she found herself on the back of that great beast, she would surely give up and climb down—he was sure of that. All he had to do was to hold out. Giving in now would be craven, and William Sturtevant had never been called craven in his life. "All right, Robbins, do as the lady says."

Robbins, with an incredulous shake of his head, cupped his hands for the lady. She placed her booted foot in the cup and let herself be heaved up. With her pulse beating rapidly, she took up the reins and looked about her. She'd never ridden a horse this size before. She seemed so high above the ground that she felt almost dizzy. Salvaje, meanwhile, was completely ignoring her. He'd lowered his head and was now calmly munching at the wet grass. If she nudged him very, *very* gently, perhaps he would not prance and rear too wildly. Slowly she lifted a hand toward his neck . . .

At that moment, the sound of wheels on gravel distracted all of them. William and Robbins looked round, and even Salvaje lifted his head. But Pippa was too terrified to turn.

"Pippa!" shouted Dolly, leaping from Oxbrough's carriage. *"Don't—!"*

"Dash it all, Pippa, have you lost your *mind*?" shrieked Sybil.

"Whoa!" shouted Oxbrough, pulling his horses to.

The noise was all that was needed to set Salvaje off. Without the prodding of a hand or spur, he reared up and set off down the path like the wind. Pippa grasped him round the neck with both arms and hung on for dear life.

The entire assemblage watched speechlessly as horse and rider disappeared round the turn of the path. "Oh, my *Lord*!" Dolly groaned as soon as she was lost from sight.

"What have I done?" William whispered in horror.

"Why on earth did she do it?" Sybil asked, appalled.

Lord Oxbrough only shook his head in wonderment. "And she insists she's not a madcap!" he muttered, amused.

Sybil stared at him. "I don't see what's funny, my lord. She may kill herself!"

"No, she won't," Oxbrough answered confidently. "She's a most resourceful girl. She'll be all right, mark my words."

"I 'ope ye don't mind me sayin' it, m' lord," Robbins interjected worriedly, "but I wouldn't wager on 'er safety. Seems t' me we oughta take one of the carriages 'n ride arfter 'er."

This was no sooner said than William dashed for his curricle. Dolly leaped up beside him, and Robbins jumped on the rear. Leaving Sybil and Oxbrough standing beside the other carriage to wait for their return, they careened down the path as fast as William could urge his horses.

They found her three miles down the path, sitting in a muddy ditch and rubbing her head. Her hat was gone, her face was streaked, her habit was in disarray, but she was apparently unhurt. The horse, of course, was nowhere to be seen. William knelt at her side. "Pippa . . . are you all right?"

She looked at him fuzzily. "My glasses . . ."

"I'll look for them," Dolly offered eagerly, relieved beyond words to see her safe.

"Can you get up?" William asked gently.

"Yes, I . . . I think so." She allowed him to help her up, keeping her lips pressed tightly together to keep from crying out. There was such a sharp pain on her right side that she feared something was broken. But under no circumstances would she admit to William that anything was wrong. "I rode him for a while, at any rate," she said shakily, smiling up at him in misty-eyed triumph. "You'll have to admit that."

"And *you'll* have to admit," he responded grudgingly, "that you were an impetuous fool. Your Salvaje is probably gone for good."

"But at least you admit that he's *my* Salvaje."

He made no answer. She threw a sidelong glance at him, but without her spectacles his face was a blur. Was he sulking because she'd won the point? She hoped not. Her head ached, the pain in her right side was excruciating, and the horse was gone. This was scarcely a triumph he should begrudge.

William, however, did begrudge it. By this foolish and destructive act, Pippa kept him from maintaining his control over the household management, over the finances and over Dolly as well. Despite the fact that Pippa's movements were hesitant and stiff (indicating that she was undoubtedly badly bruised), he felt no sympathy for her. She'd brought this on herself. She was a silly, headstrong female, and no matter what his mother said or how attractive he found her, he would not—definitely not!—ever make the girl an offer. This foolish exhibition was the very last straw.

He helped her into the carriage and climbed up beside her. Just as Robbins hopped up on the back, Dolly came running up. "I found the spectacles, Pippa, but they're badly broken. You won't be able to use them any more, I'm afraid." He dropped the mangled glasses in her lap. "Salvaje must have crushed them," he added unhappily.

She looked down at them. The frames were bent, and the lens on the left was shattered. This pathetic-looking ruin seemed a final ignominy. She'd been an idiot to have let herself be goaded into such a disastrous adventure. Not only was she painfully bruised; now she wouldn't even *see* clearly.

"I'm s-sorry," Dolly said with a crack in his voice.

She lifted her eyes from the lacerated glasses and peered down at him. Dolly's face was so woebegone with guilt and misery that even she, with her impaired eyesight, could distinguish the expression. Her heart was touched by it. She pulled off a muddy glove, reached out her hand and patted his cheek comfortingly. "Don't feel so badly, dearest. The spectacles can be replaced."

He gave her a grateful smile. "That's true. Simon can fix them."

Pippa winced. *Simon,* she thought with a stab of pain. *Simon can fix them.* It was strange that Simon's name was never mentioned unless there was some emergency, and he was needed. What was it he'd called himself last night? *Simon the Invisible,* wasn't it? She'd thought it was maudlin self-pity brought on by drink, but he'd been quite right. No one had mentioned his name all day, but now, in this emergency, Dolly had suddenly thought of him. He'd been *conjured up*, just as he'd described in his inebriated monologue: *Simon, we need you. Appear!*

She hardly heard the words Dolly spoke as he turned to William. "She looks done in," he said in a low voice. "Take her home, William. I'm going to search for Salvaje."

"Very well," William said tightly, "but I want to see you when you return. I have a few *very particular* remarks to make to you."

Pippa wanted to remonstrate. William had no right to scold Dolly about this. She'd climbed up on Salvaje's back just to prevent . . .

But the carriage began to roll. The motion sent shock waves of pain through Pippa's aching body. She was too bruised, too weary, too full of self-disgust to argue with William any more. Besides, a glance at his face showed that his mood was anything but conciliatory. His expression was stony. She could see well enough to recognize that.

She eased herself carefully back against the seat and closed her eyes. Somewhere in the back of her mind, she understood that William had closed his heart to her. He showed no inclination to soothe her or console her. There was not a sign of the suitor in him. The man who'd leaned over and planted a soft kiss on her lips only the day before was gone. She'd lost him. By falling into these Sybil-like scrapes, she'd estranged him for good.

But in the forefront of her mind, she was not concerned with William. It was Simon she was thinking of. It was Simon she wanted to conjure up here beside her. She was as reprehensible as the rest of the Sturtevants. She'd forgotten him when he had need of *her*, but now, when chaos struck, she wanted *him.* Two tears welled up beneath her closed eyelids and slid down her cheeks. *Oh, Simon,* she cried somewhere deep inside, *I'm so ashamed. I'm as bad as all the rest. But I'm bruised . . . I'm hurting . . . my glasses are broken. I need you. Why don't you appear?*

Chapter Sixteen

LADY OXBROUGH had been waiting since Wednesday to receive word from Lady Philippa about payment for the sapphire. It was not that she wished to accept payment—no indeed! It was the *gem* she wanted. But she'd been curious to see whether the Wyckfield chit really meant to deliver that enormous sum she'd pledged in her note. The shocking note the girl had left behind had said plainly that she would deliver fifteen thousand pounds on the twentieth of September. That was Thursday. Thursday and Friday had come and gone. It was now Saturday, the twenty-second, and still there had been no word. Lady Oxbrough had waited long enough.

She was certain that the young Lady Philippa and the irresponsible Sturtevant chit were the only ones involved in the theft. It was quite unlikely that the breezy but straightforward Georgina Sturtevant had had anything to do with it, and certainly the head of the family, William Sturtevant, was too upright and respectable to have sanctioned any such impropriety. No, it had to be the girls on their own.

But what was she to do about them? After careful reflection she decided that she would bring the matter to William Sturtevant's attention. He was the head of the family, after all, and he was the one who should straighten out the coil. Lord Sturtevant was the appropriate channel through which she would get her retribution. With the letter as evidence of wrongdoing, she had little doubt she would regain possession of the sapphire as soon as Sturtevant was acquainted with the facts.

Clad in her most imposing costume—a walking dress of mulberry crape covered with a matching camlet pelisse trimmed with leopard skin, and all this topped by a yellow turban made of a rich material woven from silk ribbon known as galloon—she set off at noon for Lord Sturtevant's apartments in Cleveland Street. Her appearance, she knew, was awe-inspiring. Her temper was controlled (unvengeful but firm), her purpose was clear (and quite unshakable), and her evidence was in hand (carefully tucked into her large leopardskin muff).

Lord Sturtevant's man informed her that his lordship was not at home. This gave her control a small jolt. She had purposely started out at noon to be certain of catching him at home. What sort of gentleman was it who left his bed before noon on a rainy Saturday? (Though now she came to think of it, Crippins, her butler, had told her that Basil himself had gone out early today.) She pressed Sturtevant's man for more information and learned that he'd most likely gone to his mother's house. It was there that Lady Oxbrough repaired forthwith.

She was forced to stand in Lady Sturtevant's doorway for fully ten minutes before the door was answered. The butler finally responded to her knocks but uttered not a word of apology or explanation. She'd often heard that Georgina Sturtevant ran a very loose household, but the butler's casual indifference was really the outside of enough. Her temper was growing shorter by the minute, and it was not a bit improved when she learned that

Lord Sturtevant was not here, either. "None of the family is at home, my lady," the butler told her, "but Lady Sturtevant. And *she's* in bed with the headache."

"Nonsense. Georgina Sturtevant is not the sort to nurse a sick headache," Lady Oxbrough said peremptorily, having determined in her impatience to speak to *someone* about this matter before her temper was completely lost. "Send her to me at once. I shall await her in there. That *is* the drawing room, I take it?"

Poor Latcham was no match for so authoritative and overwhelming a personage. He led her to the drawing room, offered to take her wrap (an offer which she coldly refused) and, under her imperious glare, bowed himself out and went for his mistress.

Within a few minutes, Georgina hurried in. Her eyes were circled and her hair blowzy, but she'd donned a red Florentine silk dressing gown which was, in its way, as impressive as Lady Oxbrough's pelisse, and she offered her visitor such a warm smile and sincere greeting that Lady Oxbrough's irritation weakened. "I'm sorry to have dragged you from your bed, Lady Sturtevant," she apologized.

"Do call me Georgina," Lady Sturtevant said, leaning down and taking the older woman's hand. "I'm delighted that you've come. I've wanted so often to improve our slight acquaintanceship."

"Thank you, my dear," Lady Oxbrough murmured, softened. "It's kind of you to say so, I must say. Unfortunately, my errand today may not be construed as a friendly one."

Georgina looked at her askance. "Oh?" She dropped into a chair without taking her eyes from the face of her guest. "Is there something I've done to offend you?"

"Not you, my dear, but your daughter and her friend. The Wyckfield chit."

"Heavens! *Pippa?* I might be made to believe that *Sybil*'s done something wrong—she's always been headstrong—but Pippa has always been a nonpareil. Quite above reproach."

"Not in this case, I'm afraid. I'm not certain about

your Sybil's part, but about Lady Philippa's role I can have not the slightest doubt."

Georgina raised a brow. "I can't believe that Pippa could say or do anything in the least reprehensible."

"Would stealing a jewel from my collection be considered reprehensible?" Lady Oxbrough asked flatly.

Georgina couldn't believe her ears. "Jewel? My Pippa *stole a jewel*?"

"Yes. I have uncontrovertible proof. Now, what have you to say to that?"

"I don't understand. What sort of jewel?"

"A sapphire. The Sturtevant sapphire."

"The *Sturtevant—*?" Georgina's lips turned white. She gaped at her visitor in astonishment. Then, with an "O" of comprehension, she clapped her hands to her mouth. "Oh, the *dear* girl," she muttered, tears coming into her eyes. "That she should have done such a thing for me! When I told her yesterday that the gem was missing, I never *dreamed* she would go to such lengths—"

"What are you babbling about, Georgina?" Lady Oxbrough interrupted impatiently. "You told her *yesterday* that it was missing? Ridiculous! She removed the gem from my collection on *Wednesday*!"

"Don't be silly. That's quite impossible. I didn't know *myself* that it was gone until yesterday."

"Nonetheless, my dear, she stole it on Wednesday. I must say that I have her confession. In writing!"

"Confession?" Georgina put her hands to her head in an actress-like gesture of confusion. "You're making my head swim, ma'am. What you say makes not a smidge of sense to me. In the first place—" She lowered her hands, blinked abstractedly at her visitor and then leaned forward in sudden antagonism. "In the first place," she repeated sharply, "how did the *Sturtevant sapphire* find its way into *your* collection from *my* jewel box?"

Lady Oxbrough sat back, crossed her arms over her breast and launched into an account of her entire experience with the sapphire from the day Mrs. Membry first made her the offer to the afternoon when she'd found the letter on the floor of her bedroom and the sapphire gone. Georgina, completely overset, didn't know what to make of the story. Not only was Lady Oxbrough's manner sincere, but the letter she offered in evidence was indeed written in Pippa's neat hand.

That Pippa was up to some skullduggery was patently clear. Even worse, she'd not been honest with her Aunt Georgie—a situation which Georgina would have sworn could never occur. But if the girl *had* written the incriminating letter on Wednesday, she'd known yesterday afternoon (when she'd put her arm about her aunt in loving consolation) a great deal more than she'd said. Georgina had never heard her say one dishonest word, but Pippa had certainly not been strightforward yesterday. Georgina didn't know what to make of it.

She paced about the room for many minutes in silence, trying desperately to deduce an answer from the bits and pieces of information Lady Oxbrough had supplied. Lady Oxbrough, meanwhile, watched her with a feeling of unexpected sympathy. She had not foreseen that Lady Sturtevant would react to her news with quite such excessive dismay.

Georgina stopped her pacing abruptly. "Sybil!" she said decisively.

"Sybil?"

"My daughter. She's at the bottom of all this. I don't know what sort of game the girls have been playing—or why—but the key must lie with Sybil. Ever since they were children, Sybil has been able to pull Pippa into the most ridiculous imbroglios."

Lady Oxbrough's face hardened. "I hardly think one should call an act of robbery—"

There was a sudden sound from the corridor. The outer door slammed open, its crash immediately followed by the sound of footsteps and the babble of voices. The two ladies turned their heads at once in the direction of the sounds. Out in the hallway, a man's voice could be heard above the rest. "Where's your deuced butler?" he demanded. "He's never about when he's wanted, I must say!"

"Why, that . . ." Lady Oxbrough's brows knit. "That sounds like—"

"Never mind Latcham," came Sybil's voice. "Someone send for Simon."

The drawing room door flew open, and Sybil, leaning on Lord Oxbrough's arm, came limping in. Lady Oxbrough's mouth dropped open. *"Basil!"* she exclaimed.

"Mama?" He dropped Sybil's arm and crossed to her chair. "Good heavens, what are *you* doing here?"

Sybil, turning pale at the sight of her mother's visitor, made a choking sound and dropped awkwardly upon the sofa.

Lady Oxbrough was about to ask the same question of her son when Georgina gasped. "Good God! *Pippa!*"

Every eye flew to the drawing room doorway. Framed within it stood William, leading a muddy, bedraggled Pippa into the room. From head to toe the girl's appearance bespoke calamity. Her curls were tangled and matted with mud. Her cheeks were streaked with it, too, as well as the entire right side of her riding dress. Though she held her head erect and tried to move normally, everyone could see at once that her step was the gingerly sort that one takes when badly bruised and that she was favoring her right side. Lady Sturtevant flew from her chair. "Pippa, my dearest, what *happened*?"

But Pippa's eye had fallen on the visitor. "Lady Oxbrough?" she asked in startled alarm, not quite sure of her eyes.

"Yes, it is I. Do sit down, Lady Philippa," Lady Oxbrough said, not unkindly. "You look as if you've suffered an accident."

Pippa permitted William and Lady Sturtevant to help her to the sofa next to Sybil. "It's nothing," she tried to assure them, though her voice trembled. "Just a foolish little s-spill from my horse."

Georgina turned to William with anxious eyes. "Has she broken anything?"

"I don't think so. But perhaps you ought to send someone for Simon."

Georgina clapped a hand to her head. "Oh, dear! Simon's *gone*!"

"Gone?" William asked, surprised.

"Yes. He said he was going to make some arrangements to move his laboratory to a more convenient location. I don't know when he'll be back."

Something in Pippa's chest knotted at the words. Simon was gone. The disappearing man was no longer going to make appearances at the snap of the family's fingers. He had certainly picked a fine moment for his rebellion! With every bone in her body aching, with every breath a pain, with Lady Oxbrough sitting there like a tiger ready to pounce, with a feeling deep inside her that the whole world was about to collapse, Simon was not here. "It's all right, Aunt Georgie," she managed. "I'm just a bit . . . shaken. As soon as I've had a wash . . . and changed my clothes, I'll be . . . fine." She threw a quick look in Lady Oxbrough's direction. "Would you mind awfully if I excused myself and . . . went upstairs?"

"No, of course not, love," Georgina said. "Do help her, William."

"If you don't mind," Lady Oxbrough objected, "I would appreciate the girl's presence for a moment or two longer. She says she's quite all right."

The drawing room door flew open again. Miss Townley, her face tense with agitation, burst in. "Latcham told me . . . *Pippa*! My poor *darlin'*!"

Pippa smiled at her gratefully. Ada Townley's presence brought a whiff of security with it. She was Pippa's link with her past, and her affectionate concern was reassuring. "Don't look like that, Miss Townley," she said. "I'm really quite well."

"You don't look quite well to me," the old governess muttered. "Come, let me help you upstairs."

"Just a moment, my good woman," Lady Oxbrough said in offense. "You interrupted me. I was just saying that I'd like to speak to Lady Philippa for a moment."

"Whatever it is will have to wait, ma'am," Miss Townley bristled. "This child needs her bed."

"It's all right, Miss Townley," Pippa intervened. "I'll come right up. If you'll be kind enough to ready a hot bath for me—"

"Hummmph!" Miss Townley said, glowering at Lady Oxbrough. "If that's what you wish, I'll go. But if you ain't upstairs in ten minutes, I'll be back." And she stalked from the room in disgust.

"That was not very obliging of you, Mama, I must say," Lord Oxbrough remarked after Miss Townley had departed. "What do you want of Lady Philippa that's so urgent?"

"I want her to explain *this*." Lady Oxbrough held up the fateful document which she still hoped would restore the gem to her possession.

"What is that, ma'am?" William inquired.

"Yes, Mama. What's so important that you'd keep the girl from taking her rest after what she's been through?"

Sybil, her pulse racing in guilt and fear, leaned over toward Pippa. "What *is* that letter, Pippa, do you know?" she whispered.

"Hush," Pippa muttered, feeling like Marie Antoinette at the foot of the guillotine.

"It doesn't concern you, Basil," Lady Oxbrough was saying. "But you, Lord Sturtevant, might find it interesting reading."

William, conscious of every eye upon him, crossed the room and took the letter from her hand. His eye ran over it in growing confusion. "I don't understand. What *is* this? And what has it to do with Pippa? Or with me?"

"It was *written* by Pippa," Lady Sturtevant volunteered reluctantly. "And it has to do with you, William, my dear, because the sapphire it refers to is *yours*."

"The *Sturtevant* sapphire?" he asked incredulously.

A gurgle escaped from Sybil's throat.

"Here, let *me* see that," Oxbrough said in sudden annoyance, rudely pulling the paper from William's limp hold.

"What have *you* to say to this?" William demanded, attempting to recapture the sheet of paper from his grasp.

But Oxbrough had turned aside and was quickly devouring the words. "Where did you get this, Mama? And when?" he asked when he was through.

"I found it beneath my writing table on the day of the theft." She looked up at her son with a frown of disapproval. "Though I must say, Basil, I have to agree with Lord Sturtevant. This is none of your business."

"It is very much my business. Shall I tell them, Pippa, my dear?"

Pippa blinked at him. "Tell them what?" she asked, feeling thick-headed and shaky.

He tossed the note back to William, crossed the room and knelt beside her. "Shall I tell them our little secret? About the sapphire?"

"What secret?" Sybil demanded, feeling a startled sense of outrage. "What do *you* know about the sapphire, Basil Oxbrough?"

"More than you do, Miss Sturtevant, I must say." He turned back to Pippa. "Well, my little madcap, shall I tell them?"

Pippa peered at him closely, trying to read his face. Without her spectacles, she always felt handicapped in her thinking as well as her seeing. But it was clear that Oxbrough was pushing his advantage. He was challenging her to accept his offer of marriage right here, right now! If she gave assent, he would announce their betrothal and hand over the gem. The odious fellow had kept the gem in his possession and had never even informed his mother. Lady Oxbrough had believed, all this time, that the sapphire was in Pippa's own possession!

William, meanwhile, had reread the letter and was steaming in fury. "What is the *meaning* of this, Pippa? Is it true? Did you pay Lady Oxbrough *fifteen thousand pounds*?" The enormity of the sum almost choked him.

"Well, not exactly," Pippa said faintly. "I only—"

"She hasn't paid me a penny as yet," Lady Oxbrough put in. "I've had only this promise—"

"But *fifteen thousand*?" The sum seemed to make William ill. "*Why,* Pippa?" he demanded in almost maddened confusion. "What is this all about? Why did you offer Lady Oxbrough so enormous a sum for a gem that belongs to us?"

Pippa tried to answer but could not utter a word. She cast a sidelong, helpless glance at Sybil, but her friend was staring, wide-eyed and white-lipped, at her brother's face. Sybil was terrified. Pippa could not, under any circumstances, give her away.

"Well, my dear," Basil Oxbrough murmured in Pippa's ear, "shall I save the day for you?"

Lady Sturtevant, however, was studying her daughter's face. "Don't badger Pippa, William. I think it's *Sybil* who should answer your questions."

William turned to his mother, his eyebrows lifting. "Sybil?"

Sybil drew in a gasping breath. "M-Me?"

"Yes, my love, you. I think you know a great deal about this. How did this Mrs. Membry, who sold the stone to Lady Oxbrough, get it in the first place?"

A painful flush suffused Sybil's white face. "*I* don't . . . ! What makes you think that *I* . . . ?" She threw Pippa a look of pleading desperation.

"I'm certain you know something," her mother insisted.

"Damnation, Sybil," William exploded, "your every look gives you away! Speak up at once, or—"

"William, *stop*!" Pippa put her hands to her ears, wishing only that this inquisition would come to an end. "What has Sybil to do with this? It was *I* who wrote that letter."

Basil was following the exchanges with considerable satisfaction. It seemed to him that fate was playing right into his hand. This was not unlike a game of cards. If one played one's trick at the right time, one could easily carry the day. He reached into the inner pocket of his coat and withdrew a small packet.

"Pippa, my dear," Georgina was saying, "we know you wrote the letter. What we don't know is *why*. You can't make me believe that Sybil's antics are not at the bottom of this."

"Well, *one* of you had better explain, and *at once*!" William barked, his patience at an end.

Basil had unwrapped the packet. With the sapphire gleaming in his palm, he held his hand before Pippa's face.

The sight of the stone so close at hand was too much for Pippa. Trembling with pain, fatigue and shame, she wanted only a finish to this dreadful scene. "Very well, my lord," she muttered. "Your trick." She picked up the stone, rose unsteadily to her feet and held it out to William. "Here! *Take* it! And let's have an *end* to all this."

The Sturtevants could only gape speechlessly. But Lady Oxbrough was not in the least bereft of the power of speech. "I believe," she said, rising from her chair and holding out her hand, "that the stone belongs to me. The letter is proof."

"Nonsense, Mama," Basil Oxbrough said, coming forward with a triumphant smile. "It belongs to Lady Philippa, to dispose of as she sees fit. I gave it to her myself."

"You?" His mother blinked at him in stupefaction.

"Yes. It was I who took it from your collection. You have so many stones, after all. I didn't think you'd mind if I took one of them to present to my betrothed."

"Betrothed?" Georgina sank down in her chair as if her knees had given way.

"Good God!" William muttered, staring from the gem that Pippa had placed in his palm to Pippa's face, his chest constricting as if from a blow.

"Betrothed? To *Basil*?" Sybil cried, appalled. "I can't believe it!"

"It's quite true," Basil said, smiling fatuously at all of them.

"Really, Basil," his mother said, drawing herself up in offense, "this is a very strange way of announcing it. One would think you'd been brought up in an alehouse. Not that I have any objection to the match; if this business with the sapphire had not occurred, I would have found Lady Philippa quite suitable. But to break the news in this sudden way—and without a word to me beforehand—is a most vulgar solecism. And to have removed the stone from my collection without asking is, I must say, even more reprehensible!"

"Yes, Mama, I know. I've behaved shockingly. Lady Philippa and I didn't intend to make our situation public quite so soon, I must say. I do apologize to one and all for the suddenness of our announcement. But as far as my taking the sapphire, Mama, I trust that you will not remain miffed for very long. I intend to buy you a bauble to replace it at my first opportunity."

"I suppose, Pippa," Lady Sturtevant murmured weakly, "that there's nothing left to say but to . . . to wish you happy."

"Th-Thank you, Aunt Georgie," Pippa said unsteadily. Her mind was foggy at the edges, like her eyesight. She knew she had foolishly traded her future happiness for a temporary reprieve and that, when she would have time to think, she would very much regret what she'd just done. But for the moment she didn't care to think about it. The walls of the room seemed to have turned to rubber and were bending and undulating in an alarming way. The floor beneath her feet seemed spongy and unstable, and she was certain that, if she took a step, her foot would sink into a quagmire-ish depression. Her cheeks alternately flushed and paled with waves of heat and chill. She had only one aim—to make her way out of this room and up the stairs to her bed.

But a complete reprieve was not yet to be granted. William loomed up before her glaring down at her in barely contained fury. "I shall *not* wish you happy, ma'am. There is something decidedly havey-cavey about this business, and I shall not rest until I get to the bottom of it!"

"Please, William—" Pippa pleaded with a touch of desperation.

But Sybil pushed her way between them. "I won't wish you happy, either, you *beau snatcher*," she hissed.

"Sybil!" Pippa blinked at her friend in dismay, her head too confused with sensations to understand.

"You *knew* what I'd intended in regard to Basil," she said in a choked, enraged undervoice. "I never dreamed you were such a spiteful cat! You're supposed to be my *friend*!"

"But, Sybil, I *had* to—! You don't understand."

"I understand well enough. Pippa, how *could* you have—?"

But the door burst open again. Simon, his greatcoat flapping open and his beaver in his hand, came striding in. "Mama, what's this Miss Townley's been telling—? Good Lord! *Pippa!*"

"Simon, thank *goodness* you're back!" Georgina greeted him in relief. "She's had a fall from a horse, and although she says she's quite well—"

"Quite *well*? Are you *mad*? Can't you see the girl's done in?" Without taking his eyes from Pippa's face or throwing so much as a glance at any of the others, he tossed his beaver on a chair and crossed the room toward her.

As his face swam into focus above her, Pippa felt a knot of tension melt within her chest. "Simon?" she whispered shakily. "I was so afraid . . ."

"Afraid?" He gently took her chin in his hand and looked with clinical concern into her eyes.

"I was afraid you would . . . no longer . . . materialize."

A tiny smile touched the corners of his mouth. "I'm here," he said softly.

"I'm so . . . glad . . ."

All at once her will gave way. Whether it was simple strength, a desperate spirit or mere instinct which had kept her erect during this ordeal she didn't know, but with the appearance of Simon, something within her dissolved. She felt herself sag against him, and she started to sink, very slowly, to the floor.

But without a moment of hesitation, and despite the open-mouthed stares of a roomful of observers, he gathered her up in his arms and carried her swiftly, wordlessly, from the room.

Chapter Seventeen

WILLIAM SAT at Simon's worktable, gazing abstractedly at Simon while the younger brother busily polished a piece of glass with a metal tool and abrasives taken from a row of small pots containing polishing compounds of progressive fineness. While Simon's work seemed to require concentration (he repeatedly examined the rounded glass by passing it before a candle flame and scrutinizing it closely), he nevertheless cast a curious glance at his unexpected guest every few seconds. William rarely paid visits to this attic room. He knew Simon must have surmised that something was troubling him. But Simon wouldn't attempt to hurry him into speech. If William was having difficulty in broaching the subject of his visit, Simon would be willing to wait.

William didn't quite understand why he'd come. Almost a fortnight had passed since the accident—a fortnight during which William found himself irritatingly discomposed. But what could Simon do to clarify the confusion of his mind? Simon was too absorbed in his scientific pursuits to have developed sufficient sophistication in worldly matters to help William now. Nonetheless, William had climbed up here this rainy morning to confide in Simon, as he'd often done before when all else had failed. In the past, it had done him good to unburden himself to the younger man. There was always something calm and wise in Simon's responses, even if he wasn't worldly.

Besides, there was no one else who could help him to solve the dilemma of Pippa's character. His mother's affection for the girl was so strong that she could find no fault with the girl. And Sybil was not the sort with whom one could have a serious discussion. Sybil had a grasshopper mind and a grasshopper disposition—leaping from thought to act without considering the consequences to herself or anyone else.

This latest *contretemps* had been a perfect illustration of his sister's featherheadedness. After incurring a sizeable gambling debt, she'd compounded the crime a hundredfold by evasions, lies and a series of actions which embroiled Pippa and made the situation so entangled with difficulties that he'd had the devil's own time to unravel it. It had taken all his ingenuity (and a considerable amount of money) to straighten out the tangle. And there was still one knot to be untied—Pippa's betrothal to Lord Oxbrough.

But it was Pippa's behavior that was the source of William's deepest discomfort. He couldn't determine how much of Pippa's wanton activity was inspired by her own impulses and how much by his sister's. Her stubborn insistence on riding Salvaje was certainly her own decision—and a good indication of the girl's rashness. He'd been quite revolted by that display. Then why was he still vacillating?

Simon might be able to help him. Simon knew Pippa as well as anyone in the family. And he had a keen mind and the ability to subject a problem to thorough analysis. That was why it was always helpful to talk to him.

The only trouble was that William felt embarrassed at having to admit to his younger brother that his mind was so muddled. He glanced over at Simon hesitantly. "What are you doing with that bit of glass and those strange-looking compounds?"

"I'm grinding a lens for Pippa's new spectacles. The surface of glass, you see, is full of distortions and flaws that can affect the eye's perception. I grind away at the imperfections with this metal lap. These polishing compounds, which I've graded into progressively smaller and finer grains—" But a glimpse of his brother's expression stopped him. "But you don't really want to hear me prose on about grinding lenses, do you? You've something else on your mind, I suspect."

"Yes, I have. I've been wanting to talk to you for some time . . . about Pippa."

Simon's hands ceased their motion. "Pippa?" He laid the lens and his grinding tool carefully on the table. "Her injuries are healing well, if that's what you wish to know. I spoke to the doctor about her condition this morning. There's little he can do about the broken ribs, of course, but he says they will heal by themselves in time. Her bruises are disappearing, and she seems to be mending nicely. He will probably give her permission to leave her bed in a day or two."

William shook his head. "I didn't want to speak about her physical condition."

Simon ran a hand through his disordered hair. "Are you concerned about her spirit, then? She seems in good enough spirits, I think. Couldn't you see that for yourself when you looked in on her?"

"I haven't looked in on her. Not once since the day of the accident."

Simon shot his brother a look of amazement. "Why not?"

William shrugged. "For one thing, I was—am—too angry at what she did."

"What did she do to make you so angry—let you goad her into riding that horse?"

William lowered his eyes, bit his lip and took a

troubled breath. He reached for the piece of glass and, holding it between two fingers on its outer edge, twirled it absently. "Did she tell you I goaded her into it?"

"No. Dolly did."

"I see." He studied Simon's face with a troubled, envious twinge. "Does Dolly come up here often to confide in you?"

"Sometimes."

William twirled the bit of glass nervously. "I wish he'd talk to *me* sometimes. Do I frighten the boy, Simon?"

"I don't think you frighten him. Perhaps you're too rigidly disapproving of him, that's all. If you want him to confide in you, it seems to me that all you need do is listen to him and show some enthusiasm for his pursuits."

"Yes. I'll try." Wrinkling his brow thoughtfully, he spun the piece of glass on the table like a top. "But as to the matter of Pippa, it seems to me that a woman of sense would not have permitted herself to be goaded. Even if I were at fault, that doesn't excuse—"

"But why should you be angered, in any case? She only hurt herself, not you."

William picked up the glass again and twisted it between his fingers. "But I have more than that to infuriate me. Do you know that she gave Dolly almost a *thousand pounds* to pay for that animal?"

"So Dolly said." Simon reached across the table, gently removed the lens from his brother's hand and set it aside. "But I hear that he returned the horse to his friend and returned the money to Pippa, so—"

"What difference does that make? It's the *intent* that concerns me. I *warned* her not to do it. The whole nasty business could so easily have been avoided if she'd obeyed me."

Simon shook his head. "Why should she obey you? You're neither her father nor her guardian."

"All right, all right, I'm not. But I *am* Dolly's guardian. Haven't I any rights there? But that's not the most heinous of her crimes."

"Crimes?" Simon raised a disapproving eyebrow. "Aren't you overstating—?"

"I think not. Even if you can condone—which I cannot—the matter of Dolly and the horse, the business with the sapphire is the sticking point. The fact that she even *considered* spending fifteen thousand pounds makes her seem to me to be completely impulsive, capricious and irresponsible."

"Or generous to a fault. She did it for Sybil's sake."

"Yes, I know." William dropped his head in his hands. "That's what's muddling me."

Simon stared at his brother's lowered head, sympathy warring in him with unnerving jealousy. "What do you wish me to say, William?" he asked quietly, rising from his stool. "If you find Pippa's behavior culpable, you ought to speak to *her* about it."

"How can I, when my feelings are so deucedly confused?"

"In what way confused?"

William looked up, an embarrassed half-smile turning up his lips. "I had considered the possibility, you know . . . before these indiscretions came to light . . . of offering for her. Of course, I'd dismissed the notion from my mind the afternoon of the accident, even *before* I'd learned anything about the sapphire business. Now, of course, I'm convinced that the match would be completely unsuitable—"

Simon peered at his brother closely. "Are you?"

"Completely. And yet . . . she's such a taking little thing. I find myself making excuses for her. Arguing with myself. Vacillating in a most disconcerting way."

Simon, his brow knit, wandered to the window. "It would seem to be a pointless question now, wouldn't it? She's betrothed to Oxbrough."

"Rubbish. She doesn't care a whit for Oxbrough."

"How do you know that? She accepted him, didn't she?"

"Yes, but only under duress. For that blasted sapphire. I think she'll jilt the fellow sooner or later. She needn't feel any qualms if she wishes to do so. Oxbrough deserves to be jilted."

Simon looked over his shoulder at his brother. "And are you convinced that she *wishes* to break it off?"

"I think she does. She wouldn't have permitted me to kiss her, would she, if—?"

"You kissed her?" Simon felt a pulse pound in his temple. "Have matters between you gone as far as that?"

"I don't know, Simon. I'm too muddled to know *how* far they've gone."

Simon stared out the window. "What is it you want to ask of *me*, William? I know very little of . . . of these matters."

"Yes, but you know Pippa. I suspect you know her better than any of us. What do you think of her? You suggested today that you think I've been too hasty in condemning her. But do you think she would make a suitable wife for me?"

Simon kept his eyes on the raindrops pelting down upon the street below. He was unable to make a quick response. *Be silent always when you doubt your sense,* Pope had written. What should he say to his brother? *William, you fool, why are you hesitating? Snatch up the girl while you have the chance! Don't you know how lucky—how ineffably lucky!—you are that she wants you? How can you sit there and pick away at petty transgressions when a truly glorious creature has welcomed your advances and is ready to fall into your arms? Oh, God, if I were in your place—!*

It was a long time before he could trust himself to speak. When the silence threatened to become oppressive, however, he took a deep breath and plunged in. "I can't tell you who would be suitable for you, William," he said, not turning round. "In my opinion, Pippa would make a suitable wife for any man. Nothing of what's passed has made the slightest alteration in my admiration for her, if that's what you're asking me."

"Yes, I suppose that's what I want to know. I'm glad to hear that you think her suitable—"

Simon gave a low, bitter snort. "Suitable is hardly an adequate word," he muttered.

"Then you think I *should* offer for her?"

"How can I answer? You can't ask anyone else to make a choice of that nature for you."

"Yes," William sighed, "you're right." He got to his feet and started for the door. "I know I'll have to make up my own mind in the end."

He opened the door and looked back at his brother, still standing at the window across the room, his form silhouetted by the dull, grey morning light. Nothing had been changed by their conversation. William's doubts had not really been resolved. But he felt much better than when he'd arrived. He was, somehow, closer to a decision than he'd been before. "Thank you, Simon," he said.

"What for?"

"I don't know. Just for listening." He paused, gave a rueful little laugh and shook his head in perplexity. "Women can be the very devil, can't they?"

Chapter Eighteen

PIPPA LEANED BACK against a mound of pillows which had been piled up behind her and stared moodily into the fire. Two weeks had passed since the day of her catastrophic ride on Salvaje, but few of the problems which had come to a climax on that day had yet been solved. She was forced to keep to her bed until the doctor (for whom Simon had sent as soon as he'd realized that Pippa had broken two ribs) should decree that her ribs had begun to knit. The solicitous medical man would give her no clue as to how long that would be. It was a source of extreme frustration to be thus confined. She could learn nothing of what was going on except what her occasional visitors chose to tell her.

She had one thing to be thankful for: the matter of the sapphire seemed to have been settled. Aunt Georgie, on one of her daily visits, had related to Pippa that Sybil had confessed the truth about her gambling debts.

William had given her a proper tongue-lashing, extracted from her a promise that she would never again gamble for anything but pennies, and had returned to Lady Oxbrough the five thousand pounds which she'd paid to Mrs. Membry. As far as Aunt Georgie was concerned, Sybil was chastened, the gem was back in its proper place, and the matter was closed.

Lady Oxbrough had paid a visit to Pippa's bedside twice. Each time she'd assured Pippa that she was quite satisfied. "I must say, my dear," she admitted, "that I was too greedy. Greed is, I'm afraid, a common affliction of collectors. We become too acquisitive. For that I do apologize. And while I cannot approve of your actions in attempting to remove the gem from my possession, I realize that I was at fault for not returning it to Georgina myself after Mrs. Membry sold it to me. If I had not acted improperly, you would not have felt driven to thievery. But it is a matter we should now put behind us. Basil has bought an amethyst for me which I like very well, and Birdwell and Kerr say they've located a piece of jade which just fits my specifications. My collection is growing nicely, I must say. I am quite content, all things considered. Quite content."

Pippa, however, was far from content. Her betrothal to Basil Oxbrough was a fact of her life which Aunt Georgie and Lady Oxbrough seemed to accept with perfect equanimity but which was as depressing to her as a death sentence. Basil paid daily visits to her bedside, burbling away without a qualm about his delight at the prospect of becoming "leg-shackled to a madcap." His I-must-say's set her teeth on edge, and his laughing disparagement of her attempts to convince him that she was not at all what he thought her to be drove her wild. But what she was to do about it she didn't know.

Sybil, meanwhile, had not visited her once. She was livid about Pippa's betrothal and would not respond to any of Pippa's messages. As far as she was concerned, Pippa had treacherously snatched Oxbrough away from her after she'd openly revealed to Pippa her interest in the fellow. There was nothing Sybil despised so much as a beau-snatching female, and that's what Pippa had become in her eyes.

Dolly was a constant and faithful visitor, one whom it was a pleasure to see. During the first of his visits, he shamefacedly related how he'd found Salvaje (who'd simply galloped off to Doodle's stables) and sold him back to Doodle. He'd awkwardly handed her the roll of bills. "I was childish and selfish," he confessed. "I admired that great beast so strongly that I couldn't bear not to have him. Convincing myself that I was buying him for you was the act of a spoiled child, and seeing you so badly injured cuts me to the bone. I hope you'll forgive me, Pippa, but it will be a very long time before I forgive myself."

Pippa had assured him that he was no more to blame than she herself and that she had nothing to forgive. Once he was able to dispense with his remorse, his visits became jovial and cheering.

Simon came in several times a day during the first week but never stayed long. He only checked her pulse, asked her to lift her arms to see if her mobility had improved, inquired if the doctor had called, nodded wisely and left. This week his behavior had been even more detached. He'd merely stuck his head in the door once every day, looked her over, nodded and disappeared.

But William's behavior was even more confusing. He hadn't called on her at all until today. This morning he'd stormed in, agitation marking his expression and his movements. He'd taken a seat on the side of her bed and snatched up her hand. "You can't marry Oxbrough," he'd declared without preamble. "I can't believe that your heart's engaged, and if you accepted him only to obtain that blasted sapphire, you were idiotically rash."

"Yes, but you see, William—" she'd begun.

"Hush, my dear, don't say anything. I've not had a tranquil moment since I let you ride that monstrous horse. Not a single moment in the past fortnight. I must speak my mind, or I shall never compose myself. I thought, on that afternoon in the park, that I would never make you an offer. I don't like excitement and agitation, Pippa. I'm a rational, restrained, conventional sort. I've always thought that, when I marry, I would choose a level-headed, serene, quiet woman and live a life of temperate peacefulness. But you've completely overset me. I can think of nothing else! In spite of your impulsiveness, your rash behavior, your headstrong nature, your wild scrapes—in spite of all, I've come to care for you. I'm quite unable to look at another woman. You must marry me, Pippa. You *must*."

Pippa had stared at him in amazement. "But, William, I . . . I don't—"

"No, don't say anything now. I know you're entangled in this commitment to Oxbrough. But you mustn't feel yourself bound to him. He coerced you to accept him, I suspect. It would not be dishonorable to change your mind. Ladies break with their betrotheds for much less reason than you have. Look at Sybil. She's done it three times. Break with him, Pippa. Then, when you're free, we shall speak of this again. For now, only think about what I've said. At least do that." And with a last, speaking look and a squeeze of her hand, he'd gone.

She stared into the flames glumly. She'd received two offers from two quite suitable gentlemen, but neither had offered for *her*. Their offers had been made to some imaginary female they *thought* she was—a wild, rash, impulsive, foolish madcap. That person had not the least resemblance to the Philippa Wyckfield she knew. None at all. How could she accept either one of those offers when they'd really been made to another girl? If she agreed to either one, it would be like accepting under false pretenses.

Does every man see me in that light? she wondered. *Simon, too?* The thought was depressing. Simon had been aware of all the escapades in which she'd become embroiled over the years. The foolish little romps with Sybil when she was a child, the idiotic carriage accident four years ago, the sapphire predicament, the Salvaje catastrophe, and—worst of all—her lapse of memory the night of his speech before the Royal Society. With all this accumulated evidence of misbehavior, how could he possibly think well of her?

Without paying heed to her doctor's orders, she crept out of bed and pattered across the room to the fire. Now that she was alone, clear-headed and unlikely to be interrupted, the time had come to face up to the powerful feelings toward Simon of which she'd only lately become aware: her shatteringly physical response to his drunken embrace, the quiet happiness of the hours when they'd worked together, her crushing disappointment when she'd realized she missed his hour of triumph at the Royal Society, and her desperate need of him when she'd been hurt. She stared down into the crackling flames, reliving those feelings over again. If they didn't add up to love, she didn't know the meaning of the word.

Of course it was love. It was the same feeling she'd seen in her mother's face when she looked at Thomas. She probably hadn't recognized it because she'd felt it so long and so quietly that it had simply become a part of her. She'd only realized its presence when it had begun to hurt.

With an instinct as natural and open as that which turns a sunflower to the morning light, she determined to go right upstairs and tell him what she'd discovered. She reached for her robe and, without stopping to bother about slippers, went to the door. But before she reached it, she stopped in her tracks. What if he, like the others, thought of her as a foolish little madcap? Could she bear it?

Perhaps not, she decided, but she had to tell him anyway. This amazing discovery was too overwhelming to be kept bottled inside her. Whatever the outcome, whatever the cost, she wanted Simon to know what she felt. Disregarding the remnants of pain in her side, the stiffness in her limbs and the cold of the floor against the soles of her bare feet, she pattered down the corridor and up the stairs.

Her knock was answered by a complete stranger. She gasped and started in surprise and disappointment at the sight of the grizzled, elderly gentleman who stood in Simon's doorway. "Oh!" she exclaimed. "Who—?"

"I'm Dr. Young," the gentleman said, grinning down at her. "And you must be—"

"Pippa?" came Simon's voice from behind him. "What are you doing out of bed?"

"—Pippa!" the gentleman concluded with a wink. "Just as I thought."

"Dr. Young!" Pippa said, awestruck. "Oh, I . . . I beg your pardon. I didn't mean to interrupt—"

"Nonsense. Come in, my dear," the famous scientist said, stepping aside.

Pippa, however, embarrassingly aware of her dishabille and her bare feet, took a step backward. "No, I'm . . . sorry. You must be busy—"

"You ought to be spanked," Simon said, appearing before her, taking her arm and drawing her into the room. "Didn't the doctor order you to keep to your bed?"

"Yes, but I feel quite able to move about."

Simon shut the door behind her. "Well, since you've come, you may as well say a proper hello to Dr. Young."

The elderly man lifted her hand to his lips. "So you're Pippa," he said, smiling broadly. "You don't *look* much like a mathematician."

Pippa blushed. "Simon couldn't have told you I was a *mathematician*!"

"He told me how clever you are at mathematical calculations, which is close enough. The sly dog *didn't* tell me, however, how very pretty you are. You know, young lady, that I expected to meet you before this. Simon had said you might attend the meeting at the Society."

"Yes. I was very sorry to have missed it. Simon hasn't

said much about the meeting. Was it a success?"

"In every way. The membership was universally impressed with his paper. I expect they'll soon vote him in."

Pippa's face lit up. "*Truly*? What a very great honor, Simon. Why did you never say—?"

"Time enough to say it when I'm actually accepted," Simon said, dismissing the subject.

Pippa turned back to Dr. Young. "I've wished to meet you for a long time, sir. Simon has spent hours extolling your work and explaining it to me in great detail. Despite my embarrassment at appearing before you in this shocking state of undress, I shall treasure the memory of this meeting. But I mustn't keep you any longer from your work. Please excuse me."

"No, don't go yet," Dr. Young urged. "The work we've been doing is all in your behalf, you know. I came here this afternoon to look over Simon's equipment and help him to decide what should be transported to the new quarters, but instead I find myself impressed into the very tedious task of grinding a lens for your spectacles."

"My spec—! Simon, you *didn't*—!"

Simon grinned. "Don't let him tease you, Pippa. The truth is that he insisted on helping me. Grinding lenses is a hobby with him. Here, we've finished them. Come and let's see if they'll do."

Dr. Young gave her another wink, picked up a pair of spectacles from the table and wiped them with a chamois cloth. Then he looked at them in the light. "Do you think they're right, Simon?" he asked, handing them over.

Simon examined them and nodded. "Let's see, Pippa." He positioned them on her nose. "How are they?"

It had been a fortnight since she'd worn spectacles. She'd grown almost accustomed to blur and fuzziness. She stared up at Simon's face, now sharply focused in her gaze, and felt her heart melt. How good he was! One could see it merely by looking at him. The unkempt, dark red hair that fell unheeded over his forehead, the kind, all-seeing, intent eyes, the lean face strongly lined with character, the generous mouth—anyone could see what sort of man he was. How could such a man have been invisible to those closest to him? Tears of love and gratitude burned in her throat.

Simon, reading something in her gaze, seemed to freeze. His eyes fell from her face. "Well?" he asked, suddenly awkward.

"The glasses are . . . wonderful," she said, painfully aware that he had withdrawn. "I don't know how to express my thanks. To you both."

Dr. Young had been watching the scene with interest. "You may thank us, my dear, by coming to the new quarters at every opportunity and assisting us with your calculations," he said.

Simon drew in a deep breath. "I don't think she'll have the opportunity, Dr. Young. Pippa is soon to be wed, I understand. The announcement of her betrothal to Lord Oxbrough is, my mother tells me, about to appear in *The Times*."

Dr. Young's keen grey eyes flicked from one to the other. "Really?" he asked, one eyebrow raised. "How very disappointing."

Pippa bit her lip, her color rising. *Simon must be aware that I don't intend to wed Oxbrough*, she thought in irritation. *Why did he bring up the subject at all?* Simon could be very difficult when he chose.

Simon, meanwhile, gave Dr. Young a look of amusement. "Disappointing? What a very tactless fellow you can be, my friend! You're supposed to *congratulate* the girl."

Dr. Young gave his protégé an enigmatic glance before turning to Pippa. "Of course I should. I wish you happy, my dear."

"Thank you. Now you must both excuse me. I—and my wonderful spectacles—have kept you from your work long enough. Goodbye, Dr. Young. It's been a great honor."

Simon opened the door for her. "Good evening,

Pippa. Take yourself back to bed and *stay there*. It's much too soon for you to be hopping about."

Out in the corridor she turned back to him. "Simon? Can you . . . ? Will you have time, later in the evening, to come down to . . . see me?"

His face tightened. "Is it something urgent? Unless it is, I'm afraid that Dr. Young and I will be occupied far into the night."

"I see. No, it's . . . nothing urgent. Good evening, Simon."

Pippa sat at the edge of the bed, unmoving, for more than an hour. Simon didn't want her, that much seemed clear. And the pain of it made the ache of two broken ribs seem trivial in comparison. *Why*, she asked herself forlornly, *didn't I sail with Mama and Thomas when I had the chance? I might have been happily staring out on the waves at this very moment instead of sitting here in this troublesome household moping before a dying fire and trying not to cry.*

Miss Townley entered a short while later carrying a supper tray. "Should you be sittin' up that way?" she asked.

Pippa shrugged indifferently. "I've been thinking, Miss Townley," she said, "about home. What would you say to going there?"

"Home? You mean to Wyckfield Park?"

"Yes. A rest in the country might do us both good."

Miss Townley studied her face suspiciously before replying. "Blue-deviled, are you? I don't blame you. Nothin' I'd like better than to take you to the country and cheer you up with good cookin' and proper care. When shall we go?"

"Tomorrow morning. Before anyone's up."

"Right. I'll start the packin' at once. You go to bed."

But Pippa didn't go to bed. Instead, she sat down at the little writing table in the corner and prepared a pen. Before she could permit herself to steal out of this house, she had a number of letters to write—three farewells, one refusal of an offer of marriage, and one jilt.

It would probably take her all night.

But no letter to Simon was included in the five she planned to write. She wouldn't write to Simon at all. She didn't trust herself to write to him. There was no law, after all, that required that one confessed one's love. What was the maxim that Simon had quoted a few weeks ago? Something by La Rochefoucauld. Oh, yes. *Silence is the best tactic for him who distrusts himself.* The words were very wise. Perhaps, in regard to Simon, silence was the best tactic of all.

Chapter Nineteen

SYBIL AWOKE the following morning in a paroxysm of guilt. She threw off her covers, sat up in bed and shuddered in self-revulsion. She'd treated Pippa with unforgivable shabbiness, and now her remorse was making her feel almost ill.

It was all because she'd attended a ball the night before. A most wonderful ball. It was there she'd been introduced to Leslie, Lord Wolfenden, who'd stood up with her for three dances! It had been love at first sight. She could barely contain her eagerness to tell Pippa all about it. But she and Pippa were not speaking.

She'd been a fool. Why hadn't she seen from the first that Pippa had not meant to steal Oxbrough? It was as plain as pikestaff that Pippa had allowed herself to become betrothed to Basil Oxbrough only to get back the sapphire. It was because she'd been so foolishly infatuated with Basil that Sybil hadn't been able to see the situation for what it was. But now that she'd met Leslie Wolfenden . . .

The recollection of the startlingly handsome Lord Wolfenden brought a small smile to Sybil's lips. Last night had been an evening of note. Her life would never be the same. Lord Wolfenden had been as smitten as she; he'd had eyes for no one else in the room. If she shut her eyes, she could bring his fair good looks right back to mind. How had she ever been so idiotic as to imagine that she could care for the stockily-built, too-dark Basil Oxbrough, with his haw-hawing laugh and his endless I-must-say's?

She had to see Pippa at once. She had to apologize, to embrace her friend, to share with her the excitement of her new infatuation. And after they'd talked themselves out, she would see to it that they put their heads together to concoct a scheme which would enable Pippa to jilt Lord Oxbrough (for in her new clarity of mind, Sybil realized that Pippa was not the least in love with Basil). She could barely wait to throw herself on Pippa's chest and beg forgiveness.

But it was still very early in the morning. The sounds from the corridor indicated that the servants were just beginning to stir. Pippa was probably still asleep. Perhaps she should wait until Pippa had risen.

But Sybil was not the patient sort. She couldn't wait. Dash it all, she'd had more than enough waiting in that fortnight of estrangement. She donned her robe and slippers and pattered across the hall. Her tap on Pippa's door was not answered, so she turned the knob, pushed open the door and slipped in.

There was something in her first sight of the room that gave her pause—something peculiar about its emptiness which she couldn't at first grasp. The bed was already made, the table tops were clear of books and Pippa's personal ornaments, and the miniatures of her mother and Captain Collinson, which she'd always kept on the mantel, were gone. But it was not until Sybil glanced into the dressing room and saw that the top of the dressing table held no hairbrush, no soapdish, no bottle of perfume nor box of trinkets that she realized her friend was gone. She knew without looking (though she looked anyway) that the wardrobe would be empty.

She sank on the bed, waves of guilt sweeping over her again. It was all her fault. By her selfishness and thoughtlessness, she'd driven her very best friend from the house. Only after she spent many minutes berating herself did Sybil notice the small pile of letters on the night table. She jumped up and reached for them eagerly. The very top one was addressed to her.

Dearest Sybil, Pippa had written, *I wish I could have made my adieu in person, but since you aren't speaking to me, this letter will have to do. By the time you read it, I shall have bundled up Miss Townley and all my possessions and gone off to Wyckfield Park to rest. My reasons have nothing to do with our present estrangement (which I know to be only a temporary situation), so do not chastise yourself about it. The bonds of our friendship are too strong to be severed by this ridiculous misunderstanding over Lord O.*

You'll be happy to hear that I've written to Oxbrough breaking it off. I told him that he'd shackled himself to the wrong girl. If it's a madcap he wants, I suggested that there was a certain redheaded shatterbrain, not ten yards from this room, who would suit him very well. I hope you will write and tell me how the matter proceeds.

Meanwhile, be assured that you have—now and always—the deepest affection of your loving Pippa.

Sybil, her underlip trembling pathetically, gave Latcham the other letters for delivery. Then she closeted herself in her room and cried for an hour.

Simon had not slept well. Something in Pippa's face last night, when he'd resisted her invitation to go down to talk to her, disturbed him. He hadn't intended to hurt her by that refusal but only to protect himself. Nevertheless, she *had* been hurt. The brief, almost undetectable flare of pain that had flickered in her eyes haunted him. He saw it in his dreams.

This morning he'd tried to put it—and Pippa herself—out of his mind. Simple loyalty to his brother demanded it. He packed the last of his equipment into boxes and piled them upon the other crates already waiting for the draymen. There remained only the notebooks to sort and number, and the microscopes to disassemble and crate. But he couldn't concentrate. If he didn't go down and face Pippa, he would accomplish nothing.

Steeling himself against the possibility of pain (as he always had to do when he saw her), he marched down to her room and knocked. There was no answer. "Pippa?" he called.

"If ye're lookin' fer Lady Philippa, she's gone 'ome," said Noreen from down the hall, peeping out of Lady Sturtevant's bedchamber where she'd been making up the bed.

"Gone home? What on earth do you mean?"

"T' the country, they say. Dorset."

"Are you telling me she's gone to Wyckfield Park?"

"Yes, sir. Took off wi' Miss Ada afore sunup. Gave us all a turn, I kin tell ye. Never said goodbye to a soul, neither one of 'em. Lady Philippa left letters fer th' family, acourse, 'ceptin' you, Mr. Simon. Mr. Latcham, 'e wuz sayin' downstairs on'y a little while ago that Mr. Simon'd be the most surprised of all t' learn th' news, seein' as 'ow 'e didn't get no note."

Simon peered at her with his intent stare. "I see. Well, thank you, Noreen. You may get on with your chores."

When the maid had withdrawn, Simon, not quite believing what he'd heard, pushed open Pippa's door and went in. The room looked bleak in its deserted, uninhabited state. There was not a trace of her left . . . no discarded handkerchief on the night table, no bit of ribbon on a chair, not a single hair fallen from her brush upon the surface of the dressing table. Not even a depression in her pillow where her head had lain. She'd simply and completely disappeared.

He smiled bitterly. He'd hoped that, by tomorrow, it

would have been *he* who'd done the disappearing and *she* who'd be standing forlornly in the middle of his cleaned-out laboratory looking for a trace of him. But no. She'd gone without a backward look. Without a word to him. Without even leaving him a note! *Lady Philippa left letters fer th' family, acourse, 'ceptin' you, Mr. Simon. 'Ceptin' you.*

He lifted his foot to deliver a furious kick upon the nearest bedpost, but he stopped in mid-swing. He'd be damned if he'd stub his toe for her. Not again. Instead, he strode out of the room and slammed the door viciously behind him.

Sybil, feeling purged by her bout of tears, emerged from the seclusion of her bedroom with the intention of discovering what the rest of the family was making of Pippa's desertion. She found her mother and Dolly in the drawing room, talking about the unexpected event. "I, for one, don't blame her in the least," Lady Sturtevant was saying as Sybil paused in the open doorway. "No one can have a proper rest in this upside-down household. There's always some cause here for turmoil and confusion. And you, Dolly, certainly contributed your share to Pippa's unease."

"I know," Dolly said glumly, staring at his letter. "Though she does say quite specifically that her reasons for leaving have nothing to do with me or the Salvaje affair."

"It's not your fault, Dolly," Sybil said, entering. "Dash it all, it's mine."

"Ah, Sybil, there you are. Come and sit down. I'm glad you realize *your* culpability in this matter. As I was saying to Dolly, you should have apologized to Pippa a fortnight ago. After all she'd done for your sake, the very least—"

"I know, Mama, I know." Sybil threw herself into a chair and leaned her chin on her hand. "No one feels more blue-deviled over this business than I. I was going to make it up with her this very morning. Confound it, how could I have lost my head over that pompous Oxbrough?"

Her mother looked at her with disbelief. "Are you saying, Sybil Sturtevant, that you've wearied of your infatuation with Oxbrough already?"

Sybil shrugged. "It wasn't an infatuation after all. Only a—"

Her mother held up her hands. "I know. You don't have to say it. One of your passing fancies."

"Yes. I should have realized it sooner. If I had, Pippa and I would have made up our spat and I could have prevailed upon her to remain."

Lady Sturtevant looked down at her letter. "I've been thinking, my dears, that perhaps I ought to send for the carriage and go after her. Although Pippa says here that she feels completely recovered from her accident, I cannot like her leaving us at this time. The doctor hasn't yet given her permission to leave her bed, and I shall not be easy in my mind unless I have her safe under my roof again."

"Let *me* go, Mama," Dolly offered eagerly. "You've never enjoyed long carriage rides, whereas I like nothing better. I can take the reins myself. I'd make excellent time and probably reach Wyckfield before Pippa does. Might even catch her on the road. She can't have had more than a couple of hours' start."

Sybil lifted her head, brightening. "No, Dolly. Hang it, it should be *I*. I'll go after her, Mama. It will give me the opportunity to make it up with her. And on the way I'll think of some scheme to coax her back. You know how good I am at scheming."

"Yes, we are well aware of your talents in that regard," said William, striding in without so much as a greeting to his mother. "But if anyone is going after Pippa, it's I myself."

"You, William?" Lady Sturtevant eyed her son interestedly. "Why should *you*—?"

"Because the girl's a goosecap. Just because she won't have me is no reason for her to go running off to

Dorset, and I intend to tell her so."

"William!" Lady Sturtevant started from her chair. "Are you saying you *offered* for her?"

"Yes, fool that I was. I *knew* I could never live with a shatterbrain, but I'd convinced myself that her erratic behavior was not intrinsic to her nature. I thought it only Sybil's unholy influence—"

"Thank you very much," Sybil muttered under her breath.

"—and that once I'd wedded her and taken her away from here, she'd settle down to a quiet and ordered life. But this *latest* escapade—!" He waved his letter in his mother's face. "This, Mama, is the *very last straw.* Running away like this is the very outside of enough. And we can't blame Sybil's influence this time. Sybil obviously had nothing to do with it."

"By jove, thank you again!" Sybil said, louder this time.

"But, William, I don't understand," Lady Sturtevant said, keenly disappointed. "Are you telling us that Pippa *refused* you?"

The question was overheard by Simon, just outside in the hall. He stopped in the doorway to listen to the response.

"Yes, she refused me quite bluntly," William was saying. "Claims we don't know each other—a statement I find to be ridiculous."

"Really, William, you must have misunderstood. She couldn't have said such a thing," his mother pointed out. "After all, she's been living here, off and on, since she was *ten*."

"Nevertheless, that is what she says. Here, I'll read it to you." William unfolded his letter and ran his finger down the page until he came to the relevant passage. "Just listen to this: *While I admit to a warm and sisterly affection for you and a sincere respect for your character, I do not believe we have developed, between us, that intimacy and mutual understanding which 'a marriage of true minds' requires. We don't know each other well and truly, as I believe people should who contemplate the close bonds of wedlock. I am convinced, William, that my rejection of your very flattering offer will, for that reason, give you only temporary pain. You said yourself that your feelings for me caused you nothing but turmoil and confusion. Confusion, I've learned, is not love. When you've had time for reflection, I believe you'll find that what you felt for me was little more than what Sybil calls a passing fancy.* And there you have it, Mama, in Pippa's own words."

Sybil blinked up at her brother speculatively. "How very strange. If I didn't know better, I could almost suspect that Pippa's heart was given elsewhere. *Confusion, I've learned, is not love.* What a very odd thing for her to say."

"Not so odd," her mother mused. "It's quite sensible, really, if one thinks about it. There *is* no confusion when one knows one's heart."

Simon, standing quietly in the doorway, felt his pulse begin to race. If Pippa had really meant what she'd written to William, her behavior last evening could be interpreted in an entirely new way. Is that what she'd wanted to tell him last evening—that she didn't love William after all? Could she have meant in that letter that there was no longer any confusion in her heart? Was there, suddenly, a chance for *him*? But it couldn't be. Pippa hadn't left him a note.

William, meanwhile, mulling over his mother's words, sank down on a chair. "Yes, Mama, that is an astute interpretation. I wonder if the chit is in the right of it."

"Ha!" Sybil snorted in ironic triumph. "If she is, then I'm not the *only* one in this family who is subject to passing fancies."

"Well, my love," her mother said placidly, "nobody said you were."

Dolly had had enough of this prattle. "While we sit here jabbering," he cut in, "Pippa is getting farther and farther away. Why not let me go after her?"

"No, confound it," Sybil said, jumping from her chair, "I shall do it."

"I've already told you that *I* am going myself," William said magisterially, pocketing his letter and preparing to push himself from his seat.

"*None* of you is going," Simon said from the doorway.

"Simon!" The cry came from his mother, but everyone else was equally surprised. "How long have you been standing there?"

"Long enough."

"Why didn't you say something?" his sister asked. "We never even noticed you."

"That's not unusual," Simon answered drily.

"What did you mean by saying none of us will go for Pippa?" William demanded. "What have *you* to do with this?"

"As much as you, I should think."

"He's right, William," Lady Sturtevant said. "Simon is as much a member of this family as the rest of us."

"Nice of you to acknowledge that, Mama," Simon said with a wry smile.

"Hang it, Simon, you're a part of the family, all right, but only when you choose to come down from your secluded tower," his sister accused. "I don't see why you've suddenly decided to descend and lord it over us *now*."

"I'm not lording it over you. I'm merely informing you all that I'm the one who will go after Pippa."

"I say, old man, that's not fair," Dolly objected. "I'm the best horseman in the family. Why can't I—?"

"If that's not lording it over us, blast if I know what is," Sybil muttered.

"And may I remind you, Simon, that *I'm* the head of this family?" William rose with decisive alacrity. "I have my carriage waiting, and I intend to start out at once."

"Sit down, William," Simon said with such unaccustomed firmness that William dropped down on his chair. "Did you drive over in your curricle? I'll take it, if you don't object. You can go home in the phaeton. I may catch her up by evening, Mama, but don't expect us back before tomorrow."

"See here, Simon," William sputtered, reddening, "I—"

"May I go with you, Simon?" Dolly asked, jumping up hopefully.

"Sorry, Dolly, not this time." And Simon turned to leave.

"I'll be dashed if that's not the most high-handed—!" Sybil fumed. "Why are *you* the one to take it on yourself—?"

"Yes, Simon," Lady Sturtevant inquired in placid curiosity, "why did you decide that *you're* the one to go?"

"Because I'm the one who got no letter," Simon said, turning to the upturned faces, a slight smile appearing at the corners of his mouth.

"What?"

"No *letter*?"

"What on earth is he talking about, Mama?"

"I have no idea. What *are* you talking about, Simon?"

"Pippa left me no letter. No note. No message of any kind. Don't you find that somewhat . . . significant?"

"What's so deucedly significant about it?" his sister asked irritably. "She probably just forgot about you."

"Cut line, Sybil," Dolly said, looking at Simon with shrewd approval. "Pippa wouldn't forget Simon. She spends more time with him up in his workroom than all the rest of us put together. Pippa forget Simon? Not likely. So if she didn't leave him a note, perhaps there *is* something significant in the omission."

William peered at Dolly with dawning respect. "The boy makes sense," he muttered, turning to gape at Simon. "Pippa's *always* up there with you, now I come to think of it. What *is* the significance, then, Simon?"

"Yes, Simon, my love," his mother prodded, utterly fascinated, "you must explain yourself."

"I can't, entirely. I have only the vaguest of clues. I can only say that you've all had notes, and I've had . . . silence."

"Silence?" Sybil echoed disparagingly. "What the devil is so significant about silence?"

"Perhaps nothing at all." He looked from one to the other, his smile widening. "But if I may rephrase an old maxim on the subject: *Silence is the best tactic for one who distrusts herself.*"

Sybil, after gaping up at him in confusion, sneered. "Hummph! I won't pretend to know what those words mean, but I'll wager Pippa has never even *heard* of them."

"Oh, she's heard of them right enough," Simon answered, throwing her a grin and heading for the door. "I told them to her myself."

Chapter Twenty

SHE WAS moving again. Once again Pippa Wyckfield had found it necessary to change her abode. Once again she was altering her way of life and the quality of her days. Once again she was sitting in a hired coach opposite a dozing Miss Townley with all her worldly goods piled up and tied on the carriage top, heading for another bedroom in another domicile in another place. It was small wonder she felt weepy.

She stared out of the coach window at the October landscape which the late afternoon sun had tinged with gold and permitted a few tears to fall. It had only been a month—one short month—since she'd made her last move. That last change, when she'd left her mother's house in Southampton for the Sturtevant house in London, had not been nearly as depressing as this. Then she'd entertained at least a *few* hopes of happiness. She had anticipated the bright possibilities of friendship, familial closeness, even love. This time she had nothing to hope for at all. No friends nor family waited for her at Wyckfield Park. And all chances of love were growing fainter as every turn of the coach wheels widened the distance between herself and Simon.

As a final assault on her spirits, her still-bruised body reacted to every tremor of the coach with a shudder of pain. Every roll and sway, every bump of the road, struck at her like a cruel affront. Her right side, in particular, ached torturously. She couldn't endure it much longer. She'd hoped to get as far as Andover before stopping for the night, but she'd had to order the coachman to restrain his speed, and by four they'd only managed to reach Aldershot. *Oh, well,* she thought with a sigh, *I have no reason to hurry. I may as well stop here as anywhere. Sing ho, no diff'rence, no dim-dam-diff'rence to me.*

She rapped on the roof and told the coachman, when he peered down at her from the tiny window through which they communicated, to stop at the first inn which appeared to be suitable for a pair of gentlewomen.

The coachman pulled into the yard of the Twin Chimneys, which, he told her, was as suitable as any. It was a cozy hostelry, nestled in a misty dell and boasting the most flourishing rose garden in the county. The interior, though not as pleasing to the eye as the charming courtyard, was nevertheless clean and comfortable. Miss Townley's sharp eyes had noted, when they'd alighted from the carriage, that Pippa's walk was stiff and that lines of strain were showing on her brow, and she immediately bespoke a private dining room, two bedrooms, a hot dinner to be served at seven, and tea to be served at once.

The innkeeper's wife took a liking to the elegantly modest lady who kept quietly in the background. Though the inn had no private dining rooms, she promptly shooed the two patrons lounging about in the public room into the taproom, ushered the ladies in and shut the door. The tea and simple sugar cakes the woman brought were immensely satisfying to the weary travelers even though they didn't quite revive Pippa's flagging energy. When the tea had been consumed, Miss Townley insisted that Pippa remain seated near the fire in the dining room while she saw to the stowing of their baggage and the arrangements of their bedrooms.

Left alone, Pippa wearily put her feet up on the hearth and fell into a doze. She dreamed that she was in a dark room, in which one beam of light filtered through a hole in the wall. Her eyes followed the direction of the ray to the opposite wall where the circle of light suddenly changed to a rectangle containing all the colors of the rainbow. Someone hidden by the shadows was holding a prism in the path of the light. She wheeled about. "Simon?" she asked, unaccountably frightened. She felt her way along the wall in an attempt to get closer to the hand holding the prism. "Simon?" she asked again. She was quite close now. The man in the shadows chuckled. "You make your appearances in the strangest sorts of places, I must say," said the man. It was Oxbrough, and the prism had become a sapphire, large as a ball. "Give me that!" she ordered, reaching out. "It's mine!"

The light had now become blue. She couldn't make out his face any longer. She clutched at the gem again, but the hand raised it out of her reach. In the darkness she could hear a scuffle, and a piece of glass shattered on the floor. Was it the prism? The light turned white again. "Simon?" she asked.

"You've broken the prism," another voice accused. It was William. But she hadn't broken it. She tried to explain, but William wouldn't listen. "Ask Simon," she pleaded. "He'll tell you." But William's head, silhouetted against the light, turned away from her. "You broke it!" he said, lifting the enormous sapphire high over his head and heaving it across the room. It exploded in a shower of blue sparks which hung shimmering in the air for a long moment before falling to the ground with the sound of tinkling glass.

She woke with a start. A log had fallen from the grate. She realized from the darkness outside the windows that she'd slept for a long time. It had been a mistake to permit herself to fall asleep in the chair. Every muscle in her body had stiffened. She could hardly move.

Painfully and slowly, she pulled herself up. Where had Miss Townley gone all this time? She limped to the door and peered out. There was no one in the darkened corridor. The only light came from the taproom across the hall. The clink of glasses and the sound of talk and laughter indicated that business at the Twin Chimneys was brisk tonight. But she didn't look within. Surely she'd not find Miss Townley there. Perhaps she'd gone upstairs.

With laborious effort, Pippa mounted one step and then another. Never had climbing a stairway been such an ordeal. Every movement gave her a sharp stab of pain. She had to bite her underlip to keep from crying out. Wincing, she was about to climb the third step when she felt herself lifted off her feet by two strong arms. With a gasp of shock, she turned her head to look at her attacker. Her eyes widened in utter astonishment. *Simon!*

She tried to speak, but no sound issued from her throat. Was she still dreaming? Her lips silently mouthed his name.

He shifted her weight against his chest, bringing her face level with his own. "Yes, it's I," he said, looking down at her reprovingly. "I thought I had instructed you to remain abed."

Her pulse was racing wildly. "Simon! How—?"

"Did I or did I not tell you to stay in your bed?"

A little bud of joy opened in her breast. "Yes, you did."

"Then why, ma'am, do I find you miles from home and as far from your bed as you can be? I'm not a bit surprised that you can barely climb the stairs."

"Oh, Simon," she breathed, letting her head fall on his shoulder, "I *am* glad to see you. What are you *doing* here?"

"What do you think, you greenhead?" He tightened his hold on her and began to climb the stairs.

She lifted her head and stared at him. "You didn't *follow* me here, did you?"

"No, of course not. I just happened to be strolling through the neighborhood and stopped in for a drink of Mine Host's home brew."

"Perhaps it *was* a foolish question, but why did you find it necessary to follow me?"

"I thought you might be eloping with Oxbrough, so I rushed out to stop you."

"Cawker! You knew I didn't do any such thing. I left a half-dozen notes—!"

"Did you?" He stopped his climb and looked at her pointedly. "I didn't see any."

Her eyes flickered down, and a slow flush suffused her cheeks. "Didn't you?"

He resumed his climb. "No. There was none with my name on it."

"Oh."

They came to the top of the stairway and found themselves on a little circular landing with four closed doors. "Which room is yours?" he asked.

"I have no idea. Heavens, what shall we do now? Must we go back downstairs again and ask Mine Host?"

"Not on your life." He shifted her weight to his shoulder, freeing one hand, and rapped loudly on each door in turn. For a long moment no one responded. Then the knob of the door on their extreme right turned. The door opened, and a tousled, sleepy-eyed Miss Townley peered out. "Oh, Pippa, I fell asl—Good heavens, is that—? Mr. *Simon*!"

"Good evening, Miss Townley. I'm sorry to have disturbed you. Which is Pippa's room?"

The elderly woman gaped. "Has something happened? Are you hurt?"

"No, my dear, don't be alarmed," Pippa said, smiling down at her. "I was just too tired to climb the stairs."

"I see." She looked shrewdly from one to the other. "I don't suppose you'll bother to tell me how you managed to summon Mr. Simon all the way from London to play the hero and carry you up."

"Not now, at any rate," Simon said. "I know it isn't heroic to say so, Miss Townley, but I can't play the hero much longer. This creature I'm carrying is not as light as she looks."

Miss Townley snorted and threw open the door to her right. "Take her in here, if you please."

The room was tiny, with a sharply slanted roof and a dormer window. A fire flickered cheerfully behind the grate, throwing a dim amber glow over the bed and the cupboard, the room's only furnishings. Simon, stooping to avoid bumping his head against the ceiling, carried Pippa to the bed, sat down upon it and gently laid his burden down upon the counterpane. Pippa, her head elevated by three plump pillows, gazed up at Simon with the same intensity with which he was staring at her. Almost dreamily, she lifted a hand and gently fingered his cheek. "Are you going to tell me why you came?" she asked softly.

Miss Townley, watching them in pleased surprise, realized abruptly that her presence was not required. She reached for the doorknob, backed out of the room and slowly started to pull the door closed behind her.

Simon, without taking his eyes from Pippa's face, put up a hand. "Where do you think you're going, Miss Townley?"

Pippa laughed, a low, throaty chuckle. "Yes, Miss Townley. Don't you see there's a man in my room?"

"Rubbish. No harm will come to you from Mr. Simon." And she shut the door with a snap.

There was a moment's silence. Then the door was flung open again. "But I'll be back in half an hour," Miss Townley added firmly, "so don't think I'm encouragin' any undue liberties."

They laughed long after she'd shut the door again. When at last they caught their breaths, Simon studied her speculatively. There were still tensions between them right under the surface. There were things to be asked, and answered. But he couldn't bring himself to the sticking point. He got to his feet and went to poke up the fire. "Everyone in the family sent you messages," he muttered, staring down at the flames.

"Did they? Is that why you came? To bring me messages?"

He ignored the question. "They followed me right out the door, shouting all sorts of things at me until the curricle was out of their sight."

"Really?"

"They all want you to come back, of course. Mama says she won't be easy until you're back under the doctor's care—"

"Yes?"

"—and Dolly wants you to know that he would have come for you himself if I hadn't overruled him—"

"Did you overrule him, Simon? Why?"

"—and Sybil says to tell you she's sorry about everything. Oxbrough, she says, was only a passing fancy. She's lost her head over someone else. Woolrich . . . Wolfington . . . Woolgatherer . . . some such name—"

"Incorrigible Sybil! You didn't travel all this way just to—"

"—and William, of course. William said to tell you that he thinks you may be right in what you wrote to him. But he added that he'd be quite willing to try to know you better if you haven't already lost your heart to someone else."

"Did he say that? Really?"

"Those were his very words."

"Does he suspect I *have* lost my heart to someone else?"

"Well, the family seemed to feel that there were hints in your letters . . ."

"I see. Thank you, Simon, for taking all this trouble in my behalf."

He merely grunted and turned back to the fire.

Pippa cocked her head and peeped at him from under lowered lashes. "Miss Townley has sound instincts. She has no need to worry about leaving me alone with you. You've never shown me the least impropriety, have you?"

His head came up. "Haven't I?"

"Well, only once. But you aren't supposed to have remembered that."

He came back to the bed and smiled down at her. "I remember it, all right. Vividly."

"Oh?" She lifted herself up on one elbow and looked up at him, a challenge in her eyes. "Do you have to be foxed to do it again?"

He stared at her for a moment before sitting down on the bed. "Let's try it and see," he answered, pulling her up into his arms.

It was a shocking and completely improper embrace. Pippa was certain that her newly knitted ribs would break again. But she barely felt the pain, so exhilarating was the pulsing of her blood, the warmth of his lips on hers, the feel of his face between her hands. "Is this why you followed me?" she whispered when he let her go.

He held her tightly against him, nestling her face against his neck and placing his lips on her hair. "No," he murmured.

She broke from his hold. "No? Then *why*—?"

He gave her one of his intent looks. "To ask why you wrote goodbyes to everyone but me."

"Oh." She lay back against the pillows and lowered her eyes.

"Well?" he demanded.

"I didn't . . . trust myself to write to you. I was afraid I might . . ."

"Might what?"

"Might have scribbled 'I love you' all over the page."

He expelled a long breath. "I wouldn't have minded reading such a note," he said quietly, taking one of her hands.

She smiled at him tremulously, her throat tightening with tears. "Wouldn't you, my dear?"

"Not a bit." He kept his eyes on the hand he held in

his. "I've been waiting to hear those words from you since you were ten."

"Oh, *Simon*!" She cast herself back into his arms. "Why did you never *tell* me?"

"I don't know. You seemed so . . . sisterly. I thought you loved my brother."

"I think," she whispered into his shoulder, "that I must have loved you for years. But the feeling was so . . . so natural that I never noticed. And as for William, I never really loved him at all. I only thought that I might *learn* to care for him."

"Yet you kissed him, I hear."

"Yes. But it wasn't . . . memorable."

He stroked her curls tenderly. "When did it occur to you, my love, that it was I?"

"Yesterday. No . . . the day I was flung from Salvaje's back. No . . ." She lifted her head and grinned at him. "I think it was the moment when you came back from the Royal Society, drunk as a lord and singing your dim-dam song."

He laughed and pulled her back to him. There was so much more to say. Explanations, reminiscences, revelations, plans. They would have to talk for days to cover it all. But he'd leave the talk for some other time. For now there were only a few precious moments left before Miss Townley was due to burst in on them. For those few moments, nothing would do but silence. Blissful silence.